T0395950

MURDER ON THE
GREAT NORTHERN RAILWAY

By Edward Marston

The Railway Detective series
The Railway Detective • The Excursion Train
The Railway Viaduct • The Iron Horse
Murder on the Brighton Express • The Silver Locomotive Mystery
Railway to the Grave • Blood on the Line
The Stationmaster's Farewell • Peril on the Royal Train
A Ticket to Oblivion • Timetable of Death
Signal for Vengeance • The Circus Train Conspiracy
A Christmas Railway Mystery • Points of Danger
Fear on the Phantom Special • Slaughter in the Sapperton Tunnel
Tragedy on the Branch Line
The Railway Detective's Christmas Case
Death at the Terminus • Murder in Transit
Mystery at the Station Hotel
Murder on the Great Northern Railway
Inspector Colbeck's Casebook

The Home Front Detective series
A Bespoke Murder • Instrument of Slaughter
Five Dead Canaries • Deeds of Darkness
Dance of Death • The Enemy Within
Under Attack • The Unseen Hand • Orders to Kill
Danger of Defeat • Spring Offensive

The Merlin Richards series
Murder at the Arizona Biltmore • Homicide in Chicago

The Ocean Liner Mysteries

Murder on the Lusitania • Murder on the Mauretania
Murder on the Minnesota • Murder on the Caronia
Murder on the Marmora • Murder on the Salsette
Murder on the Oceanic • Murder on the Celtic

The Domesday series

The Wolves of Savernake • The Ravens of Blackwater
The Dragons of Archenfield • The Lions of the North
The Serpents of Harbledown • The Stallions of Woodstock
The Hawks of Delamere • The Wildcats of Exeter
The Foxes of Warwick • The Owls of Gloucester
The Elephants of Norwich

The Restoration series

The King's Evil • The Amorous Nightingale • The Repentant Rake
The Frost Fair • The Parliament House • The Painted Lady

The Bracewell mysteries

The Queen's Head • The Merry Devils
The Trip to Jerusalem • The Nine Giants
The Mad Courtesan • The Silent Woman
The Roaring Boy • The Laughing Hangman
The Fair Maid of Bohemia • The Wanton Angel
The Devil's Apprentice • The Bawdy Basket
The Vagabond Clown • The Counterfeit Crank
The Malevolent Comedy • The Princess of Denmark

The Bow Street Rivals series

Shadow of the Hangman • Steps to the Gallows
Date with the Executioner • Fugitive from the Grave
Rage of the Assassin

Allison & Busby Limited
11 Wardour Mews
London W1F 8AN
allisonandbusby.com

First published in Great Britain by Allison & Busby in 2025.

Copyright © 2025 by Edward Marston

The moral right of the author is hereby asserted in accordance with the Copyright, Designs and Patents Act 1988.

*All characters and events in this publication,
other than those clearly in the public domain,
are fictitious and any resemblance to actual persons,
living or dead, is purely coincidental.*

All rights reserved. No part of this publication may be reproduced, stored in a retrieval system, or transmitted, in any form or by any means without the prior written permission of the publisher, nor be otherwise circulated in any form of binding or cover other than that in which it is published and without a similar condition being imposed on the subsequent buyer.

A CIP catalogue record for this book is available from the British Library.

First Edition

ISBN 978-0-7490-3222-7

Typeset in 11/16.5 pt Adobe Garamond Pro by Allison and Busby Ltd.

By choosing this product, you help take care of the world's forests. Learn more: www.fsc.org.

Printed and bound in Great Britain by Clays Ltd. Elcograf S.p.A

EU GPSR Authorised Representative
LOGOS EUROPE, 9 rue Nicolas Poussin, 17000, LA ROCHELLE, France
E-mail: Contact@logoseurope.eu

MURDER ON THE GREAT NORTHERN RAILWAY

Edward Marston

CHAPTER ONE

London, 1867

The hordes surging into King's Cross station were too eager to catch their trains that morning to remember that the terminus was built on the site of a smallpox and fever hospital. Desperate to get somewhere, they were in the grip of a fever of their own. The noise was deafening, the anxiety intense, the smell powerful and the jostling universal. Porters were everywhere, conducting passengers to their compartments, putting their luggage inside or, if it was too bulky, passing it up to colleagues on the roof of the carriages to be carefully stacked. Pandemonium was a daily event on the Great Northern Railway.

One porter was wheeling a large, wooden box on his trolley. It was covered in a series of thick ropes. The tall, well-dressed, broad-shouldered man who walked beside the box kept looking around to make sure that they were not being followed. When they reached the guard's van, he handed a document to the guard. As soon as he had read it, the latter stood back so that the porter could help the man lift the box aboard and stow it in a corner.

'It will be safe and sound there,' promised the guard.

'I'm travelling with it,' insisted the man.

'You'd be more comfortable in a compartment, sir.'

'It will never be out of my sight,' declared the other. 'I'm paid to watch it every inch of the way and that's what I intend to do.' Putting a hand into his pocket, he brought out some coins to tip the porter. 'Thank you.'

'God bless you, sir,' said the latter, moving away.

'Well,' said the guard, sizing the passenger up, 'if we're travelling together, I ought to know your name. I'm Tom Coveney, by the way.'

'I'd rather travel in silence,' insisted the passenger. 'You've got your job to do, and I've got mine.' He sat down in the van. 'Let me get on with it.'

The guard shrugged. 'Please yourself.'

Spring sunshine greeted the train as it emerged from the station and headed north, belching smoke and gathering speed as it did so. Locked in the guard's van, Coveney found his companion strangely uncommunicative. The man said nothing about the wooden box with which he was travelling or why he kept glancing protectively at it. In the end, the guard abandoned his attempt at starting a conversation and sat there in silence. Whenever the train stopped at a station, Coveney got out on the platform. As some passengers alighted, they were quickly replaced by new ones and another stage of the journey began. It was at Peterborough that the sequence was finally broken. No sooner had the train juddered to a halt than there was an explosion not far from the engine itself, a thunderous bang that caused panic among those on the platform. The guard leapt out of his van to investigate, trying to pick his way through the crowd of hysterical passengers who had either left the train or were struggling to board it.

His place in the guard's van was quickly taken. A man in rough clothing, and with a hat pulled down over his face, suddenly burst in and pointed a gun at its sole occupant. Jumping to his feet, the passenger reached for his own weapon, but he was far too slow. Before his hand could even touch his gun, he was hit in the chest by a searing bullet and collapsed in a heap. Putting his weapon back in its holster, the killer dragged the wooden box to the door and flung it open. He grabbed hold of the ropes and lifted the box before swinging it into the hands of a waiting companion, a sturdy man who carried the heavy load with relative ease. As panic continued to rage on the platform, the two of them disappeared through the nearest exit where a horse and cart awaited them. After the box was lifted onto the cart, the men jumped on after it and the driver snapped the reins.

The horse set off at a steady trot, leaving behind a scene of utter confusion and a dead body in the guard's van. The killer and his accomplice roared with laughter. Their plan had worked perfectly.

CHAPTER TWO

When he returned to Scotland Yard that morning, Robert Colbeck found a summons from Superintendent Tallis awaiting him. He walked swiftly to his superior's office with a quiet smile on his face. Anticipating praise for the way that he had brought his latest case to a satisfactory conclusion, he was looking forward to basking in his superior's approval. When he knocked on Tallis's door then opened it to enter the office, however, he could see that the superintendent was in no mood to congratulate him. The older man's face was puckered with concern. Evidently, something very serious had happened.

'You sent for me, sir,' said Colbeck.

'I want you and Sergeant Leeming to go to Lincoln at once,' snapped the other, reaching for a telegraph. 'Read this.'

'Who sent it?' asked Colbeck, taking the telegraph from him.

'Someone called Alexander Courtney.'

'He's the Dean of Lincoln Cathedral.'

Tallis was surprised. 'How on earth do you know that?'

'I remember reading of his appointment, sir.' He studied the telegraph. 'Why is he sending a message to us?'

'Something of great value has been stolen from a train that stopped at Peterborough on its way to Lincoln. As you can see, the man guarding the item was shot dead. We are asked to send you immediately.'

'Sergeant Leeming and I will be on the next train there, sir,' said Colbeck, handing the telegraph back. 'There's an understandable note of outrage in the summons.'

'What could the killer have stolen?'

'Let's not waste time on speculation. When we reach Lincoln, I'll send you full details as soon as possible.'

'Make sure that you do that.'

'I'll send a reply to the Dean from the telegraph station at King's Cross. I'll give him some much-needed reassurance. Please excuse me, sir. We need to be on our way.'

And before Tallis was able to speak, Colbeck left the office at speed. There was no time to waste. A new and intriguing assignment beckoned.

In Lincoln itself, Alexander Courtney was locked in conversation with Bishop John Jackson, a slim, grey-haired man in his mid-fifties who was still shocked by the crime. Dean Courtney, by contrast, was a solid individual with heavy jowls and an air of spirituality. He was quick to defend his action.

'It was important to move swiftly, Bishop,' he explained.

'But why involve Scotland Yard?' asked the other. 'The murder and theft occurred in Cambridgeshire. Is this not a case to hand to their constabulary? And surely the railway police in Peterborough station itself would wish to be involved. The crimes occurred right on their doorstep.'

'I wanted the best man and that is unquestionably Inspector Colbeck.'

'His name is unfamiliar to me.'

'He has been featured in national newspapers many times. Since he has had so many successes linked to the railway system, he is known as the Railway Detective.'

'Will such a remarkable person be available to us?'

'Even as we speak,' said Courtney, 'he is on his way here. Ten minutes ago, we received a telegraph from him, confirming the fact. Take heart. Colbeck is coming.'

'How do we break the terrible news to Gregory Tomkins?' asked the Bishop, hoarse with anxiety.

'Hopefully, we may not need to.'

'Crimes of such magnitude will certainly be reported in the press. He is bound to become aware of the fate of his masterpiece.'

'Tomkins leads a life of almost monastic dedication. I doubt if he even reads a daily newspaper. He only needs to know the full details of what happened when the villains have been arrested and condemned to death.'

'You seem very confident that they will be caught.'

'Were I a betting man – which I am not – I'd place a large wager on Colbeck. His record of success is amazing. That's why I sent that telegraph. Don't forget,' said the Dean, 'that I was on that train in Peterborough station when the explosion went off. Like everyone else, I was confused and frightened. It was only when I left my compartment and went to check on Langston that

I realised what had happened. The explosion had been set off to divert everyone's attention. When I got to the guard's van, I saw that Michael Langston had been shot dead and that the precious gift he was bringing to us had been stolen.'

'We must get it back!' insisted Bishop Jackson.

'Colbeck will find it somehow. Do as I do and place your hopes in him.'

'I find it difficult to do so. We can't rely on a detective from London. What we require is someone who can perform miracles.'

The Dean was confident. 'Such a man will be here in due course.'

Victor Leeming was no friend of railways. He resented the fact that he and Colbeck were regularly despatched to solve crimes in faraway places. It meant long, tedious journeys in noisy trains that rocked along so fiercely that he was unable to sleep. What made his suffering worse was that his companion, Robert Colbeck, was so supremely at ease when being hurled along in the compartment of a train. Because they were not alone, conversation about the case was impossible. All that Leeming could do was to examine the few facts that they had and wonder how long it would be before he was able to return to his family in London.

'Take heart, Victor,' whispered Colbeck. 'We'll be there in half an hour.'

Leeming sat up hopefully. 'In Lincoln?'

'No, in Peterborough. That's where the crimes occurred. We'll get off there so that we can find out full details.'

'Will this train wait for us?'

Colbeck shook his head. 'I'm afraid not. We'll have to catch the next one.'

Leeming rolled his eyes in despair.

* * *

When the train came to a halt in Peterborough station, the detectives were among the first passengers to alight. Seeing the stationmaster outside his office, they hurried across to him. Leeming put his valise down and took out his notebook in readiness. Colbeck explained who they were and why they needed a description of what had happened at the station earlier. Nathan Powell was delighted to help. He was a short, tubby, middle-aged man with a beard covering the lower half of his face. Powell was clearly distressed.

'Nothing like this has ever happened to us,' he moaned. 'My staff are known for their efficiency. Passengers always feel safe and well looked after here.'

'Where exactly was this explosion?' asked Colbeck.

'It was in a storeroom at the far end,' said Powell, pointing a finger. 'How anyone got inside it is a mystery. It's always kept locked and there's a railway policeman standing outside it.'

'Was he injured in the blast?'

'Yes, Inspector, and so were several passengers. It was bedlam here.'

'I daresay that everyone's attention was focussed on the blaze,' said Colbeck.

'I forced my way through the crowd to get there and joined my porters in throwing buckets of water over the flames. Passengers were screaming and struggling to move away from the fire. Most of them simply fled.'

'Did you hear a gun being fired?'

'No, Inspector. The roar of the fire blocked out everything else.'

The stationmaster was still deeply upset about the incident and tears came into his eyes at one point. He dabbed at them with a handkerchief, then continued his report. Leeming scribbled madly in his notebook. Seeing that the train was now ready to depart, Powell moved away so that he could despatch it before returning to continue his narrative. It was long and detailed. When the stationmaster's account finally ended, the sergeant had a question for him.

'How did the killer know where to find what he was after?'

'I don't follow.'

'Well, the item of luggage he was after could have been anywhere on the train. How did he find it so easily?'

'There's an obvious answer to that,' suggested Colbeck. 'Someone saw the man getting into the guard's van with it at King's Cross. He sent that information to the telegraph station here.' He turned to Powell. 'Do you have a reliable man on duty there?'

'Ralph Bickerton is very reliable,' said the stationmaster.

'Does he have a good memory?'

'He never forgets a thing, Inspector.'

'Then let's meet him,' said Colbeck.

The stationmaster led them to the telegraph station and introduced the person in charge of it. Bickerton was a stringy man in his fifties with a bald head and eyelids that fluttered like the wings of a butterfly. He was duly impressed to hear that Scotland Yard detectives were involved in the case.

'Have you been busy today?' asked Colbeck.

'I'm always busy, Inspector. I've despatched and received messages all morning.'

'Do you always read them in full?'

'Of course I do. It's part of my job.'

'I believe that a telegraph may have been sent today from King's Cross station.'

'There was more than one,' said Bickerton. 'Passengers travelling here wanted to let relatives or friends know when they were likely to arrive.'

'Did you have any unusual telegraphs?'

'Yes, I did, Inspector. One was very unusual.'

'What do you mean?'

'It was so short – only two words.'

'What were they?'

'"Guard's van".'

'To whom was the telegraph sent?'

'It was to a big, ugly man named Percy Gull. He came to the station early and kept popping in to see if there was a message for him. When his telegraph did arrive, he grinned and went straight out of here.'

'Thank you, Mr Bickerton,' said Colbeck. 'You've solved a problem for us. We need another favour. Please describe this individual to Sergeant Leeming. Every detail is vital to us. Forget about the name Percy Gull. It's clearly a false one to hide his identity. What first struck you about this man?'

'The smell,' replied Bickerton.

'What smell?' asked Leeming, notebook in hand.

'He stank to high heaven.'

'There you are,' said Colbeck with a smile. 'We've picked up his scent already.'

CHAPTER THREE

Bishop Jackson was in his office, staring in disbelief at a letter he had been given. There was a tap on the door, then it opened to admit the Dean. The newcomer saw the dismay in the other man's face.

'Has something happened?' he asked.

'No,' replied the other, 'something has not happened.'

'I don't follow.'

'Knowing the train that the detectives from London had caught, I sent Canon Smale to the station to welcome them. He waited in vain.' He waved the letter. 'This tells me that the train in question arrived on time but that there was no sign of Inspector Colbeck and Sergeant Leeming.'

'There must be some mistake,' said Courtney worriedly.

'I agree. It seems that you were the one to make it. In boasting about Inspector Colbeck's rare qualities, you raised my hopes. This missive has dashed them. They were not on the train promised. So much for your faith in Colbeck!'

'I refuse to believe that he let us down.'

'Then where is the man?'

'There has to be an explanation,' said the Dean, clearly ruffled. 'Everything I've heard about Inspector Colbeck suggests that he's a man of his word.'

'Then why have us waiting for the wrong train?'

'All will be explained in due course, Bishop.'

'I'm sure that it will,' agreed the other, tone changing, 'and I apologise for being a trifle tetchy. I've no doubt that the inspector had an extremely good reason for changing trains. It may well be that he alighted at Peterborough so that he could gather full details of what happened there earlier today.' He gave a smile of apology. 'Forgive me. I was wrong to blame Inspector Colbeck for being late when he was, in fact, only being thorough.'

Courtney nodded gratefully. 'It's the obvious explanation.'

'Let's move on to an important decision,' said Bishop Jackson. 'As we both know only too well, the Horse Fair is due to open here in a couple of days. The world and his wife will descend on Lincoln. Crowds have already started moving in.'

'I'm told that every hotel and inn in the city is fully booked.'

'I think that we can offer our visitors from Scotland Yard better accommodation than they would find in a hostelry. After all, they're here to solve a terrible crime, not to buy themselves a horse.'

Courtney was decisive. 'I'll meet the next train from London in person,' he said. 'I'm confident that Inspector Colbeck and Sergeant Leeming will be on it. They deserve a proper welcome from me.'

* * *

After what seemed like an age, they got their first glimpse of Lincoln Cathedral. As they peered through the window in their compartment, it suddenly appeared at the top of an escarpment, gazing down on the city below. Its sheer size and air of majesty took Leeming's breath away. Caught in the bright sunshine, it was absolutely dazzling.

'It looks even bigger than York Minster,' he said, mouth agape.

'William Cobbett described it as the finest building in the whole world.'

'Who was he?'

'Cobbett was a remarkable man who published *Rural Rides*, an account of his travels to various parts of the kingdom. He was very forthright in his opinions.'

'I agree with him,' said Leeming, heaving a sigh as the cathedral suddenly vanished. 'I'd love to see it properly.'

'Oh, you will,' said Colbeck. 'I can promise you that.'

The train was slowing now, bringing other things of interest into view. There was a flurry of activity in the streets. People and horses were everywhere. The market was teeming with customers. When the train finally came to a halt, the detectives were the first to get out onto the platform. They made their way towards the main exit. Colbeck was tall enough to see over the heads of the crowd. His height made him stand out from the herd. Greatly relieved, the Right Reverend Alexander Courtney spotted him and started to make his way towards him. When he eventually confronted Colbeck, the Dean's manner was effusive.

'Thank heavens you've come, Inspector!' he said, offering his hand. 'You're the answer to a prayer.'

'We responded at once to your summons, Dean,' explained Colbeck, identifying him by his apparel. 'We broke our journey at Peterborough so that we could gather full details of the crimes that occurred there.'

'I should have realised that that was what you would do.' Turning to Leeming, the Dean gave him a warm handshake. 'You are also welcome, Sergeant Leeming. The very sight of both of you lifts my spirits.'

'Two crimes were committed at Peterborough,' said Leeming. 'We know about the murder but have no idea what was stolen by the killer.'

'Lincoln Cathedral,' explained Courtney.

Leeming was startled. 'But we've just seen it through the window of our compartment. Nobody could steal anything as big as that.'

'You misunderstand me. I travelled to London with a private detective to receive an extraordinary gift. It was a large model of the cathedral, donated to us by a brilliant silversmith who was born in Lincoln and for whom the task was a labour of love.'

'It was also an act of great generosity,' observed Colbeck.

'Tomkins wanted to create the miniature cathedral before his skill began to fade.'

'Would that be Gregory Tomkins, by any chance?'

Courtney was surprised. 'You've heard of him?'

'His reputation goes before him. I've seen his work on display in the windows of a shop owned by Peat, Hatherly and Tomkins. It's quite brilliant.'

'Tomkins began his career here in Lincoln, but his fame reached the capital, and he was lured there by the promise of financial gain. He was made a partner in a respected business – but he never forgot his birthplace.'

'Tell us about this private detective,' said Colbeck.

'His name was Michael Langston, and he was highly recommended. We went to London together last night and were shown the silversmith's masterpiece before it was placed into a wooden box with a large amount of padding to protect it. Early this morning,' said the Dean, 'we caught the train back to Lincoln. Langston, who was armed, travelled with the box in the guard's van.'

'That information was sent to the telegraph station at Peterborough. We have proof of that. The killer knew exactly where to strike, taking advantage of the panic caused by an explosion in a storeroom. Everything seemed to have been planned with military precision.'

'Why would someone want to steal the silver cathedral?' wailed the Dean. 'It would have no intrinsic value to the killer. It goes without saying that the man who shot Langston dead has no acquaintance whatsoever with Christian values.'

'What he does have,' noted Leeming, 'is a source of wealth.'

'News of the theft will be in newspapers throughout the country. It will cause enormous shock and regret. Who would dare to buy such an item?'

'You would,' argued Colbeck. 'The killer and his associates intend to sell it to you.'

Courtney was shocked. 'But it came to us with no price tag. Gregory Tomkins was left a huge amount of money in the will of a rich uncle. He wanted us to share in his good fortune. That was how he was able to offer his masterpiece to us as a gift.'

'It's suddenly acquired a high value. Be warned.'

'We'd never dream of paying for it, Inspector.'

'Then you will have no chance of getting it back. You will have to deal with the thieves to bring them out into the open. It's the only way they will be arrested and made to pay for their crimes.'

Disappointed, the Dean sagged. 'I never thought of that.'

'What happened to the body of the private detective?'

'It's being held in Peterborough. It will be transferred to Lincoln so that his family can arrange a funeral. They will be devastated by news of his murder. But let me take you away from this maelstrom,' he went on, indicating the exit. 'There is a carriage waiting for us.'

'Excellent,' said Colbeck, walking beside him.

'Bishop Jackson is dying to meet you. I explained to him that you had a rare talent for solving crimes committed on the railway.'

'We've never searched for a silver cathedral before,' muttered Leeming. 'This could be our biggest test yet.'

When she arrived at the house, Lydia Quayle was given a warm welcome by Madeleine Colbeck and taken into the drawing room. The visitor studied her friend.

'You look disappointed,' she said.

'It's not because of your arrival, Lydia. That's always a pleasure. It's the fact that Robert has been sent all the way to Lincoln on what sounds like a very complex case.'

'Oh dear! It's such a long way to go.'

'His letter contained the briefest of details. A man was shot dead on the train going there and something that he was guarding was stolen.'

'How dreadful!' exclaimed Lydia.

'It's going to be a long and difficult investigation.'

'That means that Alan may be called upon again.'

Madeleine smiled. 'Yes, there's a good chance that Detective Constable Hinton will indeed be asked to help them. Robert has the highest regard for him – and so, of course, do you.'

'Don't you dare start teasing me again,' warned Lydia, wagging a finger. 'Alan and I are just . . . good friends.'

'He dotes on you, Lydia.'

'I wish that he did but work always comes first. He's desperate to gain promotion and can only spare limited time for me.'

'You're always at the forefront of his mind.'

'I hope not, Madeleine. Thinking about me would be a terrible distraction. In a murder investigation, especially, he must concentrate on the matter in hand. I accept that in the same way that you do.'

'It's something that I accepted when I married Robert. He's a wonderful husband but we only spend time together between the various cases assigned to him. He never seems to lead an investigation here in London. Superintendent Tallis always chooses to send him far and wide.'

'Yet you never seem to be lonely,' said her friend.

'I've no time for it, Lydia. As well as being a wife, I'm a mother and a daughter. That means I have a delightful child to look after and a father who is here whenever he can be to play with her.'

'How is Mr Andrews?'

'Actually,' said Madeleine, sadly, 'he's not in the best of health. He says that it's just a cold and he's afraid to give it to Helena Rose by coming here.'

'People rarely have a cold at this time of year,' argued Lydia.

'Then he's the exception that proves the rule.'

'His granddaughter must miss him dreadfully.'

'She asks for him every day. He's such an important person in her life.'

'And in yours, Madeleine.'

'Yes, of course. My father has his weaknesses, but we love

him just the same. I just wish that he wouldn't speak out of turn sometimes.'

'What do you mean?'

'Well, he does blurt things out sometimes. Last week, for instance, he suddenly asked me why you and Alan are not married yet.'

'We're not friends in that way,' said Lydia, trying to hide her embarrassment behind a laugh. 'Besides it's none of your father's business.'

'That won't stop him offering his opinion.'

'Let's change the subject, shall we?'

Yes, of course,' said Madeleine. 'It was wrong of me to tell you what he said, and I apologise.' She tugged a bell-pull to summon a maidservant. 'Time for a cup of tea, I think.'

'Oh. Yes, please!'

'I thought we'd take Helena Rose to the park this afternoon.'

'That would be lovely!'

'You are her favourite aunt, after all.'

When they met Bishop Jackson at the cathedral, the visitors were struck by his dismay at the dreadful crime that had occurred. His face was a study in grief. For his part, the Bishop was taken aback by Colbeck's educated voice and elegant appearance. He was less impressed by Leeming, whom he found a trifle coarse and decidedly rumpled. They were in the Bishop's private apartment at the cathedral. He gave them a grateful welcome.

'Thank God you've arrived, Inspector,' he said. 'The Dean has been telling me about the extraordinary reputation you have amassed over the years.'

'It pales beside your own reputation,' said Colbeck.

Jackson was modest. 'Oh, I think not.'

'Your achievements here have been remarkable. You welded together the counties of Nottinghamshire and Lincoln, stimulated the educational work of the diocese and raised the tone of the clergy. They are no mean achievements.'

'Indeed, they are not,' added the Dean, standing beside him.

'Let's concentrate on this heinous crime, shall we?' suggested the Bishop. 'Is there any hope of reclaiming the miniature cathedral and arresting those responsible for stealing it?'

'There's every hope,' Colbeck assured him. 'Remarkable as this gift appears to be, however, it's the murder of Michael Langston that must take priority. Only a brave man would have taken on such a dangerous assignment.'

'I agree,' said the Dean. 'Langston was fearless.'

'But how did anyone know that the silver cathedral was being brought here?' asked the Bishop. 'We did our best to keep everything secret.'

'How many people here were aware of what was happening?' asked Leeming.

'A mere handful of us.'

'And they were all sworn to secrecy,' said the Dean.

'That means details of its transfer here may have been leaked, by accident, in London,' said Colbeck. 'We will investigate both possible sources. Somebody found out when the gift was being brought here and it cost Michael Langston his life.'

'I need to speak to his wife and family in person,' said the Dean. 'You might care to accompany me, Inspector.'

'I'd be glad to do so,' said Colbeck. 'But let me first tell you both what we learnt from our conversation with the stationmaster at Peterborough. Sergeant Leeming took detailed notes from him.

The first thing you must know is that we are up against a cunning enemy. My guess is that the gang is probably four in number at least – one in London to send details by means of telegraph of where exactly on the train the cargo was being kept, one who started the fire at Peterborough station, the man who killed the guard and the accomplice who helped to carry the heavy box out of the guard's van.'

'Which one shot Michael Langston?' asked the Dean.

'We will find out in due course.'

'What about your theory that the gang will offer to sell it to us?'

'It's not a theory,' argued Colbeck. 'As it is, the miniature cathedral is of no use to these men. They hardly stole it to marvel at its appearance. It is a source of money to them. I suggest that you brace yourself for their demand.'

'It pains me that we will have to deal with heartless criminals,' said the Bishop.

'My sympathy is with the man who created that work of art. It must have taken ages to make it,' said Colbeck. 'How is Gregory Tomkins going to react when he hears about the theft of his masterpiece?'

The Dean sighed. 'The poor fellow is going to be horrified.'

Seven decades had taken their toll on the silversmith. The former young apprentice with boundless energy and patience had now turned into an old man plagued with ailments and whose shoulders were permanently hunched. Long white hair framed a face that was comprehensively lined. Gregory Tomkins was too tired to work a full day any more so confined his time at the shop to afternoons. When the cab dropped him off there, he raised his hat in thanks, then paid the driver before shuffling into the shop. He was welcomed by everyone working there and waved a hand in greeting. Oliver Peat, one of his partners, a short, sleek, anxious man, took him aside to whisper a warning.

'You have a visitor, Gregory,' he said. 'He's waiting in your office.'

'Is he a potential customer?' asked Tomkins, eyes kindling.

'I fear not. His name is Superintendent Tallis, and he's come from Scotland Yard to have a private word with you.'

'What about?'

'He will tell you.'

'I'm not in trouble with the police, am I, Oliver?'

Peat smiled. 'I hardly think so. You're the most law-abiding man in London.'

'Then why is he bothering me?'

'Go and find out,' advised his partner. 'He's been waiting for some time.'

'It's not illegal to be old is, is it?' asked Tomkins. 'If it is, I must plead guilty. I'm starting to feel the pangs of senility.'

'Nonsense! You have the gift of eternal youth.'

'Tell that to my dear wife!'

With a loud cackle, Tomkins went to the rear of the shop and let himself into his office. It was also his place of work and examples of his craft were everywhere. A drawing of his version in silver of Lincoln Cathedral was on the table. Edward Tallis was fascinated by its intricate detail. As the old man entered the room, the superintendent turned to him.

'You are a genius, Mr Tomkins,' he said. 'Mr Peat was right to call you a brilliant craftsman.'

'I was at one time,' agreed the silversmith, 'but the years have played havoc with my fingers and, worst of all, with my eyesight. I can only work for short, intense periods before my sight weakens. When that happens, I'm peering through a dense fog.'

'I'm sorry to hear that. As Mr Peat will have mentioned, I need to tell you something of significance. Before I do so,' warned Tallis, 'you might care to sit down.'

The silversmith quivered. 'Why? Is it bad news?'

'The worst kind, I fear.'

'Oh dear!'

'I'm afraid that it's very distressing.'

Tomkins sagged and Tallis had to reach out to support him. He eased the old man onto a chair. Before speaking, the superintendent took a deep breath.

'There is no easy way to tell you this,' he began. 'Having admired your drawing of Lincoln Cathedral, I can see how much detail you've included. The result is magnificent. Your version in silver is a triumph.'

'It went off to Lincoln early this morning, Superintendent.'

'I'm all too aware of that. Sadly, it did not reach its destination.'

'What do you mean?' asked Tomkins in alarm. 'The Dean himself came to accept it from me. He brought a private detective with him – a Michael Langston – who promised to safeguard my gift. He vowed to sleep with it last night.'

'Langston did his best to take care of it, sir.'

'What's happened? And why are you here? For Heaven's sake, man,' he went on, rising to his feet, 'tell me the truth. Is my cathedral in safe hands?'

'I'm sorry to tell you that it is not. Your masterpiece was stolen from the train at Peterborough station and Langston was shot dead in the process.'

'My God!' exclaimed Tomkins.

Unable to cope with the terrible news, the silversmith began to sway on his feet and emit a sound like the cry of a wounded animal. By moving quickly, Tallis was able to catch him as the old man lost consciousness and began to fall to the floor.

CHAPTER FOUR

Before she could go off to the park with the others, Madeleine Colbeck was diverted by news that caused a sudden change of plan. One of her father's neighbours, Kathleen Dyer, an elderly woman who used a walking stick, had made the long journey across London to inform her that Madeleine's father was ill.

'It's very good of you to tell me, Mrs Dyer,' said Madeleine, 'but I'm already aware that he has a bad cold.'

'It's worse than that now.'

'Worse?'

'As you know, we live next door to Caleb. We didn't get a wink of sleep last night because we could hear him coughing on the other side of the bedroom wall. It was a dreadful sound. When I spoke to him this morning, he looked so poorly. I told him he needed to see a doctor, but he said there was no call for that – but there was. My husband and I felt you ought to know. That's why I came here by cab to warn you.'

'Then I'll gladly repay the fare,' decided Madeleine, 'and I'll travel back with you in another cab. I hadn't realised how ill he was.'

'Caleb is a good neighbour to us. Coming here was the least I could do for him.'

'I'm very grateful, Mrs Dyer. It's obviously an emergency.'

'Oh, it is,' sighed the old woman. 'He sounded so bad in the night that I was surprised to see him still alive in the morning. I've worried about Caleb all morning. That's why I simply had to come.'

Michael Langston and his family lived in a house in the suburbs of Lincoln. When the cab stopped outside it, Dean Courtney paid the driver, then walked to the front door with Colbeck. After ringing the bell, the Dean turned to his companion.

'Leave most of the talking to me,' he suggested.

'I'll be happy to do so,' replied Colbeck.

'I've met the family before. They were delighted that Langston had been recruited for such an important task. It was a real feather in his cap.' The door was opened by a maidservant. 'Is Mrs Langston at home?'

'Yes,' said the woman. 'She and her father are in the drawing room.'

As they entered the house, both men removed their hats. After tapping on a door, the servant opened it to usher them into the room.

'You have visitors,' she explained.

Sarah Langston was on her feet at once, her face shining with hope. She was a startlingly pretty woman in her thirties. As soon as she saw the Dean, however, she was overcome by a sense of dread. Colbeck saw the look of fear in her eyes. The other person in the room was her father, a tall, slim, watchful man in his sixties, who got up to stand beside her.

'Good day to you, Dean Courtney!' he said. 'I'm hoping that you bring good news about Michael with you.'

'Alas, I do not, sir.' He indicated his companion. 'This is Detective Inspector Colbeck from Scotland Yard. We are very lucky to have his services.'

'Where is Michael?' asked Sarah. 'He should be home by now.'

'I'm afraid that your husband will not be returning, Mrs Langston,' said Colbeck softly. 'Earlier today, there was an unfortunate incident in Peterborough station. Your brave husband was shot dead.'

'Dead?' she cried, stepping back in horror.

'It's my sad duty to tell you that he died while performing an important service to the cathedral. He will always be remembered for that.'

But she was no longer listening. Eyes darting and body trembling, she was stunned by the enormity of the news. Her face crumpled. As she fainted, her father managed to catch her. Colbeck's sympathy for her welled up inside him. The woman was in despair. It made him even more determined to find and arrest the person who had killed her husband.

When the cab arrived outside her old house, Madeleine asked the driver to wait for her. After helping Kathleen Dyer out of the vehicle, she thanked her once more. The old woman let herself into her own home. Madeleine knocked on the front door of her father's house. There was no response. When she knocked louder, there was still no sound from within. Suddenly alarmed, she took a key from her reticule and used it to open the door before stepping into her former home. There was no sign of her father.

'Father!' cried Madeleine, running upstairs. 'Where are you?'

When she opened the door of his bedroom, she had the answer. Caleb Andrews was lying on the floor, wrapped up in a blanket. He did not appear to be breathing. When she knelt beside him in a complete panic, he opened a bleary eye.

'Hello, Maddy,' he said, 'I was just dreaming about you.'

During their time as detectives, Colbeck and Leeming had slept in all manner of places, but they had never enjoyed the luxury afforded by Riseholme Hall before. Built in the previous century, it was the official residence of the Bishop of Lincoln and was situated in a park in West Lindsey. Seen from the outside, it was stunning. Leeming gaped at it.

'We're going to stay there?' he said in disbelief.

Colbeck nodded. 'So it appears.'

'I thought they'd put us up in the heart of the city.'

'You're forgetting that the Horse Fair is happening very soon. That means the place will be packed with crowds. Everywhere will be fully occupied. We, on the other hand, will have bedrooms of our own and a country setting to admire when we look out of the window.'

'It's breathtaking,' said Leeming, gazing from the carriage in which they were travelling. 'Wait until we tell the superintendent about this. He'll be green with envy.'

'We're here to solve serious crimes,' Colbeck reminded him, 'not to enjoy a holiday. The murder of Michael Langston is our major concern. Watching the reaction of his poor wife to her husband's death was very painful. The sooner we identify and catch the killer, the sooner we bring her some comfort.'

'What about the silver cathedral?'

'If we find the men responsible for stealing it, we'll be praised by Bishop Jackson and thanked by the Great Northern Railway.'

'How much will the villains demand?'

'Far too much, I daresay. I've advised the Dean to draw out the process of haggling with them. It will give us the time to identify who they are.'

'At the moment, we don't have a clue.'

'Yes, we do, Victor. We suspect that these men may well have been in the army and that one of them gives off a nasty smell.'

'Well, there's no chance whatsoever of finding him when the Horse Fair is on,' warned Leeming.

'Why do you say that?'

'There'll be mountains of horse dung everywhere. The whole of Lincoln will stink like mad.'

Gregory Tomkins was slumped in a chair in his office. Edward Tallis and Oliver Peat stood beside the chair, gazing down at him with mingled fear and concern. The old man seemed to be close to his death.

'I feel dreadful at having to be the bearer of bad news,' admitted Tallis.

'Don't blame yourself, Superintendent,' said Peat. 'It was right for Gregory to know the truth as soon as possible. He strained every sinew to complete that silver cathedral. It gave him so much joy to create it. That joy has now turned to misery.'

'He will revive when the thieves are captured, and his masterpiece is in the hands of the people for whom it was intended.'

'How certain can you be that the silver cathedral can be found?'

'My best detectives are assigned to the case, Mr Peat,' said the superintendent. 'If anyone can catch the villains and reclaim your partner's masterpiece, it is Inspector Colbeck and Sergeant Leeming.'

'I am heartened by your confidence, Superintendent,' said Peat, 'but my fear is this. Will Gregory still be alive to rejoice in their capture?' He checked his pocket-watch. 'Where is that doctor? I sent for him half an hour ago.'

'Your colleague is still alive. The bad news was a terrible blow, and it will take him time to get used to it.'

'He was as distressed at the news of Langston's murder as he was at the fate of his model of Lincoln Cathedral. I was here when he met the private detective yesterday evening. Michael Langston impressed him and said that he felt it was an honour to deliver the gift to Gregory's birthplace.'

'How did news of the transfer get into the hands of criminals?'

'There was no leak at this end,' insisted Peat. 'Complete secrecy was maintained at every stage. Our staff is highly trained, I assure you. If there has been a leak of some sort, it must have happened in Lincoln itself.'

'If that is the case, Inspector Colbeck will find its origin.'

'Can you be certain that the miniature cathedral will be found?'

Tallis was positive. 'I give you my word, Mr Peat.' He glanced at the silversmith. 'What I can't promise is that the man who created it will live to celebrate its recovery.'

* * *

One glance at her father told Madeleine Colbeck that he was unwell. His face was a ghastly white and his body seemed to have shrunk. It was a lovely sunny day yet he was shivering with cold. She wrapped him up in a blanket, then started to gather his clothing up before putting it into a bag. Caleb Andrews was puzzled.

'What are you doing, Maddy?' he asked.

'You're coming to stay with us,' she told him.

'But this is my home.'

'You need looking after.'

'I don't want to be any trouble.'

'You're not well, Father. Mrs Dyer heard you coughing in the night and feared that you might be dying. She came to the house and told me how bad you were.'

'It was none of her business,' he complained.

'Be grateful to her. She did what any good neighbour would do.'

'I can manage on my own.'

'Oh no, you can't,' she insisted. 'That's why I'm taking you to our house where you'll be kept warm and seen by a doctor. Don't you dare to argue,' she warned as he opened his mouth to protest. 'We have a spare room where you'll be very comfortable.'

'Don't let my lovely granddaughter see me like this, Maddy.'

'I won't, I promise. But you need to be somewhere where we can keep an eye on you. If you stay here, you'll only upset the neighbours by coughing all night. The doctor will give you something to stop that.'

'My throat hurts,' he confessed, 'and I've got this pain in my chest.'

'The sooner I get you out of here, the better,' said Madeleine.

'Now I want you to promise me something. I have a cab waiting outside. While I load things into it, you must stay right here, all wrapped up. Do you understand?'

'I suppose so,' he mumbled.

'I want to hear you promise.'

'Leave me be, Maddy. I'm fine.'

But his body betrayed him. He started to cough uncontrollably and put a hand to his chest. The sheer volume and intensity of the sound frightened his daughter.

'I'll gather up everything we need,' she promised and rushed out of the bedroom.

When they returned to the cathedral, Colbeck and Leeming found that there was someone waiting to see them. He was a beefy man in his fifties whose uniform was a little tight for him. Rushing forward, he pumped their hands by way of welcome.

'I'm so pleased to meet you both,' he said, looking from one to the other. 'I am Richard Beard, the chief constable. I am shocked by the two crimes that have taken place and want you to know that I will do all I can to help you solve them.'

'That's very kind of you,' said Colbeck, 'and music to our ears. Chief constables usually tend to view us as interlopers.'

'Yes,' added Leeming, 'they can't wait to see the back of us.'

'That will not be the case here,' promised Beard. 'Feel free to call on me at any time. I will support you to the hilt.'

'It's an offer we will bear in mind,' said Colbeck. 'Though, given the fact that strangers are flooding into Lincoln, I daresay that your men will be at full stretch. A Horse Fair tends to attract criminals as well as those keen to buy and sell.'

'Wherever there's a crowd,' said Leeming, 'you'll always get pickpockets. As a constable in uniform, I was on duty at race meetings many times. I must have arrested dozens of quick-fingered thieves.'

'My offer stands,' said Beard. 'I have a personal interest in one of the crimes that have taken place. Michael Langston used to be under my command in the Lincoln City Police. He was a first-rate policeman.'

'Why did he leave the force?' asked Colbeck.

'There were two reasons. He hated night duty. It was understandable. Anyone with a wife as lovely as Sarah Langston would be keen to share a bed with her every night. The main reason, however, was that he felt he could make more money as a private detective. And he did,' Beard went on, 'because he had built up such a good reputation. Clients trusted him implicitly. He earnt his money without having to the pound the streets in uniform on a rainy night.' Beard shook his head sadly. 'Losing Michael deprived me of one of my best men.'

'Were you asked by Bishop Jackson to fetch something valuable from a London silversmith?' asked Leeming.

Beard shook his head. 'No, we were not.'

'Did you wish that you had been?'

'Policing this city is a full-time job, Sergeant – especially when there's a Horse Fair in the offing. If I had been approached by the Bishop, I'd have declined the offer. My officers are all needed here.'

'I feel sorry for Mrs Langston,' confessed Colbeck. 'She must wish that her husband had remained in the city force. Had he done so, he'd still be alive and well.'

'That's probably true.'

'I was there when she heard the terrible news of her husband's death. It was as if she'd been hit by a fearful blow. Having witnessed her agony, I'm determined to find the man who shot Michael Langston.'

'Count on my help,' Beard assured him. 'We'll catch him between us.'

Having examined him carefully, Dr Phelps put a tablet into a cup of water and held it to the silversmith's lips. Within minutes, Gregory Tomkins began to feel drowsy. Oliver Peat and Edward Tallis had watched the treatment being administered.

'How long will he sleep?' asked Peat.

'Several hours,' replied the doctor. 'The tablet can't take away the memory of the murder, but it will ease the pain slightly.'

'Do we need to take him home?' said Tallis.

'There's no need,' Peat told him. 'We have a spare bedroom for emergencies here at the shop. I think that the shock Gregory was given qualifies as an emergency. It shook me, I can tell you.'

'I'll leave these tablets with you, Mr Peat,' said the doctor, handing him a small box. 'If he starts to brood on the murder, give him another one in a mug of water. As you can see, their effect is almost immediate.'

'Word needs to be sent to his wife. She must not be left in the dark.'

'Quite so,' said Tallis. 'His absence will distress her.'

'I'll go to Gregory's home myself and explain the situation,' volunteered Peat.

'That's very good of you, sir,' said the doctor. 'It's in his best interests to be kept here for a night. I'll check on him first thing in the morning to see if he has come to terms with the profound shock he suffered.'

'I feel guilty for having passed on news of the murder,' said

Tallis, 'but Tomkins deserved the truth. I hadn't realised that it would have such a powerful effect on him.'

'Working on that cathedral became an obsession for him,' recalled Peat, sadly. 'Gregory worked on it until he dropped. He told me that he wanted it to be a thing of beauty – and that's exactly what it was. Not any more,' he sighed. 'It will now be linked in his mind to the murder of a brave detective who gave his life while trying to protect it.'

'The killer will pay for his crime,' insisted Tallis. 'Mr Tomkins may be able to draw some satisfaction from that.'

'I doubt it, Superintendent. Having worked beside him for some many years, I know Gregory well. He will blame himself for what happened. If he hadn't had the idea of creating Lincoln Cathedral in silver, then Michael Langston would still be alive. How can Gregory ever forgive himself for the man's death?'

Madeleine Colbeck was glad that her daughter had gone off to the park with Nanny Hopkins and Lydia Quayle. It meant that Helena Rose was unaware that her grandfather had moved into the house. Her mother decided that it was far better for her to be kept in ignorance of the old man's condition. By the time that her daughter came back from the park with the others, Caleb Andrews was tucked up in the spare bed. He continued to have occasional bouts of coughing, but the sound did not reach all parts of the house.

When the doctor was sent for, it was some time before he was able to come. Dr Hilliard was a spry gentleman in his sixties with a white beard and a pair of spectacles over which he peered at the patient.

'There's nothing wrong with me,' complained Andrews.

'Then why can I see so many worrying signs?' asked the other. 'Your face is ashen, your eyes bloodshot and your body tense. Mrs Colbeck tells me that you've had a bad cold. If your coughing was loud and long enough to wake the neighbours, there is something seriously wrong, Mr Andrews. Do you understand?'

'I feel much better now.'

'Well, you don't look it. A cold would give you the cough that I heard when I came along the landing but something more serious has infected your lungs. I need to give you a thorough examination,' said the doctor, taking a stethoscope from his bag. 'Let me listen to that chest of yours.'

'There's nothing wrong with my chest,' insisted Andrews, drawing back. 'I've picked up a cold, that's all. Let me have a couple of days in bed and I'll be fine.'

'Don't you want to know what's wrong with you?'

'It's easing all the time.'

'Well, it doesn't sound like it. Your voice is so husky.'

'Just leave me be, Doctor.'

'Your daughter summoned me, and she was right to do so. You've had a hard life, Mr Andrews, and it's taken its toll. Driving a steam engine means that you inhaled coal dust all day for many years. That was bad for you.'

'I got used to it.'

'Let me listen to your chest,' said Dr Hilliard, fixing the stethoscope into his ears. 'That's the best place to start.' As he bent over the patient, he made Andrews flinch. 'Now, now, sir. You must cooperate. I'm here to help you. Don't you wish to get better?'

'Yes, I do,' murmured the other, closing his eyes and bracing himself. 'Do what you need to do. But I still say it's only a cold.'

As the doctor bent over him, Andrews began to cough so loudly that the man pulled back quickly to get out of range. The rasping sound went on for minutes.

Colbeck and Leeming were delighted to have met the chief constable and to find out that he was happy to help them in every way. Richard Beard was unusual in that respect. Most people in his position resented any interference from Scotland Yard because it suggested that their individual forces were incapable of solving a major crime. In a previous case, Colbeck and Leeming had been hampered by the lack of help from the police in Shrewsbury. It was a relief to know that Richard Beard was keen to let his men assist the detectives in any way required.

'It's such a boon to have a chief constable on our side for once,' said Leeming.

'Quite so,' agreed Colbeck, 'but we must remember that his officers will be fully occupied during the Horse Fair. Their ability to assist us will be limited.'

'In other words – we're on our own.'

'We must bear in mind the fact that the crimes took place in Cambridgeshire. The chief constable there might not be so amenable.'

'We can but hope.'

'Let's turn our attention to the suspects,' suggested Colbeck. 'I still think that they might well have been in the army.'

'You reckoned there'd be a gang of four men. One of them, we know, gave off a terrible smell. That's unusual for someone who was once in the army. Soldiers are usually people who wash themselves thoroughly every day.'

'I agree, Victor. That's why I think there's another explanation for the stink.'

'Such as?'

'Perhaps the man works on a farm,' said Colbeck. 'We were told that he had rough clothing and a battered hat. If he'd come to the station from his farm, his boots might have been caked with manure. In the confined space of the telegraph office, he would have given off a powerful stench.'

'Do you think his farm is within easy reach of Peterborough?'

'It's more than likely. That's where the silver cathedral may be hidden.'

'How do you know that?'

'It's because I believe that Percy Gull, as he called himself, was the man who killed Michael Langston and stole the gift from the guard's van. When he was given the information he needed by telegraph, he was delighted. He knew exactly where to strike. We need to find out his real name and where he lives.'

'Searching Lincolnshire is a big enough problem for us,' protested Leeming. 'It's one of the largest counties in the country. Do we have to include Cambridgeshire as well?'

'It may well come to that, I'm afraid. That means we need help.'

'Detective Constable Hinton?'

'When we finish here at the cathedral, we'll walk to the station and send a telegraph to Superintendent Tallis. We need two men at least – Alan Hinton and Eric Boyce. We know that they work well together.'

They were about to move off when Leeming stopped and turned to Colbeck.

'I've just thought of something,' he said. 'If one of the men we're after is a farmer, he'll be very interested in horses. Do you think he might turn up at the Horse Fair?'

'I think there's a very good chance that he might well do so. Let's get down to the railway station to send a telegraph to the superintendent,' said Colbeck, heading for the door. 'He needs to be kept informed of any developments.'

CHAPTER FIVE

As soon as they arrived at Scotland Yard the next morning, Alan Hinton and Eric Boyce were summoned to the superintendent's office. Both men were tall, slim and angular but the resemblance between them ended there. Hinton was a keen, experienced, fearless detective whereas Boyce was a quieter, more thoughtful character. He was happy to let his colleague do most of the talking.

'You sent for us, sir?' asked Hinton.

'Yes, I did,' replied Tallis. 'Whatever cases you're working on, I want you to forget them. You're needed in a murder investigation.'

Hinton's eyes lit up. 'Would that be with Inspector Colbeck?'

'If you'll shut up and listen, I'll tell you. As soon as I finish giving you your orders, I want the both of you on a train to Lincoln. A valuable gift to the cathedral was stolen yesterday and the private detective guarding it was shot dead at Peterborough Railway Station.'

'What was this valuable gift?'

'You'll find out when you get there.'

'Where will we stay?'

'Colbeck will tell you that. When you get to King's Cross, let him know the likely time of your arrival by sending a telegraph to him at Lincoln Railway Station. If you do that, he and Sergeant Leeming will be there to welcome you when you arrive.'

'It's a long way to go,' said Boyce anxiously.

'The distance is irrelevant. We pursue criminals wherever they are. It's a difficult case. That's why the inspector asked for you by name.'

Both men smiled.

'There's no need to take pleasure from the summons. Be warned. It's a dangerous assignment. To that end, I'm issuing the pair of you with weapons.'

'Thank you, sir,' said Hinton.

'You'll be hunting armed men who will fight back. My advice to you is simple. If it comes to a gun battle – shoot first.'

Lydia Quayle was so shocked to hear what had happened the previous day that she returned the following morning to see how Caleb Andrews was faring.

'He's still alive, thank God!' said Madeleine.

'That's a relief,' said Lydia.

'I was terrified by what Mrs Dyer told me yesterday. My father was seriously ill. It was my duty to fetch him.'

'I agree. Was he ready to leave his own home?' asked Lydia.

'No, he wasn't,' said Madeleine. 'I almost forced him to come. He hates relying on anyone else.'

'But you're his daughter.'

'He values his independence, Lydia. Also, he hates doctors. I had to warn Dr Hilliard that he might be awkward.'

'How did the doctor react?'

'He laughed and told me that he's used to awkward patients. After examining my father, Dr Hilliard confided that I'd rescued him just in time. Had he been left on his own, he would have finished up with a far worse condition – something close to pneumonia. Anyway, he gave my father a box of pills and a miracle happened.'

'Mr Andrews jumped out of bed and danced around the room?'

Madeleine smiled. 'No, Lydia – but he stopped coughing then drifted off to sleep.'

'Rest is the thing he needs most, I daresay.'

'He slept soundly last night because he was exhausted. I didn't hear a peep from him. He looked almost normal this morning.'

'He's receiving medical attention – that's the main thing. It sounds to me as if calling on Dr Hilliard may have saved his life.'

'Mrs Dyer deserves all the praise,' said Madeleine. 'She came here to raise the alarm. That's the value of having a good neighbour.'

'She obviously came here just in time. Your father needed medical attention desperately. I imagine Helena Rose was delighted to hear that he was spending the night under the same roof.'

'That was her immediate reaction. Then I explained to her that he was ill and unable to see her. She was so disappointed to hear that.'

'Will she be able to see him today?'

'Not until Dr Hilliard has been. He'll be here this afternoon to check on his patient. We must rely on his advice.'

'I do hope that he does allow your daughter to see her grandfather.'

'So do I,' said Madeleine. 'She's making a card for my father and will be so upset if she's unable to give it to him in person. She's spent hours drawing a picture of a steam engine for him.'

'She's obviously following in your footsteps.'

'Not exactly, Lydia. It's a very strange steam engine, to be honest. It has six huge funnels and is nothing like the ones that Father used to drive.'

'He'll be grateful nevertheless, I daresay.'

'Yes, he'll probably tell her that she is the real artist in the family.'

'She has a long way to go before she can challenge you, Madeleine. When it comes to paintings of steam engines, you have few rivals.'

After a comfortable night and a hearty breakfast, Colbeck and Leeming made their way to the railway station in Lincoln. As they had hoped, there was a telegraph awaiting them. It gave them the time of the train on which their colleagues would be arriving.

'The superintendent has agreed to your request,' said Leeming gratefully.

'That makes a change.'

'As long as he doesn't turn up here himself.'

'There's no chance of that happening, Victor. He's needed at Scotland Yard.'

'We've a few hours to wait before their train arrives. Could we stretch our legs and see a little of the city?'

'I was about to make the same suggestion.'

As they headed towards the exit, Colbeck looked up at one of the station clocks then took out his pocket-watch and glanced at it.

'That clock is two minutes late,' he said.

'Are you sure that your watch is on time?'

'I'd swear to it.' He looked around. 'What have you noticed about the city today?'

'It's full of manure. People keep coming with horses to sell. We've seen hundreds already.'

'Wait until the fair opens. Huge crowds will descend on Lincoln.'

'I just want Hinton and Boyce to get here. We need their help.'

'They'll be here on time,' promised Colbeck. 'Meanwhile, we can enjoy a stroll through the streets. It's a beautiful city and we must seize every opportunity we can to enjoy its sights.' They left the station and strode out into the street. 'It's going to be a sunny day, I fancy.'

'I hope so.'

'Let's hope that this good weather lasts throughout the Horse Fair.'

Unaware that they were being talked about, Alan Hinton and Eric Boyce were seated beside each other in a second-class compartment of a train. It had maintained a good speed from London and arrived at Peterborough station slightly ahead of time. Both detectives stared through the window.

'This is where it happened,' whispered Hinton.

'Yes,' said Boyce, excited by the thought of reaching the murder scene at last. 'I daresay that we'll get to know this place very well.'

'I hope that the local police won't be as unhelpful as they were in Shrewsbury.'

'Everything worked out for the best in the end,' recalled Boyce. 'After the murder was solved, the superintendent met the chief constable in person. I'm told that he and his old army friend got on very well. I just wish that that could have happened earlier.'

'I get the feeling that this case will be even more of challenge.'

'It's why we were sent for,' said his colleague. 'They need help.'

'I could do with some action – and it will be good to have a change from London.'

'It will be even better to be so far away from the superintendent.'

'Yes,' agreed Hinton. 'We work best when we don't have him barking at our heels. And there's nothing so reassuring at having a loaded gun apiece. I'm keeping my fingers crossed that we'll have a chance to use them.'

Patrick Farr was a stocky man in his forties with an ugly face that featured a broken nose and two piggy eyes. His friend Silas Weaver was even bigger. Well over six feet in height, Weaver had wide shoulders and muscular arms. It was he who had carried the heavy wooden box from the guard's van to the waiting horse and cart. In the safety of the farm, they could now study their prize in detail. They were in the barn where the stolen box had been locked up for the night, buried under a tarpaulin. Farr used a knife to cut through the ropes protecting the box. He then needed a crowbar to get at their prize. Once the box had been opened, they had to take out the thick padding wrapped around the silver cathedral. When the cloth was finally peeled off, the object was exposed in all its glory. Both men were startled.

'Jesus!' exclaimed Farr. 'Just look at that, Silas.'

Weaver goggled. 'I've never seen anything like it.'

'This will make all of us rich. I'll be able to give up farming and start to enjoy life. We should have done something like this years ago.'

'It's beautiful, Pat. Look at the details. It must have taken years to make.'

'Years to make,' said Farr, grinning, 'but only minutes to steal. If you ask me, the effort was well worth it. Luckily, everything went to plan. We got what we were after, and nobody has the slightest idea who we are or where we're hiding.'

'Except that you're not hiding. This is your own little farm. You live here.'

'Only until we get them to buy this cathedral back.'

Weaver frowned. 'What if they refuse to pay up?'

'Don't be stupid, man. Of course they'll pay up. We're dealing with the Bishop and the Dean. This is a gift they'll treasure. They'll beg us to sell it back to them.'

'How much is it worth?'

'Its price will be high enough to mean no more farming for me. I'll buy a nice house in Lincoln and become a well-behaved citizen.'

'What about the others?' asked Weaver.

'What about them?'

'We were promised equal shares for all four of us.'

'That's what will happen,' said Farr. 'Now let's wrap up the cathedral to keep it warm. It needs to be in perfect condition so that we can demand a high price.'

'Don't hide it away,' pleaded Weaver. 'It's so beautiful. I need time to take it all in.' His eyes glistened. 'Give me time to gloat!'

Caleb Andrews was beginning to enjoy the pleasure of being looked after. In his own home he had been cold, lonely and miserable.

He was now in a bedroom with a fire in the grate and servants to call on. The only disappointment was that he could not hug his adorable granddaughter. Dr Hilliard had given him strict orders. During the visit he made earlier, he had warned the patient that he must not infect anyone else in the house. To that end, servants who brought him food took the precaution of covering their faces while they were close to him. Helena Rose was not even allowed into the room.

'When can I see her, Maddy?' he asked. 'I'm her grandfather.'

'You heard what Dr Hilliard said,' she reminded him. 'You have a very nasty infection. It's bad enough for an adult but it would be even worse if it spread to a child. Helena Rose is as impatient as you are but— well, you'll both have to wait.'

'Seeing my granddaughter is the best medicine possible.'

'Then it's a treat you'll have when the time is ripe.'

'But I feel so much better, Maddy – and why are you standing so far away from me? It's unnatural. I've got a cold, that's all. It's not leprosy.'

'I'm following the doctor's orders,' said Madeleine. 'Those pills he gave you have already put some colour back in your cheeks, but we mustn't expect a miracle cure. Just lie back and relax. Enjoy a rest for once.'

'I've rested too much already. I want to get up and do things.'

'Well, you must be patient, Father. It may be a week or more before you're fit enough to get up. Dr Hilliard warned you that you had to follow his orders. Do you really want to spend a whole night coughing again? Apart from anything else, it must have been very painful.'

'It was, Maddy – but my throat feels better since I started taking those pills the doctor gave me. Anyway, let's stop talking about my problems,' he said. 'How is Robert getting on with his latest case?'

'It could take a long time to solve,' she said with a sigh.

'Do you have any details?'

'Only the few that came in a letter earlier today. He and Victor are in Lincoln, trying to find the people who stole a model of the cathedral made of silver. The detective who was taking it north from London was shot dead in Peterborough station and the little cathedral was stolen.'

'Does Robert have any theories about the killer?'

'I'm sure that he does but he's keeping them to himself. What's making the case even more difficult is that a Horse Fair opens in Lincoln tomorrow. According to Robert, the city is already awash with horses.'

'Horse Fairs are a nightmare,' complained Andrews.

'Why do you say that?'

'It's because I remember driving hundreds of horses to fairs in the past. The animals made a dreadful noise, and they left a terrible mess in the stock wagons. Then there's all the crime that takes place,' he added. 'Horse Fairs are a honeypot for villains.'

When the train finally arrived at the station, Colbeck and Leeming were there to welcome their colleagues from Scotland Yard. As the newcomers left their carriage, they were instantly spotted by their superiors. By dint of waving both arms like the sails of a windmill, Leeming managed to attract the attention of Hinton and Boyce.

'There they are,' said Hinton, picking them out in the crowd.

'I'm so glad that we got here at last,' said Boyce. 'I thought the journey was going to last forever.'

'It was well worth the effort, Eric. I feel it in my bones.'

They made their way towards the two people waiting to shake their hands and give them a cordial welcome. At Colbeck's suggestion, all four of them went into the refreshment room and sat down at a table.

'Thank you so much for coming,' said Colbeck. 'The superintendent will have told you something about the crimes we're here to solve.'

'We only know that something was stolen and that the man hired to bring it to Lincoln was shot in the process. The murder,' recalled Hinton, 'happened at the railway station in Peterborough.'

'That's where you'll be going tomorrow,' said Leeming.

'Yes,' added Colbeck. 'You'll spend the night here, then return to Peterborough in the morning and get in touch with the chief constable. Meanwhile, you are probably hungry after a long train journey. I suggest that you have something to eat here before we take you to Riseholme Hall. Bishop Jackson has agreed that you can stay there with us tonight. I think you'll find it a much higher class of accommodation than anything we usually enjoy. Don't you agree, Victor?'

'It's wonderful,' said Leeming. 'I slept like a log.'

'What sort of a man is the Bishop?' asked Hinton.

'He was born to take on the role,' replied Colbeck, 'and is highly respected.'

Leeming grinned. 'I'm surprised that he has any time to be a bishop.'

'Why is that?' asked Boyce.

'It turns out that he has ten daughters and one son. People joke about it. Most of the Bishop's energy must go on looking after his family.'

* * *

Having wrapped the silver cathedral up with great care, they put it back in its box and replaced the wood that had been levered off. Though rough and ready as a rule, both men handled the gift with great care. It was, after all, the key to their future.

'Will you really sell the farm?' asked Weaver.

Farr was decisive. 'I'll be glad to get rid of it,' he said. 'Farming is hard work. You're always at the mercy of the weather. I promised my father I'd keep the place going but he died years ago so I can change my mind. What about you, Silas?'

'I fancy a move to London. I'm fed up with country life.'

'That makes two of us.' Farr looked down at the box, then patted it. 'This has changed our lives. I never thought that something religious would be useful to us. Stealing it is the best thing we ever did.'

'We're not only thieves,' warned Weaver. 'We had to commit murder to get what we wanted. That means the police will be hunting us.'

'They haven't a clue who we are or where we live.'

'I won't feel really safe until I'm a long way away from here.'

'Lincoln will suit me,' said Farr. 'I'm not a church-going man but I might just wander into the cathedral one day, knowing that one of its treasures made us rich.' They shared a laugh. 'Meanwhile, we have to keep it safe and wait for my cousin to arrive.'

'Yes, he'll know what to do.'

'Jerry will have some idea of how much we ought to demand from the cathedral.'

'What if they won't pay up?'

'They've got no choice,' Farr assured him. 'They'll be dying to get it back.'

* * *

After their meal in the refreshment room, Colbeck led the newcomers to the West Front of the cathedral. Alan Hinton and Eric Boyce stood there and marvelled at the façade. Rising above it and piercing the sky were two massive towers topped by pinnacles.

'The Dean told us about the treasures of the cathedral,' said Colbeck. 'There's a whole list of them.'

'He went on and on for ages,' sighed Leeming.

'I hadn't realised it was so big,' admitted Hinton.

'And imposing,' said Boyce, eyes widening in awe.

'The oldest treasure,' continued Colbeck, 'is from the end of the tenth century. It's a collection of the homilies of the Venerable Bede. Almost two hundred parchment folios have survived. Dean Courtney told us about the other priceless items, including the paten belonging to Bishop Robert Grosseteste. It dates from the thirteenth century. The Dean was especially proud of that treasure.'

'What about the latest addition to the collection?' asked Hinton.

'That is temporarily unavailable – until the thieves issue their demand.'

'Is that what they will do, Inspector?'

'Why else steal it if not to offer it back at a high price? It's only a matter of time before the bargaining will start.'

'What do we do until then?' wondered Boyce.

'We keep searching for clues,' said Colbeck. 'Sergeant Leeming and I will do so here while both of you will be asking questions in the place where it was stolen.'

'Do we stay in Peterborough?'

'Yes, that will be your base, but I fancy that you'll need to explore the county before you find a trace of the killer. The chief constable here is very amenable. I can't promise that you'll get the same kind of help from his counterpart over the border.'

'How do we travel, sir?'

'You may well have to hire horses.'

'If you stay here for the Horse Fair,' joked Leeming, 'you can buy a horse apiece.'

'On police pay?' asked Hinton with a dry laugh.

'I like horses but, for some reason, they don't like me. I have difficulty staying the saddle. I hope that neither of you has that problem.'

'We'll manage,' said Hinton, 'won't we, Eric?'

'Yes,' agreed Boyce. 'I've always liked riding.'

'Let's take the pair of you out to Riseholme Hall,' suggested Colbeck. 'We can then give you all the details that we've so far amassed. Also, you will be able to inhale good, clean, fresh air. All you can smell here is the stink of horses. They've invaded the city in their hundreds.'

Jeremy Keane was a short, slim man in his forties who seemed unable to relax. Even when sitting in a first-class compartment of a train, he was constantly fidgeting. His fellow travellers lost count of the number of times that he adjusted his coat, pulled down the cuffs of his shirt and brushed off non-existent dust from his trousers. There was something else they noticed. Keane had a quiet smile on his face. From time to time it blossomed into a full grin as if he were congratulating himself on a remarkable achievement.

When the train finally reached Peterborough, he was among the first to alight. Too short to see over the heads of the people thronging the platform, he headed for the nearest exit. The strong hand of Patrick Farr soon landed on his shoulder.

'Welcome to Peterborough, Jerry!'

'Thanks, Pat,' he replied, shaking the other man's outstretched hand. 'It's great to see you again.' He lowered his voice. 'How did everything go?'

'Exactly as we planned.'

'I knew I could rely on you. Where is it?'

'Safe and sound at the farm.'

'I can't wait to see it.'

'I've got a trap waiting. I'll drive you out there.' He lowered his voice. 'We did it, Jerry. We stole it in broad daylight. We're going to be rich.'

'Not until we can squeeze the money out of the cathedral.'

'That's your job.'

'I'll get a small fortune out of them,' boasted Keane. 'Because of the risks we took, we deserve every penny we can get.'

'We can rely on you, Jerry. You've got the gift of the gab.'

'Where's Silas?'

'He's waiting out at the farm.'

'Did he obey his orders?'

'He obeyed them to the letter – and so did Tim Redshaw. He planted that bomb here at the station. All four of us made a great team.'

'I need to talk to you about Redshaw.'

'Why?'

'I've been thinking,' said Keane, as they headed towards the exit.

'About what?'

'The numbers.'

'I don't follow.'

'We agreed to divide the takings into four.'

'It's only fair, Jerry.'

'If we split the money between three of us, we'd each get a much larger slice.'

'We can't cut out Tim,' argued Farr. 'What he did was dangerous. He expects to get paid for the risks he took.'

'Oh, he'll get his reward, don't worry,' said Keane with sly grin. 'But it may not come in the shape of money.'

CHAPTER SIX

Dinner at Riseholme Hall that evening was an unexpected luxury for them. The four detectives dined in a private room where good food and wine were served, and where they could feast their eyes on exquisite furniture and beautiful paintings. Victor Leeming nevertheless found a cause for complaint.

'It's a bit creepy in here, isn't it?' he said, looking around.

'I find it a positive treat,' observed Colbeck. 'Bishop Jackson lives in style. I do admire his choice of paintings.'

'They're far too religious for me. I've never seen so many angels. I keep expecting them to burst into song. That would put me off my food altogether.'

'If you don't like art of such quality, Victor, there's something wrong with you.'

'I prefer your wife's paintings, Inspector. They're so easy on the eye.'

'You can't expect Bishop Jackson to hang a series of railway scenes on his walls,' said Colbeck, laughing. 'They'd be ludicrously out of place. Much as I admire Madeleine's work, it would not fit in here. Anyway,' he went on, 'let's remember why we find ourselves in Lincoln. There's a dangerous killer to catch and a silver cathedral to reclaim.'

'Why did the crimes happen in Peterborough?' asked Hinton.

'Good question, Alan.'

'Because the men involved lived near the railway station,' suggested Leeming.

'That's true,' agreed Colbeck. 'It means that they knew the station well enough to plan their crime in such a way that nobody was aware of it.'

'How many of them were there?' asked Boyce.

'Three at least. The gift inside that box was made of solid silver. It would probably have taken two men to carry it. A third man would have set off the explosion, then joined his friends on the vehicle that carried them away from the station. That's your starting point tomorrow,' advised Colbeck. 'They would have needed a cart to transport anything so heavy. It must have been waiting outside for them. I want the two of you to question every cab driver who was there at the time. One of them must have seen the box being carried out of the station and lifted onto a cart.'

'What about the man who sent that telegraph from King's Cross?' asked Leeming. 'He passed on vital information.'

'My guess is that he may well be the leader of the gang. He somehow became aware of when the item was being transported to Lincoln and told one of his henchmen where on the train it was being kept. In other words,' said Colbeck, 'he is directly involved in the crime.'

'Does that mean we search for him in London?' said Hinton.

'There's no point, Alan. He's much more likely to have joined his friends in Cambridgeshire by now. I daresay that he can't wait to feast his eyes on that silver cathedral. Also, of course,' added Colbeck, 'he'll want to handle negotiations with the Dean and the Bishop.'

Jeremy Keane had been to his cousin's farm several times in the past, but his latest visit had a special significance. He was there as the leader of a gang that had just had a signal triumph. It was something to celebrate. As he gazed lovingly at the glistening cathedral, he raised his glass of beer in triumph.

'Here's to a wonderful future for all of us!' he said.

'Hear, hear!' chorused the others before taking a long drink.

'How much do each of us get?' asked Weaver.

'You'll have to be patient, Silas.'

'I was the person who carried that bloody thing out of the station. It felt as if it was made of lead.'

'It's a brilliant mixture of sterling silver and silver plating. Sterling silver is a precious metal and highly expensive. At a guess, I'd say that most of the model has a coating of silver plate over a metal such as copper or nickel.'

'How much is it worth?'

'A lot of money,' said Farr. 'You'll get your share. Won't he, Jerry?'

'Yes,' said Keane. 'We'll all get exactly what we deserve.'

'It's a pity that Tim Redshaw isn't here to celebrate,' noted Weaver. 'We'd never have managed without him. It was Tim who set off that explosion at the station.'

'Yes,' agreed Farr, 'he did what he was told to do – just like the rest of us. But it was my cousin, Jerry, who made it all possible. He handed that silver cathedral to us on a plate.' He raised his glass. 'Thanks, Jerry.'

'Thanks, Jerry,' added Weaver.

'I got lucky, that's all,' explained Keane. 'Some useful information happened to come my way, and I made full use of it. When I knew the date when the item was being taken to Lincoln, I devised a plan. I wrote to my cousin and asked Pat if he'd like to join me.'

Farr grinned. 'I jumped at the chance!'

'I told him to recruit two men he could trust. One of them had to be strong – that was you, Silas. The other had to have used explosives – that was Tim Redshaw.'

'I knew he'd been in the army,' said Farr, 'and had fought in the Crimea. Also, he's had a bad time lately and is desperate for money. Tim was the ideal choice.'

'He did what was needed,' agreed Keane. 'It's what all four of us did. There's only one person that worried me.'

'Who do you mean, Jerry?' asked his cousin.

'The man who drove you away from the station in his cart.'

'Oh, don't worry about Dan Hufton. He won't say a word,' promised Farr. 'Dan has got no idea what we were up to. He was just pleased to get paid for driving his cart a couple of miles.'

'He'll have read about us in the newspapers.'

'Dan can't read. He's old, half-blind and lives alone with his wife. That's why I chose him. You can forget about Dan Hufton. He's no problem.'

'I hope you're right,' said Keane.

'What do we do next, Jerry?' asked Weaver.

'We contact the cathedral and make our demand.' Putting a

hand inside his coat, he brought out a sheet of paper and unfolded it. 'This is a rough idea of what we can expect to get.'

He handed the paper to his cousin, who read the letter with Weaver peering over his shoulder. They were astounded by the amount of money being demanded in return for the silver cathedral.

'Will they pay hundreds of thousands of pounds?' asked Farr in amazement.

'Oh, yes,' replied Keane, with a confident smile. 'They're desperate to have their precious cathedral back – at whatever cost.'

After kneeling in prayer at the altar rail, John Jackson went into the vestry and found the Dean waiting for him. One thing dominated the Bishop's thoughts.

'Have they been in touch?'

'No,' said the other, shaking his head. 'They're deliberately keeping us waiting.'

'Why?'

'I've no idea, Bishop. Perhaps they just want us to suffer.'

'We've had enough pain as it is. I keep blaming myself for sending only one man to bring that precious gift here to the cathedral.'

'You were not to know that thieves were waiting to steal it.'

'I feel so responsible for Langston's death.'

'It's a burden we must both share. I was on that train, remember. I've been reproaching myself for not being with him in the guard's van. While I was sitting comfortably in a compartment, he was at the mercy of a killer.'

'How could they possibly know that the silver cathedral was on the train?'

'I'm hoping that Inspector Colbeck will be able to answer that question in due course. Meanwhile, I've agreed to let him offer a substantial reward for information leading to the safe return of the stolen item and the capture of those who stole it.'

'How much will that cost?' asked the Bishop anxiously.

'It will be a fraction of the amount demanded from us for the return of the miniature cathedral. Colbeck has been in touch with the stationmaster in Peterborough, asking him to put up posters advertising the reward. He has also written to the county's leading newspaper to give prominence to the appeal. It will contain the description of the main suspect given to Colbeck by the man on duty in the telegraph station in Peterborough.'

'He is taking sensible steps, but he is also revealing that we did not take adequate care to transfer the gift from London safely. Because of decisions we made, a private detective was shot dead and the item he was guarding was stolen from the guard's van. In other words, Dean, we failed abysmally.'

'I accept that.'

'People are bound to criticise us.'

'Their anger will subside when they see the silver cathedral on display here.'

'If that ever happens,' said the Bishop gloomily. 'How can we trust such evil men to keep their word? They might take their money but give us nothing in return.'

'Don't be so defeatist. Inspector Colbeck has been in a similar situation before. He has dealt with thieves offering to return a stolen item for money. Those men are still languishing in prison.'

'In this case, they deserve to be hanged.'

'They will be, I assure you.'

'I wish that I had your confidence in the inspector.'

'He is our only hope,' said the Dean. 'With extra men at his disposal, he is confident that the balance will shift in our favour.'

'I will pray that you are right.'

Preparations for the Horse Fair had been going on for weeks before the event. Streets had been swept, house fronts had been cleaned or even painted, and every attempt had been made to brighten the face of the city. Fairground amusements were set up to attract visitors and to bring even more colour to the occasion. Horse owners from as far away as Ireland, France, Germany and Belgium flocked to the event. It was expected that somewhere between eight and nine hundred horses would be sold on the first day alone. As they made their way to the railway station, the detectives marvelled at the scene of activity. Horses stood on both sides of the High Street from the Stonebow to the railway crossing. Many of them were having their coats brushed to smarten their appearance. A symphony of neighs and whinnies filled the air.

'I've never seen anything like it,' confessed Eric Boyce. 'I'm sorry that we will have to miss all the fun.'

'You'll have fun of your own in Peterborough,' said Colbeck. 'You'll be hunting down vicious criminals.'

'When we have something to report, we'll contact you by telegraph.'

'Please do that.'

'Take your last smell of horse manure,' advised Leeming as he stepped around a pile of it. 'You're going to somewhere where you can breathe more easily.'

When the four of them reached the station, more passengers from an incoming train were surging out to enjoy the Horse Fair.

Bright sunshine welcomed them. The two younger detectives were among the few people who caught a train that was taking them away from the city. Colbeck and Leeming waved them off.

'They're lucky to escape,' observed Leeming. 'Lincoln has been invaded.'

'The city is ready for them, Victor. It's at its prettiest and most welcoming. Let's see if the Bishop and the Dean are caught up in the excitement, shall we?'

Caleb Andrews had stopped complaining about being moved out of his own house and had realised how much better off he now was. Waited on hand, foot and finger, he quickly adapted to his situation. He tried to persuade himself that he was on holiday and not recovering from a virus that had given him a painful chest and a persistent cough. Treatment by Dr Hilliard had eased his discomfort considerably. He was once more able to speak in a voice that no longer sounded like the croak of a frog.

'I can't thank you enough for bringing me here, Maddy,' he said.

'You've changed your tune,' she teased. 'I had to force you to leave your own house. You kept saying that there was nothing wrong with you.'

'I like my independence.'

'According to Dr Hilliard, liking your independence could have been the death of you. Remember how old you are. You're less able to fend off diseases.'

'When can I see my granddaughter again?'

'When you're less likely to pass on the infection to her,' said Madeleine. 'She's as eager to meet you as you are to see her again. Meanwhile, you'll have to communicate another way.'

'It was so good of her to draw this picture for me,' he said, picking it up from the bedside table. 'I've never actually seen a steam engine with six tall funnels, but it's brought me a lot of pleasure. It may be that Helena Rose is not going to take after you and become an artist. She's going to copy her grandfather and work on the railway.'

Madeleine laughed. 'We have other plans for her future.'

'Any word from Robert?'

'The mail hasn't come yet.'

'I feel sorry for him having to travel on the Great Northern Railway.'

'He had no choice,' she pointed out. 'It was on one of their trains that the murder occurred.'

'The guard should have done his job properly.'

'How do you know that he was at fault?'

'Because he's typical of the GNR. They don't employ the right sort of people.'

'If he'd stayed in the guard's van, he might have been killed by the man who shot the private detective. Robert put no blame on the guard or on the railway company.'

'That's because he doesn't know the GNR as well as I do.'

She grinned.

'What's so funny?'

'You are,' she said, laughing. 'Because you worked for the LNWR you can't resist sniping at every other railway company. In my opinion that's a good sign. It proves that you really are getting better.'

When they got to the cathedral, Colbeck and Leeming found that they had arrived at a critical time. A demand had been sent by the men who had stolen the miniature cathedral. It had been addressed to Dean Courtney. When the detectives were admitted to the Bishop's office, they found that he had just seen the amount demanded. It was as if he had just received a hefty blow and was still groggy. Colbeck was worried.

'Are you all right, Bishop?' he asked.

'No, I am deeply shocked by the letter that the Dean received today. It makes the most extortionate demand.'

'See for yourself, Inspector,' said the Dean, handing him the missive. 'I had braced myself in advance, but the figure stated here is far bigger than any that I envisaged.'

'Does that matter?' asked Colbeck.

'Yes, it does. It proves that they are out to inflict the greatest possible damage on our financial resources. Not content with killing the person we employed and stealing the work of art he was bringing to us, they're determined to bleed us dry.'

'There's no cause for alarm,' suggested Leeming. 'The amount will not be paid.'

'We simply have to give them the impression that you will comply with their outrageous demand,' added Colbeck. 'It's the only way to lure them out of their hiding place. That's when I and my men step in.'

'These villains will stop at nothing,' warned the Bishop.

'We will all be armed.'

'What if they outnumber you?'

'We have the advantage of surprise,' said Colbeck, 'and that is priceless.'

'So what do you advise us to do, Inspector?'

'Make them wait. Tell them that it will take time for you to amass the amount of money required. They will be angry but there's nothing they can do about it. Tell them a lie about the precarious state of cathedral finances.'

'We can't stoop to dishonesty,' said the Dean, shocked.

'You don't have to,' replied Colbeck. 'I will happily do it for you.'

When they reached Peterborough station, the first thing that the detectives did was to congratulate the stationmaster. Taking Colbeck's advice, he had put up posters that offered a reward to anyone with information that would lead to the arrest of the gang who had committed the dreadful crimes. The detectives then went to the cab rank outside and asked the drivers in turn if any of them had seen a large box being carried out to a waiting cart on the previous day. Most had not but one driver did recall seeing a hefty man heaving a wooden box onto a cart then climbing up beside it with his companion. The cart had left the railway station at speed.

After thanking the helpful cab driver, they asked him to take them to police headquarters. During the journey, they had their first glimpse of Peterborough. It was market day and crowds were milling among the various stalls.

'This looks like a nice place to live,' said Hinton, approvingly. 'The cathedral is smaller than the one in Lincoln, and they haven't been invaded by hundreds of horses.'

'What sort of man is the chief constable?' asked Boyce. 'That's the only thing I want to know.'

'Leave the talking to me, Eric.'

'Why is that?'

'It's because I've had more practice at it and because you are much better at weighing somebody up. You're a good listener.'

'I don't usually have a chance to do anything else.'

'Is that a complaint?'

'No, it's an observation.'

The cab eventually dropped them off outside a building with a uniformed policeman coming out of it. After paying their driver, they went into the police station to be confronted by the duty sergeant, a whiskery individual of middle years with eyes that ignited at the sight of them. Before Hinton could introduce them, the man spoke.

'I know who you are,' he said with an edge of hostility. 'Inspector Colbeck wrote to warn us that he was sending you here. I don't know why. The crimes were committed on our patch. It's up to us to solve them.'

'Perhaps we should speak to someone more senior,' suggested Hinton.

'The chief constable will tell you the same thing.'

'Nevertheless, we wish to meet him.'

'Follow me.'

Coming out from behind the desk, the sergeant led them down a corridor to a room at the far end. After tapping on the door with his knuckles, he opened it and led the visitors into the room. Seated behind a large desk was a chunky man in his fifties with an almost academic air about him. He looked up from the document he had been reading.

'These are the detectives sent by Inspector Colbeck,' announced the sergeant.

'Thank you, Sergeant Wilkes. That will be all.'

'Yes, sir,' said the man before leaving the room and closing the door behind him.

'Welcome, gentlemen,' said the chief constable, rising to his feet. 'One of you is Detective Constable Hinton, I believe.'

'That's me, sir,' volunteered Hinton.

'Then you must be Detective Constable Boyce,' said the man, shifting his gaze to his other visitor. 'I'm pleased to meet you both. Why don't we all sit down?'

'Thank you, sir,' said Boyce, lowering himself onto a chair.

'My name, as you know, is Marcus Napier, and I am not only chief constable of Peterborough – I hold the same office for the county of Northamptonshire. That may seem strange to you, but the Liberty of Peterborough and City Police have more in common, historically, with Northamptonshire than with Cambridgeshire. I'll spare you the full details.'

'I'm sure that we'll pick them up as we go along, sir,' said Hinton.

'Quite so. We came into existence rather late,' explained the other. 'It was not until March 1857 that the Liberty of Peterborough Police was formed. It consisted of one chief constable, my predecessor, three sergeants and sixteen constables.'

'Is that all?' asked Boyce, shocked.

'I'm afraid so – but we have steadily grown since then. Obviously, we are unable to compete with the Metropolitan Police, but we are not rank amateurs floating in the backwaters. It's important for you – and Inspector Colbeck – to know that we have dealt with cases of murder, arson, armed robbery and other serious crimes. In most cases we have achieved an arrest. Do you hear what I am saying?'

'Yes, sir,' said Hinton. 'You are not amateurs.'

'When the law is broken in this city, we do something about it. Make that clear to Inspector Colbeck, please. We insist on being involved.'

'He is counting on the fact. Without local help, our investigation would be hampered from the very start. What we were sent here to discuss is the way in which you can best assist us. Were he not waiting for a demand to be sent by the villains to the cathedral, the inspector would have come here in person.'

'I look forward to meeting him.'

'If we join forces,' said Boyce, 'we will be far more effective.'

'I'm glad that you understand that. Let's turn to practicalities. What are your orders and where do you intend to stay?'

'We will be based in Peterborough,' explained Hinton, 'so we will need accommodation. We'll also need transport so that we can go further afield. That may involve hiring horses.'

'We may be able to help you with both of those things.'

'We'd be eternally grateful, sir.'

'It's what allies do for each other, isn't it?' said Napier. 'Do not think that the men at my command are all like Sergeant Wilkes. He is good policeman but is possessive by nature. In his opinion, we should be solely in charge of this case while you are left to twiddle your thumbs in Scotland Yard.'

Boyce laughed. 'There's no thumb-twiddling allowed when Superintendent Tallis is on duty,' he said. 'He keeps our noses to the wheel.'

'Then he's a man after my own heart,' declared Napier. 'I'm sorry that he's not here so that I can tell him that to his face.'

Edward Tallis was an impatient man at the best of times. As he stood on the platform at King's Cross station, he was angered by the news that the train to Lincoln would be fifteen minutes late. Even such a small delay was unacceptable. Important events were happening in the northern city. Tallis felt it vital that he should be involved in them.

* * *

Despite her age, Alice Tomkins was very active. She was a tall, willowy woman with a fierce pride in her husband's skill as a silversmith and a readiness to support him in every way. From the moment when he had been brought home, she had become a nurse as well as a wife, seeing to his needs and following the doctor's orders to the letter. Her husband was increasingly impatient. When Alice went into the bedroom, he was struggling to get out of bed.

'Don't you dare get up, Gregory,' she said, easing him back between the sheets and pulling the blanket over him. 'Remember what the doctor said. You need rest.'

'How can I rest when my mind is on fire?' he asked. 'I put every effort into making that silver cathedral. It was an obsession for month after month.'

'You don't need to tell me that. Every time you came back home, you were exhausted – and your eyes were troubling you.'

'I was being reminded how old I was, that's all.'

'I've been begging you to retire for years.'

He smiled fondly. 'Do you really want me hanging around the house all day and getting under your feet?'

'If it keeps you alive then yes, I do,' she said. 'I want you to have the rest that you richly deserve. You're a master of your trade. Enjoy your fame.'

'How can I do that when my masterpiece has been stolen? When I heard the news, I felt like a mother whose baby has been stolen. That cathedral meant more to me than anything else I've made over the years. Working on it was a joy. Then the moment I sent it off to Lincoln, the man guarding it was shot dead and my gift to the cathedral was stolen. Think how Michael Langston's family must feel.'

'I mourn with them, Gregory.'

'Superintendent Tallis promised that his officers would catch the killer and reclaim my model, but it has lost its pristine condition now. Grubby hands have been all over it. There's a danger that it may have been damaged. When it left London, it was a work of art. All it will become now is a means of squeezing money out of the cathedral.'

'You must stop worrying about it,' she urged. 'It's bad for you. Remember what the doctor told you. It's a source of pain and regret. Don't punish yourself by thinking about it.'

'I can't help it, Alice. Working on that cathedral helped me to stay alive. It gave me a purpose. It reminded me that I was still a gifted silversmith.' He shook his head sadly. 'I'll never be able to make anything as beautiful as that again.'

As tears streamed down his face, she put her arms lovingly around him.

'You've had a wonderful career, Gregory,' she told him. 'Every silversmith in London is aware of your amazing talent. You have nothing to prove. You have won many awards during your career. Remember that. It's time for you to rest and look back fondly on your achievements.'

'If only I could do that, my love,' he sighed. 'But there's an ugly blotch on my reputation. I'll be remembered as the silversmith whose work brought about the untimely death of a private detective who was guarding something I created.' He spread his arms. 'How can I ever forget that, indirectly, I killed him.'

CHAPTER SEVEN

By the time that Edward Tallis finally arrived in Lincoln, the Horse Fair was bigger and noisier than ever. Glimpsing the crowds through the window of his compartment, he felt his hopes fade. The last thing his detectives needed was the noise, distraction and commotion in the streets. It was an enormous handicap to a murder investigation. The telegraphs sent to him from Lincoln by Inspector Colbeck had warned him of the difficulties they faced. Tallis had responded to the request for help by sending two experienced detectives, but he now felt the urge to be involved himself. It had, after all, fallen to him to pass on the dreadful news to the silversmith that his greatest achievement had been stolen by thieves who had shot dead the man guarding it.

It was as if he had just plunged a knife into the heart of Gregory Tomkins. The bruising memory had stayed with Tallis. To make amends, he felt moved to get directly involved in the search for those responsible for the crimes. Like the silversmith, he was a man with a waning talent. While it was still serviceable, he was keen to put his experience at the service of Tomkins. It was his duty.

When his train came to a halt in the station, he was part of a huge crowd that headed for the exits. As soon as he left the building, however, he became keenly aware of the size, noise and abiding stink of the Horse Fair. Crossing to the cab rank, he spoke to a driver who was smoking a pipe as he leant against a wall.

'Take me to the cathedral,' ordered Tallis.

'How am I supposed to do that?' replied the other. 'Every road is blocked. If you want to get there, you'll have to fight your way through all those horses.'

Alan Hinton and Eric Boyce were in luck. Although the duty sergeant at the police station had little respect for the Scotland Yard detectives he regarded as intruders, he obeyed his orders to help them. Sergeant Wilkes not only found them a place where they could stay, he even told them where they could hire horses. It meant that they had somewhere to leave their luggage and a way of travelling around the county. As they rode their horses out of the city, they were keenly aware of the difficulties that lay ahead.

'They could be anywhere,' said Hinton.

'Remember what that cab driver told us,' Boyce reminded him. 'When that cart left the station, it followed the road that went to the south.'

'There's more than one road that does that.'

'Then we need to rely on people we pass. Someone must have seen something. That cart was unusual. It was carrying a large wooden box and had two men sitting beside it.'

'Don't forget the old man driving it.'

'That cab driver we talked to said that he'd seen him before,' recalled Boyce. 'That means the old man might be a regular visitor to Peterborough.'

'I think the best suggestion came from Inspector Colbeck,' said Hinton. 'He felt that the men we're after might have come from a farm.'

'This county seems to have nothing but farms.'

'Then we have to call on them one by one.'

'That could take ages,' complained Boyce.

'So? It's a fine day and these horses seem biddable enough. I don't know about you but I'm enjoying being in the saddle for a change. There we are,' said Hinton as he spotted something ahead. 'There's a roadside inn. We can ask there if anyone saw a cart going past with two men and a large wooden box on it.'

The three men were in the farmhouse owned by Patrick Farr, seated in the kitchen and reflecting on their achievement.

'What you haven't told us,' said Silas Weaver, 'is how you knew the silver cathedral would be travelling to Lincoln by train.'

Jeremy Keane grinned. 'It's a secret.'

'We'd like to know the details, Jerry.'

'I keep my ears open. That's all I can tell you. When I hear something that sounds as if it might be useful, I do my best to find out the full details. Once I've done that,' said Keane, 'I work out how many men I need to help me.'

'First of all,' said Farr, 'I got a letter from Jerry, saying he knew a way we might be able to make a lot of money. Could I get two reliable men? Yes, I could, I told him. So I picked you, Silas, and Tim Redshaw. I vouched for the pair of you.'

'Thanks, Pat,' said Weaver.

'Tim jumped at the offer – and so did you.'

'All that happened then,' said Keane, 'was that you obeyed my orders. While I took care of things in London, you were to get ready in Peterborough.'

'We took no chances,' recalled Farr. 'We walked through what we had to do twice in a row. We got used to coping with the crowds who pour off a train. Tim Redshaw loved the rehearsals. He worked out how to get into the storeroom and set off that explosion as a train pulled into the station.'

'You left nothing to chance,' said Keane approvingly. 'That's why everything went like clockwork. Each one of you kept his nerve. That was crucial.'

'What about Dan Hufton?' asked Weaver.

'All he did was to give us a lift on his cart,' argued Farr. 'Dan was too old and too stupid to do anything else. He knew nothing about our plans because he couldn't be trusted. Dan drinks like a fish. If he'd had enough beer inside him he'd have boasted about what we had just done.'

'That would have been fatal for all of us,' noted Keane. 'As it is, we're sitting here in the safety of my cousin's farm and waiting for word from the cathedral. I made it clear to them that we needed a definite answer by tomorrow.'

'What if we don't get the amount you demanded, Jerry?'

Keane grinned. 'Then we'll have to increase the price, won't we?'

Colbeck and Leeming were at the cathedral, discussing the situation with the Dean. They could see how rattled he had been by the excessive demand. The detectives did their best to raise his spirits.

'Don't lose heart,' advised Colbeck. 'At least they've come out of hiding.'

'Yes, but we still have no idea who they are,' protested Courtney.

'They're hardened criminals,' said Leeming. 'They'll stop at nothing.'

'Do they actually mean to hand over the silver cathedral?'

'We can never be sure with men like these,' said Colbeck. 'We must see what they suggest is the way to exchange the money. That's the moment when we have the best chance to arrest them.'

'If only we had more men at our disposal,' complained Leeming. 'The chief constable is supporting us to the hilt, but he can't spare many of his officers to help us. They're too busy hunting pickpockets at the Horse Fair.'

Courtney was about to say something when there was a knock on the door. It opened to admit a young man in a cassock. None of them really noticed him because he had a companion in tow. Superintendent Tallis had arrived. He was flushed, weary and panting. He dropped his valise to the floor.

'Thank heavens!' he said. 'What a climb up that hill! I thought I'd never get here.'

Lydia Quayle was alone in the drawing room of her house, reading a letter from her younger brother, Lucas. He was her main contact with a family that she had effectively left in the wake of her father's murder. Relations with her other siblings were uncertain and she rarely corresponded with any of them. She lived in a different world now with a different set of friends and different objects in life. Her most important relationship now was with Madeleine Colbeck. It was forged during the investigation into her father's murder. It had been led by Robert Colbeck and the killer was eventually arrested and hanged. But Lydia had never forgotten the help that Madeleine had offered during the dark days when the loss of her father had preyed on her mind.

As she reflected on what she had lost when she moved to London, she was reminded of the things that she had gained. Having escaped from the companionship of a possessive older woman, Lydia felt that she had at last achieved freedom of movement. It was exhilarating. She had money to buy a comfortable house and to hire reliable servants. Best of all was the fact that she was now an unofficial member of the Colbeck household with the status of favourite aunt to the delightful Helena Rose. Putting the letter aside, she rose from her chair and went into the hall. She was just in time to see the front door being closed from outside with great care. Her immediate reaction was that one of her servants had gone out. Then she remembered that she was, in fact, the only person in the house.

A sudden fear gripped her. Had there been an intruder on her property? Rushing to the front door, she flung it open in the hope of seeing who had just left. But there were several people walking past in both directions, making it impossible for her to identify the person she was after. Lydia was almost paralysed by uncertainty. Had she really seen her front door closing or had she simply imagined it?

Now that he had been introduced to the Dean and offered a chair, Edward Tallis had been able to get his breath back. He offered no explanation for his unheralded arrival. All that he could talk about was his walk from the railway station.

'The city has been overtaken by animals,' he complained. 'They're blocking the High Street and making a fearful noise.

When I tried to climb up here by means of another route, I found it blocked by herds of sheep and cattle. What on earth is going on, Dean Courtney? Are farm animals being given precedence over human beings?'

'You have arrived on the first day of the Horse Fair,' explained the Dean. 'That means we have to put up with a degree of inconvenience.'

'I'm sorry that you came at the wrong time, sir,' said Leeming. 'To be honest, we were not expecting you.'

'Nevertheless,' said Colbeck, stepping in to divert the superintendent's glare away from Leeming, 'we are delighted to see you. Events have moved on since my last telegraph to you. We have received a demand from the men in possession of the stolen cathedral.'

'It is wickedly excessive,' explained the Dean.

'May I see it?' asked Tallis.

'Yes, of course. It's right here.'

He handed a sheet of paper to the superintendent. Startled by the amount of money demanded, Tallis did not notice how neat the calligraphy was. He gave the letter back to the Dean.

'There's no mention of how the money is to be handed over.'

'They just want an agreement at this stage,' said Colbeck. 'Once the money is promised, they will explain how and when it will be exchanged for Gregory Tomkins's masterpiece. The silversmith must have been profoundly shocked that his work of art was stolen.'

'I was there when he heard the grim news,' said Tallis. 'It shook him rigid. Someone had stolen what was almost certainly the last example of his mastery as a silversmith. Tomkins was in despair. In fact,' he continued, 'it was seeing the effect of the news on him that gave me the urge to take an active part in the search for the villains behind the crimes.'

'I'm glad to hand over control of the investigation, sir.'

'No, no, Inspector,' continued Tallis, 'I have not come to displace you. This case is yours. I am here merely to take orders from you.'

Leeming grinned. 'Does that mean I'm senior to you as well, Superintendent?'

'No, it doesn't,' growled Tallis.

'What is the next step?' asked Dean Courtney.

'Inspector Colbeck must answer that. He is still in charge.'

'In that case,' said Colbeck decisively, 'this is what we must do . . .'

The Green Man was a small, cluttered inn that catered for travellers on the road to Sawtry. It had a pleasing atmosphere and a friendly landlord with a big belly and red cheeks. What he told them was that he had been outside the inn two days before when a cart rumbled past with a large box on it. Seated beside it were two big men who looked as if they might be farmers.

'It must be them,' decided Boyce.

'What was the driver like?' asked Hinton.

'He was an old man who seemed half-asleep,' said the landlord. 'He didn't even see me. I hoped they might stop for a tankard of beer apiece, but they didn't give us a second glance. They obviously had somewhere to get to.'

Madeleine Colbeck had not been expecting a visit from Lydia Quayle, so it was a pleasant surprise when the latter turned up. Having opened the front door herself, Madeleine embraced her friend warmly and invited her in. She then saw the look of anxiety in Lydia's eyes.

'Has something happened?' she asked.

'I don't know,' admitted Lydia. 'That's part of the trouble.'

'Come into the drawing room and tell me all about it.'

'I will, Madeleine.'

They were soon sitting side by side on the sofa. Lydia took a deep breath.

'I'm frightened,' she said, grasping her friend's hand.

'What's the problem?'

'The truth is that I don't really know. What I can tell you is that it was very upsetting and made me wonder if I'd been seeing something that never actually happened.'

'You're not making much sense, Lydia.'

Her friend took a deep breath before speaking again. 'I'll try to be as calm as I can,' she said, 'but the truth is that I feel so . . . uneasy.'

'Why?'

'Earlier today, I was alone in the house because my cook and maidservant had both gone out shopping. I was reading a letter from my brother, Lucas. When I went into the hall, I saw the strangest thing.'

'What was it?'

'The front door was being closed very carefully by someone outside the house. It really shook me. I thought that I was completely alone in here. Evidently, I was not.'

'Could one of the servants have slipped back to the house?'

'They were not due to return from the market for at least an hour. My home had been broken into, Madeleine. The thought made me shudder.'

'What did you do?'

'Well, when I finally pulled myself together,' said Lydia, 'I opened the front door in the hope of seeing the person who had left so silently.'

'And did you catch a glimpse of this person?'

'I may have done but he or she was part of a crowd going past the house in both directions. I began to wonder if I'd made a mistake. Perhaps there had been nobody there, after all.'

'What did you do next?'

'I did my best to pretend that the front door had never been open at all. I was misled by a trick of my imagination. Then I made a cup of tea and tried to shrug the whole thing off. But it was no use, Madeleine. I saw what I saw. I was certain of it.'

'It must have been very upsetting.'

'I was shaking all over,' said Lydia. 'If someone had been in my house, he had to be a burglar. I flew into a panic. I didn't know whether to call the police or check to see if anything had been stolen.'

'That's what I'd have done in the circumstances. I'd have been anxious to know if anything valuable was missing.'

'In the end, that's what I did myself. I even grabbed a walking stick so that I had something with which to defend myself. Then I began my search upstairs, going from room to room. Anything valuable is kept in a safe in the wall of the master bedroom. It's hidden behind a large mirror.'

'And?'

'The mirror was still in place and the safe untouched.'

'What about windows? Had any of them been tampered with?'

'No, they hadn't. I checked every one of them, then came

downstairs to begin a search of the ground floor. I was very thorough. I searched everywhere in vain. You can imagine how desperate I felt.'

'If it put your mind at rest, it was the right thing to do.'

'But it only made things worse. That's what upset me the most. The thought that a stranger might – just might – have been inside my bedroom, examining things that I hold dear, sitting on my bed perhaps and letting one of my necklaces run through his fingers. I thought my mind was about to explode, Madeleine. The only thing I could think of was to come to you as soon as possible.'

'I'm so glad that you did.'

'It's left me so utterly confused. Am I going mad or did I really see someone shutting my front door from outside?'

'Close your eyes and take a deep breath,' urged Madeleine, holding her friend's hands in her own. 'Go on. That's it. Keep your eyes shut tight until I tell you to open them. Do your best to clear your mind.'

'I'll try,' whispered Lydia. 'I'll try anything you suggest.'

Early hopes were eventually dashed. Having ridden for hours, Alan Hinton and Eric Boyce came to a point where three different roads led south. They discussed which road they should take for some time before agreeing that they had failed. During their time in the saddle, they had called on several farms without gathering any information about the men on a cart with a large wooden box. The truth had to be faced.

'This road is getting us nowhere,' decided Boyce.

'Shall we try the road in the middle?' asked Hinton.

'It'll be like all the others, Alan. It will take us nowhere. Besides,

I've been in the saddle for long enough and so have you. Let's go back. Agreed?'

Hinton was disappointed but realistic. 'Agreed,' he said.

Back at the cathedral, Edward Tallis had recovered from his exertions among farm animals and listened to a more detailed account of what his detectives had been doing since their arrival. Since the Dean was no longer with them, the three of them felt able to talk with more ease. Colbeck asked about the silversmith.

'What sort of a man is Gregory Tomkins?'

'I think he's a mere shadow of the master craftsman he used to be. The loss of his latest work was devastating. In donating it to the cathedral here, he would have been applauded for his kindness and his skill. Instead of that, he is sitting at home in a daze, wondering if he will ever see one of his finest works again.'

'The theft must have shaken him to the core,' said Leeming.

'He is more upset at the death of the private detective guarding it than he is at his own loss. Tomkins ought to be able to look back on a wonderful career but the shadow of Michael Langston's murder will obscure it from him.'

'The only way to dispel that shadow is to catch the men behind these crimes,' said Colbeck. 'With each new piece of evidence turning up, I'm getting an idea of just how callous the members of the gang are.'

'I'm certain that their leader lives in London,' said Tallis.

'How do you know, sir?' asked Leeming.

'Think it through, Sergeant. How could the men who stole that precious item possibly know when it was likely to arrive at Peterborough station? They must have had an associate in London who discovered when and how it would be despatched. My first thought was that someone working alongside Tomkins had to be involved but that is clearly not the case,' affirmed Tallis. 'I spoke to both of the man's partners, and they assured me that everyone they employed had been sworn to secrecy.'

'What about Mr Tomkins himself?' asked Colbeck.

'He is above suspicion.'

'You've told us how old and uncertain he is. Could he have let the information slip out accidentally while drinking with friends in a public place? After all, it's something to be proud of. Tomkins has created an object that is going to join other treasures in one of the country's finest cathedrals. Most silversmiths would be tempted to boast about it.'

'That's true,' conceded Tallis.

'If the theft and murder were planned in London, isn't that where you should be, sir?' asked Leeming. 'That's where the gang leader needs to be hunted – not here in Lincoln.'

Tallis stiffened. 'Are you daring to tell me what to do, Sergeant?'

'No, no . . . it was just a suggestion.'

'It's a fair point, Superintendent,' said Colbeck. 'I agree that these crimes involve someone based in the capital, a man who somehow found out when the silver cathedral was being sent here by train. We know that he alerted the person whom we believe was the killer by sending him a telegraph to Peterborough station. My guess is that this individual has now joined his confederates in Cambridgeshire. You've seen the demand that was sent here. The man who wrote it has an educated hand.'

'He's certainly not a farmer,' said Tallis. 'Horny hands could not produce calligraphy like that.'

* * *

Jeremy Keane strutted arrogantly through the streets of Lincoln with his cousin. Patrick Farr could not resist looking at the various horses being offered for sale. Prospective buyers were careful. If they took an interest in a particular animal, they would insist that someone would take its reins and run it up and down the High Street at speed to prove that it was sound in wind and limb. Only when they were convinced that the horse was worth buying could the haggling begin. Money was changing hands at a fast rate.

Patrick Farr sighed. 'I'll miss the annual Horse Fair,' he said. 'I've been here so many times over the years.'

'You won't need to own a horse when we get our money,' promised Keane. 'You'll be able to afford a cab to take you wherever you wish to go. Your farming days will be over, Pat. You'll be a new man.'

'A new man in need of a new wife,' said his cousin. 'I've been very lonely since Nancy died. It's time I stopped mourning and started to enjoy myself again.'

'And who have you got to thank?'

'You, Jerry. You made it all possible.'

'I'd always known that you were a man who took chances if the stakes were high enough. That's why I involved you. I can't say that I've had hired someone like Weaver but – since you picked him – I relied on your judgement.'

'Silas does what I tell him, and we needed someone strong enough to lift that box out of the guard's van.'

'I agree,' said Keane, 'but that's all he did. Does Weaver really deserve a quarter of the money by proving that he has big muscles?'

'I thought that was what we agreed, Jerry.'

'It was – at the start. But we're the people who did the important things. I planned the whole thing, and you had the nerve to shoot that private detective dead. In other words, we should get a larger share than either Weaver or Redshaw.'

'They'll be very upset if that happens.'

'No, they won't,' boasted Keane. 'I showed Weaver the amount I demanded from the cathedral, but I increased the figure before I sent it to the Dean. Weaver doesn't know that. The same goes for Redshaw. All he did was to set off an explosion. Do you think that's worth a quarter of all we get?'

'It's what I promised him.'

'I still think we should cut him out altogether. That way, Redshaw gets nothing at all, and Weaver is getting a much smaller amount than either of us.' He nudged Farr with his elbow. 'We're cousins, after all. It's only fair that we should look out for each other.'

'Yes,' said Farr, undecided. 'I suppose that it is.'

CHAPTER EIGHT

Lydia Quayle was grateful that she had made the decision to turn to her friend. She felt so much better after she had spent time with Madeleine Colbeck that she reached out to give her an involuntary hug.

'Thank you so much,' said Lydia. 'I'm really glad that I came here.'

'You know that you're always welcome. If you wish, I'll come back to your house with you, and we'll have another search. There must be an explanation of why someone had been inside it.'

'Save yourself the time, Madeleine. I've calmed down now. Besides, you're needed here to look after your father.'

'I know but he's still upset that he can't see his granddaughter and annoyed that Robert has not sent us enough details about the crime that he is now investigating. My father thinks that he could offer some advice.'

'I'm not sure that your husband would welcome that,' said Lydia. 'Advice from hundreds of miles away from someone who has probably never been to Lincoln is useless. All that your father can offer is wild guesswork.'

'That won't stop him trying to solve the crime,' said Madeleine. 'It gives him something to occupy his mind and a chance to mock the Great Northern Railway.'

'I don't think that the railway company can be blamed for what happened.'

'Try telling that to my father!'

'Anyway,' said Lydia, 'I must be off. I've taken up far too much of your time.'

'That's nonsense. Since you've come all this way, I insist that you stay for dinner. You can have the pleasure of reading a bedtime story to Helena Rose and have a glance at my latest painting.'

Lydia smiled. 'I'm very tempted, Madeleine.'

'Good – that's settled.'

'You're such a wonderful friend.'

'I could say the same about you. Look at the way you were so upset when you discovered that someone had copied a painting of mine and tried to pass it off as her own work. I was so glad that you brought it to my attention.'

'I was outraged on your behalf.'

'The problem was eventually solved,' said Madeleine. 'Over dinner, we can talk at length about the shock that you had earlier. It really jolted you. I hope that I've been able to calm you down a bit. And don't forget that you've got a bedtime story to read to your favourite niece. You need all your concentration to do that.'

* * *

Edward Tallis was beginning to regret his decision to go to Lincoln. The long train journey had tired him and the walk uphill to the cathedral had almost exhausted him. While he was grateful to hear full details of the investigation, he was made aware of how impulsively he had behaved. He had not realised that the Horse Fair would have increased the city's population so markedly and filled every available room in its hotels and inns. But for the Bishop's hospitality, he would have had nowhere to sleep that night. As it was, he, Colbeck and Leeming were driven to Riseholme Hall to enjoy its many comforts.

'What sort of man is Bishop Jackson?' he asked.

'He's very able and very industrious,' replied Colbeck.

'I hope that I get the opportunity to meet him.'

'I'm sure that you will, sir. As you know, it's the Dean who effectively runs the cathedral, leaving the Bishop free to attend to his many duties.'

'Yes,' said Leeming with a chuckle. 'He needs to find time to spend with his children – all eleven of them.'

Tallis was astounded. 'Eleven children?'

'Ten daughters and one son, sir.'

'It's not a laughing matter, Victor,' said Colbeck. 'It's to Bishop Jackson's credit that he has achieved so much since he came to Lincoln and has earnt the respect of everyone in the county.'

'How has he reacted to the loss of a wonderful gift,' asked Tallis, 'and the murder of the man employed to bring it safely to its new home?'

'The crimes have shocked him, sir. He has visited the home of the private detective involved and offered what comfort he could to the man's wife and family. And he listened to the Dean's plea that we should be sent for. Both men believe that we will be able to identify and arrest the villains responsible.'

'Quite right, too,' agreed the superintendent. 'We must pursue them relentlessly. I have been in touch with the managing director of the Great Northern Railway to assure him that we are fully involved in the search for these wicked men. By the way,' he went on, 'what happened to the two men you requested? Hinton and Boyce were despatched immediately. I hope they have been a useful addition to the investigation.'

'Indeed, they have,' said Colbeck. 'They are currently in Cambridgeshire, pursuing lines of enquiry there. When they return to Peterborough, I hope that they will send news to us of their search by means of a telegraph.'

Alan Hinton and Eric Boyce ate their meal in the Dog and Badger, a small but hospitable tavern in Peterborough. The food was good and the beer serviceable. Their only regret was that they had nothing to celebrate. Boyce was downhearted. His face was a picture of sorrow.

'Cheer up, Eric,' said Hinton. 'We'll have better luck tomorrow.'

'It's not luck we need, Alan. It's a miracle.'

'We took the wrong road, that's all. We'll explore a different one next time.'

'I hope we don't have to spend too much time in the saddle. When we got back here and dismounted, my body ached all over.'

'I got off lightly, then. All I had was a sore backside.'

'That message we sent from the telegraph office in Peterborough was not worth reading. It will upset the inspector when he sees it.'

'We tried our best. He'll appreciate that.'

'At least we escaped the Horse Fair. That's one thing to be

thankful for. With all those people and horses there, we could hardly move.'

'It couldn't have worked out better for the men we're after,' said Hinton. 'The city is full to bursting and the police can't possibly control the numbers. If they try to hand over that silver cathedral in return for a lot of money, the villains can disappear in the crowd. The Horse Fair is an absolute gift to them.'

'Then we should be back there. If there's to be an exchange of money for the silversmith's gift, every pair of eyes will be needed. Instead of riding aimlessly around the next county, we should head back to Lincoln in the morning.'

'But we were told to search Cambridgeshire.'

'I say we go back early tomorrow.'

'I'd prefer to stick to our orders.'

'Do you want another day in the saddle and a sore bum?'

There was a long pause. 'Let me think about it,' said Hinton.

By the time that the detectives had been driven to Riseholme Hall, there was a marked improvement in the superintendent's condition. He was conducted on a brief tour of the house by Bishop Jackson himself. Colbeck and Leeming were left alone to talk about the unexpected arrival of their superior.

'I'm worried about him,' confided Colbeck.

'I'm always worried about the superintendent,' said Leeming. 'We work so much better when he is not taking charge of an investigation.'

'You heard what he said, Victor. We are making the decisions in this case.'

'Yet we're still in his shadow. That scares me.'

'I'm more troubled by his appearance,' admitted Colbeck. 'The walk up the hill really took the wind out of him. He was short of breath and white with fatigue.'

Leeming grimaced. 'I feel like that most of the time.'

'And something else worried me. He's lost some of his habitual authority. Can you ever remember him letting us control an investigation when he was directly involved in it? That's most unusual. Then there's the reason he gave for coming here.'

'He said he was moved by the effect of the crimes on the silversmith. He felt very sorry for the old man and wanted to help get the stolen cathedral back.'

'You call Gregory Tomkins "old" but the superintendent is probably a trifle older. That's another factor to consider. His age means that he's lost a lot of his energy.'

'I haven't noticed it,' complained Leeming. 'Whenever he tells us off, there's still that same bitterness in his voice.'

'I disagree,' said Colbeck. 'For the very first time, I'm troubled about him. It's not just his rush to get here and that testing climb up the hill that's wearied him. He's lost his old vigour. Time has finally caught up with him.'

'He seems like the same old superintendent to me – nasty, testy and very angry.'

'I dispute that portrait of him. In my view, he's a shadow of the man we know and that presents us with a real problem.'

'Does it?'

'Yes, Victor. It's all very well feeling the urge to get involved in the investigation. It shows that he really cares about the silversmith. In practical terms, however, he won't be able to help us very much. In fact, I suspect that he's going to be far more of a hindrance.'

* * *

Edward Tallis was never entirely at ease when talking to senior figures in the Anglican church. He had nursed for years an underlying resentment of bishops who sat in the House of Lords, feeling that they should not be allowed a say on decisions that affected the entire population of the country. At the same time, however, he had respect for men who had devoted their lives to spiritual matters, and in Bishop Jackson, he found someone who had done just that. As the two of them paced around the building, he was interested to hear how the cathedral was run, and why the Bishop was so proud of his achievements there.

'The major credit must go to Dean Courtney,' confessed the Bishop. 'He has taken so much pressure off me. Look at this crisis that we face, for instance. When I first heard of the calamity, I had no idea what to do next. I was therefore relieved when the Dean told me that he had made direct contact with you and requested the services of Inspector Colbeck.'

'It was a sensible course of action.'

'I realise that now, Superintendent. I had a few doubts at first but, having met your detectives, I am so glad that you were able to send them here.'

'They are highly experienced and, as it happens, have dealt with a cathedral before.'

'Which one, may I ask?'

'York Minster. What took them to the city was an explosion in the railway station there. I know that Colbeck had to speak directly to the Bishop more than once. I'm pleased to tell you that the problems were eventually solved and that Colbeck was praised for the way that he had dealt with a whole gamut of crimes.'

'I pray that he can do the same thing here.'

'Some of his methods may seem rather strange,' confessed

Tallis, 'but they almost invariably achieve results.'

'That's reassuring to hear, Superintendent.'

'How well did you know Gregory Tomkins?'

'I was lucky enough to meet him when I first became Bishop,' said the other. 'That would be fourteen or fifteen years ago. Tomkins had made some silverware for the cathedral. It was of the highest quality. Then, alas, he moved to London to develop his craft in the capital. But he never forgot the place where he was born.'

'When I met him, he talked so lovingly of Lincoln.'

'I sincerely hope that he will one day visit us again.'

'He will not do so until his latest creation is recovered and the villains who stole it are made to pay the penalty for their crimes. When that happens – and it will, I earnestly hope – Gregory Tomkins will be eager to return to his birthplace.'

The silversmith had felt well enough to get out of bed that day. Still in his dressing gown, he sat in a chair in the drawing room with his wife. Tomkins looked proudly at the examples of his work that were dotted around the room. A large silver cup occupied pride of place of the mantelpiece.

'What are you thinking?' asked his wife.

'I'm thinking that I really did have exceptional skill at one point in my life.'

'You still do have it,' she insisted. 'You may be slower now but you're as talented as you always were. Your standards are still very high.'

'No, they aren't. They're in decline.'

'Nonsense! You are the best silversmith in London.'

'Then why don't I feel that I am? This last year has been marked by a series of losses. My body is starting to ache all over, my eyesight has got much worse, and my confidence is fading with every day. Most troubling of all is that I'm losing my touch.'

'I've seen no sign of it.'

'That's because I've hidden the truth from you, Alice. I'm starting to lose my nerve. The effort of finishing the cathedral has sapped the last of my stamina.'

'Remember what that superintendent said,' she urged. 'He called you a master craftsman with a touch of genius. I agree with him.'

'It's wonderful of you to remind me of that, my love, but you have to face the ugly truth. My touch of genius has left me. My fingers no longer obey me and it's a real effort for me to sit down in my workshop. As far as my career is concerned,' he went on, sadly, 'Gregory Tomkins is extinct. Do you mind being married to an empty husk of a silversmith?'

'I love you whatever happens because you're my wonderful husband.'

Putting her arms around him, she kissed him softly on the cheek.

Dining with Madeleine Colbeck had been the ideal tonic for Lydia Quayle. She was able to read a story to Madeleine's daughter, enjoy a long chat over a delicious meal and even snatch a few words with Caleb Andrews. When she left the house, she had forgotten all about her earlier qualms. The sensation of pleasure, however, did not last. As soon as the cab drew up outside her house, her fears returned with full force. Earlier that day, a stranger had been inside the building. After leaving the cab and paying the driver, she steeled herself to study the house. A light in a window on the ground floor told her that someone was at home. Walking to the front door with some trepidation, she took out her key and inserted it into the lock with a trembling hand. When the door opened, she needed a few moments before she felt able to enter the house.

As soon as she had closed and bolted the door behind her, she was startled by the sudden appearance of her cook. Martha had come out of the kitchen.

'Oh, good evening, Miss Quayle,' she said. 'I was just about to go to bed.'

'Where is Pamela?'

'She went upstairs hours ago. The note you left said that we didn't need to stay up for you and Pamela was very tired. Is there anything I can get for you?'

'No, no, I've not long had dinner.'

'Then it's probably time for me to go to bed as well.'

'Just a moment,' said Lydia, 'I'd like a word with you.'

'As many as you wish,' replied the cook happily.

Martha Grey was a tubby woman in her early forties with rosy cheeks and an almost permanent smile on her face. As well as doing all the cooking she had many other duties, and Lydia had found her supremely reliable.

'What time did you leave the house earlier on?' she asked.

'It must have been close to three o'clock this afternoon,' replied Martha. 'We did the shopping at the market then had a long walk in the park. When we got back, you'd gone and left that note for us.'

'Did anyone else come into the house?'

'Of course they didn't – we've had no visitors here all day. Why do you ask?'

'When I was on my own, I had the feeling that someone left the house and closed the front door very quietly after them.'

'Well, it wasn't me or Pamela. I can tell you that. We'd have been at the market.' Martha narrowed her eyes. 'Are you quite certain about this, Miss Quayle?'

'Yes – and it's very upsetting.'

'I agree. I hate the idea that someone sneaked into the house. We don't want to be burgled.'

'Nothing was stolen a far as I can see.'

'That's a relief. You must have disturbed the intruder. I'm so glad you didn't have to confront him.'

'So am I, Martha.'

'The idea that we had a stranger in here is shocking. It makes me shudder.'

Early next morning, Victor Leeming was sent to the telegraph office at the railway station to see if there was any word from Hinton and Boyce. When the message was handed to him, he was dismayed to learn that the two men had achieved very little on the previous day and had decided to come back to the maelstrom that was Lincoln's Horse Fair. Returning to the cathedral, Leeming handed the telegraph to Colbeck. As he read it, the inspector noted a piece of good news to set against the fact that his men had failed to achieve their objectives.

'They were given help by the chief constable,' he said. 'It's encouraging to hear that we have an ally in Peterborough and not a rival.'

'But they're coming back empty-handed,' observed Leeming sadly.

'We'll find work for them to do.'

'Since they failed so badly, we ought to have gone to Peterborough ourselves.'

'Our place is here, Victor. Now that a demand has been sent to the Dean, he needs us on the spot. It may be our only chance to catch the men we're after.'

'It won't be easy with the streets filled by horses. The villains will be able to use the animals as a shield they can hide behind.'

'You're forgetting about the box in which the silver cathedral is travelling. Tomkins told the superintendent how bulky it was. No matter how many horses have poured into the city,' said Colbeck, 'they can't hide a large wooden box.'

After taking their last look at the model of the cathedral, they wrapped it carefully in its padding, lowered it into the box then nailed it safely in place. Jeremy Keane tried to lift it but found it too heavy and lowered it immediately to the ground.

'It weighs a ton,' he protested.

Patrick Farr laughed. 'Now you know why we needed Silas's brawn. He carried it as if it was as light as a feather and swung it onto the back of the cart.'

'Can he be trusted?'

'He's as silent as a grave, Jerry.'

'I don't want him getting drunk and boasting to his friends that he helped to rob a train. I prefer a man who knows how to keep his mouth shut.'

'Then that's what we've got in Silas Weaver. He's not very clever, maybe, but he does what he's told no matter how dangerous it is.'

'He seemed a bit simple to me.'

'No,' insisted Farr, 'he's just very shy, that's all. When I told him what your plan was he said you must be a genius. Silas is in awe of you, Jerry. That's why he didn't say very much when he met you.'

'What will he do when he gets his share of the money?'

'Move to London with his wife and enjoy city life for a change.

Don't have any qualms about Silas. He won't let us down.'

'It's reassuring to hear that, Pat.'

They were interrupted by the sound of the knocker on the front door. Someone was using it with some force. The noise startled Keane.

'Who the devil is that?' he asked.

'Calm down, Jerry. There's no need for alarm.'

'You told me we'd be completely safe here.'

'And that's exactly what we are,' soothed his cousin. 'The only person who knocks on the door that hard is Tim Redshaw. He likes to let people know that he's arrived. I told him you'd come here after we'd stolen the silversmith's cathedral.' Farr moved to the door. 'I'll let him in. It's only fair that you meet the fourth member of our gang.'

Madeleine Colbeck was so worried about her friend that she took a cab to Lydia's house. When she rang the bell, the door was opened by Pamela, a slender woman in her twenties who gave the visitor a welcoming smile.

'Good morning, Mrs Colbeck,' she said. 'It's so nice to see you again.'

'Thank you, Pamela.'

'Miss Quayle is in the drawing room.'

She stood back so that Madeleine could enter the house, then she closed the front door. Before the maid could announce the visitor's arrival, Lydia came out of the drawing room with a smile on her face.

'I thought I heard your voice,' she said, embracing her visitor. 'What a lovely surprise to see you again!' She turned to Pamela. 'I think that a tray of tea is in order.'

'I'll get it at once,' replied the woman before heading for the kitchen.

'So,' asked Lydia, beaming at her visitor. 'What brings you here, Madeleine?'

'I'm worried about you.'

'I feel so much better this morning.'

'What you told me yesterday was very upsetting. I hated the idea of you being given such a shock – especially in your own home.'

'Let's take a moment to talk about it, shall we?' suggested Lydia.

They went into the drawing room and sat down opposite each other. Madeleine was pleased to see that her friend seemed to be much calmer.

'Did you talk to the servants about what happened?' she asked.

'Yes, I did. Martha was still up when I got back last night. To be honest, I believe that she thought I was imagining the whole thing. What was the man after?'

'But you can't be certain if it was a man.'

'That's true. What I can be certain of is that I was very disturbed. It doesn't really matter if it was a man or a woman – an intruder had been in the house. That was enough for me. I was rattled.'

'I don't blame you. That's why I came.' She glanced towards the hall. 'I must say that Pamela gets prettier every time I see her.'

'Yes, it's rather unfair on Martha. She's a kind-hearted woman and a wonderful cook but she has got heavier and heavier. When Pamela stands beside her, she puts Martha in the shade. It's not fair.'

'How do they get on together?'

'Extremely well, as it happens. Martha is like a mother to her. Pamela is the daughter that she never had. Between them, they pamper me.' Lydia smiled. 'I rather enjoy that, to be honest.'

'You deserve pampering.'

'Oh, I don't know about that.'

'And you deserve help from me to discover who could possibly have got into this house without you even noticing it – and what he or she was doing here.'

'The nagging fear hasn't really gone away.'

'Let's think about motive,' suggested Madeleine. 'That's what Robert always asks. What reason could a man have to sneak into your house?'

'Perhaps he just wanted to give me a scare.'

'I can think of a very different reason.'

'What is it?'

'When the door opened for me today, I was reminded how pretty Pamela is. The wonder is that she seems to be unaware of it. Suppose that she has caught the eye of a man. Pamela would certainly turn heads as she walked down a street.'

'But she's such an innocent young woman.'

'Her innocence might be an attraction to certain men,' suggested Madeleine. 'Whenever she leaves the house, she's bound to get admiring glances.'

'To be honest, I don't think she would even notice them.'

'That doesn't mean they don't exist, Lydia. I speak from experience.'

Her friend was startled. 'You do?'

'It was at a time when I was rather innocent myself,' confessed Madeleine. 'I had no idea that a certain person had taken an interest in me. It was someone I knew, a young man who had worked with my father. He was too shy to declare his feelings for me, so – whenever he was off duty – he followed me from time to time if I left the house alone.'

'Were you aware of his interest?'

'No, Lydia, I wasn't. But there were fleeting moments in public when I felt that something wasn't quite right. I just couldn't decide what it was.'

'That must have been worrying.'

'It was and it wasn't. There was no sense of danger. And when I discovered who this person was, I was not upset. After all, I was the daughter of an engine driver so, if I did marry, the chances were that I'd be the wife of someone like the very man who had taken an interest in me.'

'What happened?'

'My father was attacked by men who robbed the train he was driving, and that's how I met Robert. He led the investigation into the crime and we . . . we were drawn towards each other as a result. I've been happily married ever since.'

'Why have you never told me about this man who followed you?'

Madeleine shrugged. 'I suppose that it's something I'd rather forget. It's only because we were talking about Pamela that the memory came back to me.'

'You think that she's being followed by a man?'

'It's a possibility.'

'If she is, Pamela wouldn't be aware of it. Usually, when she goes out of the house, she's with Martha. So are you saying that this man got into the house somehow? Why on earth would he go to such lengths?'

'Men can behave in strange ways sometimes, Lydia. If he had seen Pamela leaving the house with Martha, he might have chosen the moment to break in.'

'There was no sign of forced entry – and what could he possibly want?'

'Simply being in her room would be enough. I take it that it would be very different from Martha's.'

'Yes, the cook has a much larger room.'

'I think it's important not to alarm Pamela by suggesting that someone sneaked into her room. But you might ask her casually if anything is missing. If an admirer did get in there, I think he'd be tempted to steal something that reminded him of Pamela. That might be what he came for.'

'You've got me really worried now,' said Lydia.

'I didn't mean to do that. It's just a guess on my part. Who knows? The person you heard leaving your house might have been a woman, after all.'

'But how on earth did she get in here?'

Madeleine pulled a face. 'I wish I knew.'

CHAPTER NINE

When they met in a private room at the cathedral, Colbeck was not impressed by the fact that the two detectives he had sent into the neighbouring county had come back with such scant new evidence.

'Why didn't you continue your search there today?' he demanded.

'We thought we'd be of more use here, Inspector,' explained Hinton. 'If the missing model of the cathedral is to be exchanged for money, we felt that we wanted to catch the men who stole it in the first place.'

'No date has been set for the exchange,' said Colbeck.

'But we could use extra help,' argued Leeming. 'Since you gave us bad news, I'll give you some in return. Superintendent Tallis is here in Lincoln.'

'That's all we need!' sighed Hinton.

'He won't be pleased that you've gathered no new evidence.'

'We did gather some information,' said Boyce quietly. 'We spoke to a cab driver who remembered seeing a man carrying a large box out of the station shortly after an explosion had gone off there. The man and his companion jumped onto the back of a waiting cart and it set off in a southerly direction.'

'Then there's the stationmaster in Peterborough,' added Hinton. 'We made a point of speaking to him before our train back here arrived. There'd been a good response to the posters he put up in the station. Lots of people came forward to talk about what they saw on the day of the crime. We jotted down the information.' Taking out his notepad, he put it on the table. 'You might care to look at it, Inspector.'

'Tell us about the chief constable,' said Leeming.

'He's launched his own investigation,' replied Boyce. 'Any evidence gathered will be sent to you here.'

'What sort of man is he?' asked Colbeck.

'He's exactly the sort of man you'd expect,' said Hinton, 'and he was very helpful. He's heard of you, Inspector, and said that he hopes to meet you one day.'

'Then he didn't feel we were mounting an investigation that should really have been left to him?'

'He just wanted the men involved caught and punished. What happened at Peterborough Railway Station caused a real shock. There was, however, a point that he felt he ought to make. His police force has dealt successfully with many major crimes in the past. We were asked to respect their record of success.'

'That's fair enough,' agreed Colbeck.

'What's been happening here, sir?' asked Boyce. 'Apart from the arrival of the superintendent, that is.'

'As you can see, the Horse Fair has brought the city alive. There's a festive atmosphere and the streets are full of people. Inevitably, there's a lot of crime taking place. Whenever there are big crowds, thieves have a field day.'

'You just have to watch where you're going, that's all,' said Leeming. 'Otherwise, you're bound to step into some horse manure.'

'What about a demand for money in return for the silver cathedral?' asked Boyce. 'How much are they asking for?'

'A small fortune.'

'Will the Bishop pay the amount?'

'He has already agreed to do so in principle,' Colbeck told him. 'It's the only way to get the gift back.'

'And to bring the villains who stole it out into the open,' said Leeming.

'When will the exchange be made?'

'We're still waiting for details from them,' said Colbeck. 'I'm sure they will arrange things so that they are in no danger of capture. Our job is to ensure that we arrest every one of them.'

Timothy Redshaw was a thickset man with the look of a soldier about him. He stood up straight, spoke crisply and looked people in the eye. Redshaw managed to impress Jeremy Keane to the point where the latter began to revise his earlier decision to pay the man nothing for his part in the theft of the silver cathedral.

'What do you do for a living, Tim?' he asked.

'I work as a gamekeeper on an estate.'

'How long were you in the army?'

'Six years,' said Redshaw. 'Luckily, they coincided with the Crimean War.'

Keane was surprised. 'You call that lucky?'

'I thrive on action, Jerry. Besides, I learnt how to stay alive in combat. It was a valuable lesson.'

'You look as if you're in good condition.'

'I have to be if I want to catch poachers.'

'Tell him about that young couple you discovered in a ditch, Tim.'

Redshaw grinned. 'They were stark naked and getting to know each other very well. When I fired over their heads, they raced away without a stitch of clothing on. I was in luck. The man had left his wallet behind,' recalled Redshaw. 'I was twenty pounds better off. That will teach them to trespass on the estate.'

'What was the woman like?' asked Keane.

'She was a lot faster than the man. When they made a run for it, she was yards ahead of him. The clothes she left behind fitted my wife, so it was a good day for us.'

'But not as good as the day when you distracted the crowds at the railway station. Pat tells me your timing was perfect.'

'It was,' Farr chimed in. 'The moment the train came to a halt, there was an explosion you could have heard a mile away. Tim did a wonderful job.'

'I obeyed orders,' said Redshaw. 'I called today to see when exactly I get paid for what I did at the station.'

'It will be very soon,' promised Keane. 'I sent our demand to the cathedral, and they've agreed to pay every penny. All we need to do is to arrange how we collect it.'

'I'd like to be there when it happens,' volunteered Redshaw. 'If I'm going to get a lot of money, I'm ready to earn it in any way necessary.'

'I like your attitude, Tim.' Keane turned to his cousin. 'I'm going to rethink what I said earlier, Pat. This man is one of us. We can make good use of him in Lincoln.'

After Madeleine left, Lydia Quayle resolved to question Pamela again without putting any sort of pressure on the woman. She bided her time. It was shortly after luncheon that she had a chance to talk to the young woman.

'I take it that Martha has told you about that problem I had yesterday.'

'Yes, she did,' said Pamela.

'When I was alone, I had the feeling that someone left the house and closed the front door with extreme care.'

'Martha told me that you opened the door but the person who'd been in here had been lost in the crowd.'

'What annoyed me the most is that I couldn't decide if it was a man or a woman who had somehow managed to break into the house.'

'Are you certain a stranger was in here?'

'Someone was, Pamela. I'm sure of it.'

'Does that mean this person was a burglar?' asked the maid in alarm.

'I wish I knew. My initial fear was that he or she had broken in to find out if there was anything worth stealing. That thought really upset me.'

'I'm not surprised.'

'Nothing was taken as far as I know. There are some very expensive ornaments in my bedroom, but they are still there. What about your room, Pamela? Are you aware of anything that seems to be missing?'

'No,' said the other. 'To be honest, there's nothing worth stealing.'

'Was anything out of place when you went to bed?'

'No, I'm very careful to keep every item where it should be. If something had been stolen, I'd have spotted it immediately.'

'Then I'm sorry to have wasted your time.'

Pamela was disturbed. 'How did this person get into the house?'

'I wish I knew.'

'And what was he after?'

'We may never know,' said Lydia. 'But I'm taking no chances. I've got a locksmith coming today to change the lock on the front door. If we've had someone in here, I want to be sure that he won't be able to do the same thing again.'

'That's very wise.'

'If a man could get in here during the day, he could do the same thing at night. That thought is frightening.'

'Do you think I should have a lock on my door?' asked Pamela, worried.

'I think that we all should as an extra precaution. When we go to sleep it's vital that we have complete security. We need to feel safe.'

Colbeck was relieved. When he had gone through the respective notepads given to him by Hinton and Boyce, he had found a sizeable amount of useful new evidence. As he returned the notepads to the two detectives, he told them to stay in Lincoln so that two extra pairs of eyes were available for the moment when the money was handed over to the gang in return for the silver model of the cathedral. Colbeck anticipated problems.

'We can't expect these men to honour their word,' he warned.

'What do we do, Inspector?' asked Hinton.

'Keep your weapon loaded. It may well be needed.'

'Who is going to hand over the money?'

'I am,' said Leeming proudly. 'The Dean is going to provide me with clothing that makes me look as if I'm part of the cathedral staff.'

'It would be unfair to use someone actually employed here,' said Colbeck. 'The strain on them would be immense. Victor has been in situations like this before and will keep his nerve.'

'Will you be armed, Sergeant?' asked Hinton.

'Oh, yes,' replied Leeming. 'They won't expect someone in holy orders to have a gun tucked away somewhere.'

'What about the superintendent?' wondered Boyce. 'Will he be involved?'

'I'll do my best to keep him out of the way,' said Colbeck. 'He's tried to offer me advice, but I've overruled him. Since he put me in charge of this investigation, he must obey my orders.'

'Why did he come here?'

'He was moved by the plight of Gregory Tomkins. It was the superintendent who broke the terrible news of the crime to him. The silversmith was mortified. He had worked for several months on his gift to the cathedral and – in a flash – it disappeared.'

'The news must have hit him like a thunderbolt,' said Hinton.

'It did,' agreed Colbeck. 'Mr Tomkins is old and his days as a silversmith are numbered. The model over which he laboured for so long is probably the last major work that he will create. He was inspired by his love of Lincoln, the place where he was born and where he developed his extraordinary skills. What he really wants is to be able to hand over his masterpiece to Bishop Jackson and take part in a service during which the gift is blessed. That means he will be able to die happy.'

'The superintendent heard him say those exact words,' noted Leeming.

'I just wish that Tallis wasn't here,' said Hinton. 'I feel that we're being watched by him – watched and judged.'

'That could work the other way, Alan,' suggested Colbeck. 'You'll be in the perfect position to show your merit to the superintendent and, possibly, earn some sort of promotion. How does that sound?'

Caleb Andrews was feeling better. He was coughing less and able to get a good night's sleep. He hoped that it was only a matter of time before the doctor allowed him to see his granddaughter again without danger of giving her an infection. When Madeleine went into the bedroom, she took the letter that had arrived that morning from her husband and read bits of it to her father. He was dismayed.

'It sounds to me as if we may not see him for days,' he complained.

'Reading between the lines,' she said, 'I get the impression that he'd rather not have the superintendent breathing down his neck.'

'I don't blame him. I met the man once. I'd hate to work under him.'

'Robert pointed out that the very fact that Superintendent Tallis came to Lincoln shows you how serious a case it is. A huge amount of money is involved.'

'Yes, but they won't actually lose it, will they?'

'That depends on what happens. Robert's job would be so much easier if there was no Horse Fair. He says that the chaos there might work in favour of the men who stole the silver cathedral.'

'I hope not,' said Andrews. 'Anyway, putting Lincoln aside for a moment, I wanted to ask you about Lydia. You've been so worried about her. Were you able to put her mind at rest when you called on her this morning?'

'No, I wasn't,' confessed Madeleine.

'Why not?'

'A stranger somehow got into her house. Lydia doesn't know if it was a man or a woman. Either way, it really upset her. She's having the lock on the front door changed.'

'That's a good idea.'

'I hope that it reassures her. She was so edgy when I spoke to her.'

'I know what Lydia needs,' he declared.

'Yes, it's peace of mind.'

'The only way she'll get that is if she has a man in the house. Tell her to marry Alan Hinton and her troubles will be over.'

Madeleine laughed. 'It's not as simple as that, Father.'

'Why not? She likes him, doesn't she?'

'Yes, of course. Lydia is very fond of him.'

'Then what's holding them up?'

'Lydia comes from a wealthy family,' she replied 'Ordinarily, she'd never even meet someone like Alan. I'm sure that he'd love to get closer to her but he's only a detective constable. He doesn't have the kind of income that allows him to marry someone like Lydia.'

'He doesn't need it,' said Andrews. 'Lydia probably has enough money for the two of them. It would certainly make her feel safer. Tell her I said so. If she has a detective living with her, she can forget about having intruders there.'

Madeleine laughed. 'You can't make big decisions for other people, Father. It may well be that Lydia prefers to live alone. Alan is a good friend,' she said. 'If he was a husband, she'd worry like mad every time he goes off on a dangerous assignment.'

'You don't worry about Robert, do you?'

'Of course I do – but I've learnt to live with the problem. I just keep praying that he will not be injured in any way. I couldn't bear that.'

As a rule, Lydia never took much interest in what her servants were doing. Martha and Pamela both had a list of duties, and they tackled them systematically. Neither of them needed to be scolded or even corrected. So quiet and efficient were they that there were times when Lydia did not even realise that they were in the house. Things had now changed. In view of what Madeleine had told her, Lydia took more interest in Pamela. The maidservant went about her work dutifully, unaware that her employer was trying to keep an eye on her.

Until Madeleine had mentioned the fact to her, Lydia had not really noticed how attractive Pamela had become. The servant had a slim figure, and a strikingly pretty face beneath her well-groomed fair hair. She moved with natural grace. What Pamela lacked was a proper education, but she had learnt quickly since joining the household and could speak politely. It was the reason that Lydia was happy for her to answer the front door when anyone called at the house. She now studied Pamela more carefully and saw that the woman was bound to collect some interest from men when she was out in public. Had an unknown individual been attracted to her? At all events, one thing was certain. Pamela was completely unaware of whom such a person could be.

Victor Leeming was seething with embarrassment. Under the watchful eye of Dean Courtney, he was trying on a series of cassocks to find the one that fitted him best. They were in the vestry at the cathedral with Edward Tallis. The superintendent was quick to notice that Leeming was not wholly committed to wearing his disguise.

'What's the trouble, man?' he demanded.

'I'm not sure, sir,' replied the sergeant.

'There's no need to look so uncomfortable. Act as if you really are a member of the cathedral clergy. Show some dignity. Move around as if you're proud to be in the service of the Almighty.'

'I'm doing my best, sir.'

'Well, it's not good enough. When you deal with these men, you must look as if you are a genuine member of the staff here. Stop slouching. Move around as if you belong in a place of worship.'

'But I don't, sir,' admitted Leeming. 'I'm like a fish out of water. Why can't we use a real chaplain from the cathedral?'

'It's because we would be putting his life in danger.'

'What about my life?' muttered Leeming.

'You know how to take care of yourself in a dangerous situation,' insisted Tallis. 'We can't ask a member of the cathedral clergy to face these vile criminals. That's far too risky for someone on the Dean's staff. The situation calls for an experienced detective. I thought you'd jump at the chance to have such an important role.'

'I do jump at it, Superintendent. I was happy to agree to it at first. It was only when I saw how I looked in a cassock that I changed my mind. Also, there's another problem. These men will be armed. If I'm to meet them face to face, I'd like a weapon of my own.' He patted his garment. 'Where on earth can I hide it if I'm wearing this?'

'May I make a suggestion?' asked the Dean.

'Please do,' invited Tallis.

'It's clear that the Sergeant feels rather uncomfortable in that cassock.'

'I certainly do,' agreed Leeming.

'Walk around the cathedral with me. Observe the way that I behave in this illustrious setting. We'll go side by side down the nave at a steady pace. Keep your head down and your mind on something spiritual. I'm quite sure that you'll soon get the hang of it, Sergeant.'

'I very much doubt that,' said Leeming.

'Dean Courtney has given you excellent advice,' said Tallis. 'Obey it. You leave me as a detective sergeant anxious about carrying out a role that makes you feel ill at ease. Come back to me as if you have been a member of the cathedral staff for years.'

'Let's go, shall we?' said the Dean, indicating the door.

Jeremy Keane had been pleasantly surprised. Given the opportunity of meeting Timothy Redshaw, he had been delighted by the man's obvious qualities. Redshaw was tough, down to earth and ready to obey orders. Instead of being deprived of his share of the stolen money, Keane decided, Redshaw should be given the chance to earn an even bigger amount. If anyone deserved a smaller share, it was Silas Weaver. Apart from his impressive strength, he had little to contribute. There had to be a way of reducing the amount of money he was given so that the other three men involved in the crime could each get more.

For his part, Redshaw wanted to know more about Keane. But for his leadership, there would have been no theft. Redshaw could see that Keane was a very clever man, able to devise a plan that had worked to perfection. He pressed the Londoner for more detail.

'What made you organise everything so carefully?' asked Redshaw.

'Valuable information came into my hands,' replied Keane.

'How?'

'I work in the jewellery trade, Tim. While gifted people like Gregory Tomkins make wonderful items, I prefer to buy and sell them. It's less difficult and can be more rewarding. I mixed with the jewellery fraternity all the time,' said Keane, 'and got to know all the key figures in it. The big bonus of my work was that I heard the latest gossip.'

'What do you mean, Jerry?' asked his cousin.

'People like to boast about their work to make themselves feel important. I met a couple of them in the Red Fox, a pub in the jewellery quarter. They worked a few blocks away from the premises of Peat, Hatherly and Tomkins. I'd passed on a lot of gossip to them in the past, so they probably felt they owed me something in return.'

'What did they tell you?' wondered Redshaw.

'They boasted about being under the same roof as Tomkins, one of the finest silversmiths in the country. I heard that he'd been working on something special. It was a gift for a cathedral – that's all they told me. Well, I knew that Tomkins was born and brought up in Lincoln, so it was easy to guess which cathedral it was.'

'But how did you find out when the gift would be transferred there?'

'That took me weeks,' confessed Keane. 'I had to buy those two men a lot of beer before I got the truth out of them. I couldn't believe that the only security they had for the silver cathedral was a private detective. Imagine the carelessness. There was only one man guarding something so priceless!'

'Have you ever done anything like this before, Jerry?' asked Redshaw.

'If you're asking if I've broken the law before, the answer is yes, I have. There's a lot of loose money in the jewellery trade.' Keane's grin broadened. 'Stealing some of it has been my hobby for years.'

When there was a lull in their work, Martha and Pamela sat down in the kitchen to enjoy a cup of tea together. The latter was curious.

'Do you think that we had a stranger in the house?' she asked.

'That's what Miss Quayle believes.'

'Could she have made a mistake?'

'It's possible, I suppose, Pamela.'

'How on earth could he or she get in here?'

'Who knows?' asked Martha. 'The one thing I'm certain about is that he must have sneaked in somehow when we went off to the market. In other words, he must have been watching the house.'

'The very idea makes me shiver!'

'He must have been here when Miss Quayle came back. I suppose that he waited for a chance to escape then took it.' Her brow crinkled. 'There is one other possibility.'

'What is it?' asked Pamela.

'I wondered if it had been someone who used to work here. Her name was Kitty. When she left, you replaced her. If I'm honest, I was glad to see Kitty go.'

'Why was that?'

'She worked hard but she was very sly. I never trusted her. There were times when she was given a key to the house so that she could let herself back in.' Martha lowered her voice. 'What if she had another key cut?'

'But it's years since she worked here.'

'Kitty could have been biding her time until we'd forgotten about her. She – or a man close to her – watched the house to see when it would be empty. Then one of them let themself in.'

'Yet nothing was stolen.'

'Perhaps one of them got in to see exactly what could be taken. Thieves do this kind of thing, I'm told. They have a good look inside a house to decide exactly what they want. Then they come back and steal it.'

'Can you imagine this woman involved in burglary?'

'Frankly, I can. There was something odd about Kitty. I never trusted her.'

'Did you mention her to Miss Quayle?'

'No, she's probably forgotten that the girl used to work here. I certainly did. It's only because we had the lock on the front door changed that I remembered that Kitty used to have a key to the house from time to time.'

'Where is she now, Martha?'

'She's in service somewhere in London, I daresay. And she certainly knows how to attract men, I can tell you that,' said the cook darkly. 'Kitty was spiteful. She's the sort of person who'd bide her time before she had the chance to get her own back on someone who once got rid of her.'

Colbeck was amazed at the transformation. When he entered the cathedral, he saw the Dean walking slowly down the nave with a companion. At first glance, he assumed that the other man was a member of the clergy. The two figures walked with a measured tread between the ranks of chairs. It was only when they got closer that Colbeck was able to identify the Dean's companion. It was Victor Leeming.

'I didn't recognise you,' said Colbeck, smiling. 'You looked completely at home here.'

'Well, I don't feel at home,' complained the sergeant.

'I really thought that you were a member of the clergy.'

'No, thank you, sir.'

'Sergeant Leeming is a quick learner,' said the Dean. 'The longer we walked side by side, the more he adapted to being in a cathedral.'

'It's a good sign,' noted Colbeck. 'If he can convince me that he works here, he'll certainly be able to fool the men who will come to get their money in exchange for the stolen cathedral.'

'There's only one problem,' said Leeming.

'What is it?'

'Well, I was wondering where I could hide a gun in this cassock. Then I realised something. If I was stupid enough to fire a shot in the middle of a Horse Fair, I'd start a stampede. Just imagine all those animals galloping through the streets.'

'It's a terrifying thought,' said Colbeck.

'We must avoid a stampede at all costs,' agreed the Dean. 'It would ruin everything.' He stood back to appraise Leeming. 'You've improved already, Sergeant. Anyone would think that you were completely at home in here.'

There was a note of desperation in Leeming's voice. 'Can I take this cassock off now, please?'

It was impossible for Patrick Farr to visit a Horse Fair without being fascinated by the animals on show. Jeremy Keane and Timothy Redshaw left him to study them and made their way up to the cathedral. They looked at it from all angles, wondering where best to organise the exchange. Having received their money, they would hand over the gift from Gregory Tomkins. It was vital to ensure their escape.

'What are we going to do, Jerry?' asked Redshaw.

'Make the exchange at midnight,' replied the other. 'We need darkness to make certain that we can vanish quickly with the money.'

'Where will we take it?'

'We'll find a hiding place just outside the city. We'll divide the money there before we make our way back to Pat's farm to celebrate.'

'No more working as a gamekeeper!' said Redshaw.

'Don't be so rash, Tim,' urged the other. 'You must keep your job for a while. If you leave it suddenly, you'll arouse suspicion. I've told my cousin the same thing. He must not put his farm on the market for months.'

'He'll be itching to do so.'

'Pat will have to be patient. That goes for all of us. There are Scotland Yard detectives looking for us, remember. They're clever devils. We must carry on our lives as if nothing has happened or we'll give the game away.'

Redshaw was impressed. 'You've thought of everything, Jerry.'

'I hope so.'

'What if the Dean tries to set a trap for us?'

'Then he'll be making a terrible mistake,' warned Keane with a grim smile.

CHAPTER TEN

Thanks to the doctor's pills, Caleb Andrews had felt markedly better that day. He felt able to get out of bed, dress himself and venture downstairs. The first person to welcome him was his granddaughter, who clapped her hands with joy. Helena Rose had drawn another steam engine for her grandfather. She had included the right number of funnels this time. When she showed him the drawing, Andrews praised her accuracy.

Alone with his own daughter later on, he thanked her effusively for bringing him to the house.

'I'm sorry I was so stubborn, Maddy.'

'I'm used to it.'

'What a terrible thing to say about me!' he cried with mock outrage.

'It's the truth. You like to have your own way. If I hadn't come to fetch you, you'd have got worse and worse.'

'I realise that now.'

'We had to rescue you before you got really ill.'

'Thank heaven you did just that! I know I was against the idea at first, but it saved me from getting seriously ill. That doctor was wonderful. He spotted the problem at once and gave me the pills to cure it. My chest is fine now,' he went on, tapping it with the flat of his hand. 'I feel as if I'm thirty years younger.'

'Well, don't try to prove it. You're staying with us until I'm a hundred per cent certain that you're fit enough to go home.'

'Don't be so bossy.'

'You need more rest.'

He snorted.

'And we can do without rude noises.'

'Any more news from Robert?'

'Yes,' she replied. 'A letter came early this morning. He feels that the gang are just about to arrange a time to hand over the item they stole – if they get the money that they've demanded, that is.'

'How did they know when it was travelling to Lincoln?'

'Robert is still trying to work that out.'

'I blame the Great Northern Railway.'

Madeleine laughed. 'You'd blame everything on them.'

'They should have employed a guard who took more care of a precious object, and they should have made sure that nobody else realised that the train was carrying something made of solid silver.'

'I'm sure that they tried to hide that fact.'

'Then how did the gift come to be stolen? A man was shot dead on that train, Maddy. His life was far more important than a model of Lincoln cathedral. The Great Northern Railway should have protected its passengers properly.'

'The same could be said of the company you worked for,' she argued. 'The London and North Western Railway has had its share of crime. You were a victim of it once, Father – or had you forgotten?'

'I could never forget it, Maddy,' he said seriously. 'I was badly injured when those men climbed onto my footplate. It took me a long time before I could go back to work. Mind you,' he remembered, 'there were compensations. As a result of that attack on me, I got myself a son-in-law who catches villains on the railway system, and, in due course, the most beautiful granddaughter in the world.'

No matter how much she tried, Lydia could not put the incident out of her mind. It kept her awake at nights. Someone – male or female – had managed to get into her house. Even though there was a new lock on the front door, she did not feel safe. When she saw Pamela taking a break from housework, she took the opportunity to speak to her.

'I do wish I knew who got in here the other day,' Lydia said.

'Martha and I were talking about that,' replied Pamela. 'She wondered if it might have been a woman called Kitty.'

Lydia frowned. 'Kitty?'

'She worked here, didn't she?'

'Ah, yes, she did. I'd rather forgotten her. Frankly, I was glad to get rid of the woman. She always had such a resentful look about her. You've been much more pleasant and hard-working than Kitty.'

'Martha told me that she sometimes had a key to the front door.'

Lydia was jolted. 'Yes, she did. I'd forgotten that.'

'Might she have been the person you heard closing the door?'

'I suppose that it could have been – but it's a long time since Kitty worked here. On the other hand, she was the sort of person who nursed grievances. I upset her a few times when I had to speak sharply to her.'

'Was she the kind of woman who'd want to get revenge?'

'Now that you mention it, Kitty was exactly that kind of woman. Why on earth didn't I think of her before?' asked Lydia. 'It's typical of her that she kept the spare key to the front door. It meant that she could let herself in here whenever she wanted.'

'Yet she never stole anything.'

'We don't know that for certain, Pamela.'

'Martha wondered if she came into the house to see what was worth taking then reported back to a male friend who would burgle the place. Luckily, you've changed the front door lock so he won't be able to get in.'

'You've made me really anxious now,' admitted Lydia. 'I have enough trouble sleeping as it is. Thinking about Kitty will mean that I won't get a wink of sleep.'

'I didn't want to upset you,' said Pamela. 'It was just a guess on Martha's part. Kitty may not even live in London now. I'm sorry I mentioned her name to you.'

'I'm not,' said Lydia softly.

The letter from the leader of the gang arrived for the Dean when he was talking to Inspector Colbeck at the cathedral. Having opened and read it, he passed it to his companion. Colbeck read the orders with care. He was impressed.

'The exchange is to be made in two days,' he noted. 'That's clever of them. They're using darkness to conceal themselves and to limit our chances of catching them easily.'

'What they don't say is how they are bringing the wooden box,' said the Dean.

'They'll need a cart to do that.'

'Yes, the model will be far too heavy to carry.'

'Yet one of them was strong enough to lug it out of the train,' remembered Colbeck. 'My detectives told me that a cab driver at Peterborough station had seen a man put it on the back of a cart then climb aboard with his accomplice before being driven off.'

'What do you make of their request about the money, Inspector?'

'They want it inside saddle-bags. That means they'll be riding horses so that they can make a quick exit when they have their money. The wooden box will have been brought on a cart. They're happy to abandon that.'

'What do you make of their demand?'

'It's written by the same person who wrote to you earlier. He is clearly an educated man and wishes to leave nothing to chance. He's taken care not to tell us the exact location where he wants to make the exchange. In other words,' said Colbeck, 'he's giving us no chance to arrange a welcoming committee. We're up against a man who thinks about all eventualities.'

'Do you still believe that he's a farmer?'

'No, I don't. He's their leader and comes from London. He obviously has friends near Peterborough on whom he can call. I'm certain that he supplied information about the time that the train carrying your gift from Gregory Tomkins would arrive at the station. This man obviously watched the box being loaded onto the train in question.'

'He seems fiendishly well-prepared,' said the Dean.

'I've spent most of my career arresting men of that calibre,' said

Colbeck. 'They always make a fatal mistake at some point. We just need to bide our time. I'll pass on the news to Sergeant Leeming.'

'How will he react?'

'I should imagine that he will be delighted. Since he will be handing over the saddlebag at midnight, nobody will see him properly in the darkness.'

Back at the farm, Jeremy Keane was in the kitchen with his cousin. Patrick Farr downed the last of his tea then put the cup aside. He was troubled by doubts.

'When we hand over the box,' he said, 'they'll have torches outside the cathedral at the place where it happens. Our faces are going to be seen, Jerry.'

'Not if we're wearing masks, Pat,' replied Keane. 'I got a woman friend to make four of them out of an old scarf because I knew they'd come in useful.'

'I'd never have thought of that.'

'Then it's good that you let me do the thinking. I knew that you could steal that box from the guard's van and bring it here. But the difficult bit is exchanging it for the money. They'll do everything they can to arrest us. I want to make that almost impossible for them.'

'I wish I had your brains.'

'You did your share. I relied on you to recruit two good, reliable men who were ready to break the law. You found Weaver and Redshaw – and they both obeyed my orders. I've got my doubts about Weaver but not about Redshaw. Tim is a very useful man. I'm sorry I had qualms about him.'

'Nothing frightens Tim. He's as brave as they come.'

'I'll make good use of that bravery.'

'How much have you told this woman friend of yours?'

'All that she knows is that I'm hoping to go back home with a lot of money.'

'Wasn't she curious?'

'I'm sure she was but she has the sense not to ask questions. She just does what I tell her. When I asked her to make those masks, she didn't wonder why. She could see that it was important, so she simply did it.'

'I need to find myself a woman like that.'

'That won't be difficult,' said Keane, grinning. 'You'll be rich, Pat. That means you can pick and choose.'

'It's no fun sleeping in an empty bed,' moaned Farr.

'Those days are over. If we get our money from the cathedral, we can all start to enjoy much better lives.'

As time passed, Gregory Tomkins seemed to be getting worse. He had lapsed into a deep pessimism. His wife did her best to remain hopeful, but her husband's behaviour was trying. Wrapped up in his dressing gown, Tomkins was sitting in an armchair in the drawing room and staring unseeingly out of the window. When his wife put a cup of tea on the table beside him, he hardly noticed her.

'Try to think positive thoughts, Gregory,' she advised.

'What?' he asked, taken by surprise.

'I can see from the look on your face that you're still brooding.'

'I can't help it, Alice.'

'Yes, you can. You used to boast that the secret of your success was that you had the gift of concentration. It meant that you could spend long hours working. All that effort you put in was bound to have its effect on you.'

'I keep thinking about my model of Lincoln Cathedral.'

'That's the worst thing you can do.'

'It's gone, Alice. I might as well face the truth. It's gone forever.'

'I have more faith in Inspector Colbeck.'

'What can he do?' asked Tomkins. 'The men who stole my masterpiece are mindless ruffians. They don't even recognise the significance of what they've done. They've probably never been anywhere near the cathedral and – even if they had been there – it was not to get on their knees and pray. They're despicable heathens.'

'Inspector Colbeck will catch them somehow.'

'He's met his match at last.'

'I don't believe that.'

'Then why have we had no news from him?'

'Try to be patient, Gregory.'

'How can I be patient when my mind is in turmoil?' he asked.

'You heard what Superintendent Tallis told us. He went up to Lincoln himself to help in the search. He was full of praise for the inspector. You ought to feel reassured by what he told us.'

'I'd love to feel reassured. The only way that that could happen is if my work was standing in its rightful place in the cathedral. But it's probably not even in the county, let alone on display. What if those thieves have damaged it deliberately? That's my fear, Alice. All those months of dedication on my part were a waste of time.'

'I've never seen you work so hard and so relentlessly. It was frightening.'

'It was my farewell to a lifetime as a silversmith,' he said. 'Instead of being a monument to my career, it's hidden away somewhere in the neighbouring county.'

'Stop punishing yourself with such thoughts.'

'I can't help it, my love.'

'You've done nothing wrong.'

'Then why do I feel so guilty?' asked Tomkins. 'Why do I feel that I should have been sitting with that brave private detective in the guard's van? I should have had a gun and helped him to fight off those dreadful men.'

'You're too old to do such things. You keep mourning the loss of your cathedral and so do I. But I also think about the detective's wife and family. Imagine how terrible a blow it must have been for them. You've lost a work of art,' she told him. 'Mrs Langston has lost a dear husband.'

He nodded penitently. 'You're right to scold me, Alice. I see everything from my point of view. Michael Langston was a hero. He guarded my cathedral with his life. I should remember that. As soon as I feel well enough,' he promised, 'I'll go to Lincoln in person to express my condolences to his wife and family.'

'I'm sure that they will appreciate that, Gregory. And while you're in Lincoln,' she said confidently, 'you'll be able to thank Inspector Colbeck for catching the men who stole the most beautiful thing you ever made.'

Madeleine Colbeck was delighted by the unexpected arrival of her closest friend. Then she realised that Lydia Quayle was in a state of anxiety. She took her visitor into the drawing room and sat beside her on the sofa.

'Has something happened?' she asked.

'I think so,' replied Lydia. 'We might have discovered who sneaked into my house recently. It was Martha's suggestion, and I believe she may be right.'

'Who was the man?'

'I'm now fairly certain that it was a woman.'

Madeleine was surprised. 'Really?'

'Do you remember a maidservant I once had by the name of Kitty Piper?'

'Yes, I do,' said Madeleine, 'but I can't say that I do so fondly. There was something odd about that woman.'

'It's the reason I was glad to let her go.'

'Whenever Pamela opens your front door, I get a welcoming smile. I never got that from Kitty. She was always rather cold.'

'I was glad to see her go, Madeleine. And I was lucky to find a replacement for her very quickly. Pamela is a delight to have in the house. Kitty was not.'

'Why did your cook suggest her name?'

'Martha remembered that Kitty had a key to the front door. I gave one to Kitty and to Martha so that they could come and go as they wished.' She lowered her voice. 'What if Kitty used her key to get into my house?'

'Didn't she hand it back before she stopped working for you?'

'Yes, of course, but she could easily have had another one cut beforehand.'

'What reason would she have to come back to you house?'

'Knowing Kitty,' said Lydia, 'I suspect that it was to get her revenge. We were never on the best of terms. Of course, it may be that she didn't come in person. Perhaps she had a male friend. Kitty was something of a flirt. Martha told me that, when they were out together, Kitty always got a lot of attention from men.'

'Was it a male friend who let himself into your house with Kitty's key?'

'I'm beginning to think that.'

'How upsetting that must have been!' said Madeleine. 'No

wonder you were so shaken by the experience.'

'I'm so relieved that it must have been Kitty.'

'And this was Martha's suggestion, was it?'

'Yes, and I'm glad that she made it. To be honest, I'd forgotten that I'd ever employed Kitty. I was so glad to get rid of her that I put her out of my mind.'

'And suddenly, she's back.'

'She is – or a man she knows is.'

'Yet nothing appeared to be stolen, Lydia.'

'That doesn't make it any less criminal. Using her key, he let himself in, found his way around the house and made a list of things worth stealing.'

'In that case,' said Madeleine, 'you need to keep all the interior doors locked when you go to bed.'

'But he won't be able to get in with Kitty's key again,' Lydia reminded her. 'It won't fit the front door any more.'

'That should reassure you.'

'It should,' agreed Lydia, 'but it doesn't somehow, and I don't know why.'

'What are you afraid of?'

'I'm afraid of a woman who used to work for me getting some sort of revenge. There's one thing of which I'm certain, Madeleine.'

'What is it?'

'Whoever broke into my house . . . will try to do so again.'

Madeleine enfolded her friend in her arms.

Alan Hinton and Eric Boyce had been sent into the city in search of the most likely place that would be chosen by the gang to collect their money in return for the silver model of the cathedral. At that moment, Lincoln was bursting at the seams. The detectives had to imagine what it would be like at midnight and what sort of exit would be chosen. After a lengthy spell dodging crowds, horses and farm animals, the two men rewarded themselves with a hot pie from one of the stalls set up for the Horse Fair. They found a quiet spot behind a booth and munched their food.

'How long is the superintendent staying?' asked Hinton.

'Why not ask him, Alan?'

'It's because I don't want my head bitten off.'

'Then ask the inspector,' suggested Boyce. 'He is supposed to be in charge of the investigation and will know what the superintendent's plans are.'

'I think Tallis would be more use in London. That's where the crime was plotted.'

'It's also where the silversmith works. He must have some idea who got hold of the details about the time when his gift would be brought by train to Lincoln.'

'From what I heard, the silversmith is too distressed to remember anything.'

'That's a pity!'

'The theft of his work may well be the death of him.'

'What a terrible shame that would be!'

'How much money is the gang demanding?'

'Far too much, I expect,' said Boyce. 'They want to make a killing. Most people would think twice about taking money from a cathedral. I mean, it's . . . well, it's indecent, to say the least. Don't they have any standards?'

'No,' decided Hinton. 'I think we're better off agreeing that these men are rotten through and through. Theft and murder mean nothing to them. They're just necessary steps to making them rich.'

A group of horses trotted past, making them stand back quickly out of the way.

'If I ever come here again,' promised Boyce, 'it won't be when the Horse Fair is on. It's like being in the middle of a cavalry charge.'

'There are compensations, Eric.'

'I can't see any.'

'Then take a bite of your pie – they're delicious.'

Edward Tallis had spent a long time in the cathedral on his own. When he came out at last, Colbeck was waiting to speak to him. He noticed that the superintendent had his valise with him and that he was limping badly.

'Have you hurt yourself, sir?' he asked solicitously.

'It's my own fault. At my age I shouldn't spend so much time on my knees. Getting up again was agonising.'

'I didn't know that you went in there to pray.'

'I wasn't praying,' explained Tallis. 'I went in there to clear my mind and to get some help.'

'Were you seeking divine intervention?'

'Don't be ridiculous! I've never fooled myself that the Almighty would be interested in anything I had to say. It was Gregory Tomkins who sent me there. In the calm of the cathedral I could think properly about him.'

'And what conclusion did you reach, sir?'

'I decided that I must be on the next train back to London.'

Colbeck was surprised. 'What made you reach that decision?'

'I can't stop thinking about the silversmith. Tomkins was utterly shocked by the theft of his work, and even more horrified at the murder of the man guarding it on the train. Tomkins is in pain,' said Tallis. 'I came here in pursuit of the men responsible for the crimes, yet they were planned in London. That's where their leader lives and where he somehow got hold of the information about the day and time when the silversmith's gift was being brought here by train.'

'It would be very helpful to know how those details leaked out.'

'Then that's what I'll try to find out in London.'

'We'll have to manage without you, sir.'

'I'm in the way, Inspector. I felt glad that I came and had the opportunity of meeting the Bishop and the Dean, but my place is in London, searching for the man who somehow got hold of information that enabled him to devise a plan to seize the silver cathedral with the help of associates in Cambridgeshire.'

'You've made the right decision, sir,' said Colbeck.

'I'm sorry that I seem to be deserting you.'

'And I'm sorry that you are leaving us with sore knees.'

'It serves me right,' admitted Tallis with a grin. 'I'm old enough to know better than to kneel down for such a long period.'

'I wish you well in your quest, Superintendent. Forget about us. First of all, you should speak to Gregory Tomkins. Now that he has had time to recover from the shock of what happened, he may be able to help you. Good luck, sir.'

'Thank you. I may need it.'

Silas Weaver walked side by side with Patrick Farr around the latter's farm. Both were keenly aware that they might not be doing that for much longer.

'You'll be very sad to leave this here, Pat,' he said.

'I'll be sad because I've built the place up, but I'll be glad as well. Getting up at the crack of dawn to supervise the milking is something that's always an effort. There's also the smell of the farm. It's got into my clothes,' complained Farr. 'I'd love to wake up in a house where I can start the day with a hot bath then put on a clean suit.'

'You talked about finding yourself a new wife?'

'That's at the top of my list.'

'What sort of woman are you looking for?'

Farr laughed. 'One who does whatever I tell her.'

'They're the best kind,' said Weaver with a throaty chuckle.

'My first wife died before we could have any children. I'm hoping for better luck next time. It would be nice to be a family man everyone respected.'

'You're well-respected in the farming community.'

'It's time for a change, Silas – a complete change. But what about you? Do you still think of moving to London?'

'Yes, I do,' said Weaver firmly. 'I've got friends there – people with the same interests as me.'

Farr laughed. 'The only things you're interested in are getting drunk and watching wrestling matches.'

'It's the world I came from. I was fourteen when I discovered the magic of a pint of beer and, as you know, I had quite a reputation as a wrestler. I loved taking on another man in front of a baying audience. It was exciting.'

'Then you got married and stopped fighting.'

'My wife didn't like the people I was mixing with.'

'Does that include me?'

'No, of course not, Pat. You employ me here on the farm. Molly's grateful to you.'

'What have you told her?'

'Nothing,' said Weaver. 'I know when to keep my trap shut.'

'Molly must never know where the money came from. You understand?'

'Of course . . .'

They stopped near a fence and paused to survey a field. A small flock of sheep were grazing happily in the sunshine. Spring lambs were frolicking. Weaver smiled fondly at the scene, but Farr turned away abruptly.

'Let's go back into the farmhouse,' he suggested. 'I'm putting this world behind me for good. The only time I want to see a lamb is when it's on the plate in front of me with plenty of spuds and veg beside it.'

The four policemen met in a tavern near the cathedral. As Hinton and Boyce sat down at the table, Colbeck told them that Superintendent Tallis had gone back to London.

'That does surprise me,' said Hinton. 'I thought he'd want to be here when the gang handed over what they'd stolen in return for a huge amount of money.'

'He changed his mind,' explained Colbeck. 'Because he wants us to wind up this investigation, he's gone to find out who gave vital information to the leader of the gang. Once we know that, our task will become much easier.'

'That'll be a relief!' said Leeming.

'You're going to hand over the money, aren't you?' asked Boyce.

'Someone has to.'

'Victor will be dressed in a cassock,' explained Colbeck, 'so that he looks as if he's a member of the cathedral clergy.'

'That means you'll come face to face with them,' said Hinton.

'I was looking forward to that,' confessed Leeming, 'but I'm not so sure now. These men are ruthless. There's no telling what they'll do.'

'Whatever it is,' said Colbeck, 'you'll be equal to the challenge.' He turned to the others. 'I told you to find the most likely place where the handover might take place.'

'We've spotted a few places,' said Hinton, taking a sheet of paper from inside his pocket and laying it on the table. 'This is a rough map of the city.'

Leeming laughed derisively. 'It's nothing like Lincoln!'

'Look more closely,' advised Colbeck. 'It is fairly accurate. All the main features are there – if a little hazy. What are those three stars on the map?'

'They're the three places the gang might choose,' said Boyce, using a finger to point. 'At the moment, all three are hidden but it will be different at night when all these people have gone off to where they're sleeping. This is our favourite,' he went on, jabbing a finger on the map. 'It's fairly close to the cathedral but it gives them an easy escape route out of the city.'

'That's a good point, Eric,' said Colbeck, 'but the other places you picked out have their advantages as well. Each one gives them different advantages. We must bear in mind that, once they have their money, they'll want to ride quickly away. That being the case, perhaps they'll choose the place right next to a gate out of the city.'

'It's what I'd choose,' decided Leeming.

'Don't change sides, Victor. Remember that you're handing over a saddlebag filled with money. You're one of us,' said Colbeck. 'We're there to arrest these men. And we'll have a better chance of doing that if we know exactly where they'll be.'

'That's true, Inspector.'

'And we won't be entirely alone,' Colbeck reminded them. 'The chief constable is going to give us some additional men. I've asked for them to be out of uniform so that they won't be recognised for what they are. Right,' he added, reaching for his tankard and raising it high. 'Here's to the success of our venture!'

Edward Tallis was on a train that would take him back to London. He had ample time to reflect on the progress of their investigation. In giving Colbeck control over him while he was in Lincoln, Tallis had not only been acknowledging the man's natural superiority as a detective, he had become keenly aware of his own declining power. He had also come to rue the time when he had to climb all the way up to the cathedral, he had scolded himself for doing anything as reckless as getting down on his knees. It was not a religious impulse that made him do it. He was responding to a need to be alone in a quiet place where he could review the situation at leisure and think kindly about Gregory Tomkins, the tormented silversmith. It was only when he tried to get up again that he realised what a terrible mistake he had made.

Seated in a crowded compartment, he was suffering pain in his knees and a jabbing sensation in his back. The jolting of the train made the agony more intense.

He scolded himself for acting on impulse and making the long journey to Lincoln. It had taught him his physical limitations and had cruelly reminded him of his age. He was no longer the thrusting former soldier who had made such a good impression on the commissioner at Scotland Yard. The truth had to be faced. Tallis was in decline. It was not only his body that had lost its former power. His mind was also faltering at times. Occasional losses of memory were starting to trouble him, and his concentration was less intense. As he felt another pang in his shoulder, and an answering jab in both knees, he had a sudden, frightening thought.

He might well be involved in his very last investigation.

CHAPTER ELEVEN

Alice Tomkins was struck by the dramatic contrast. When her husband had finished work on the latest example of his brilliance as a silversmith, he had been in state of euphoria. Everything was different now. In the wake of its theft, he was completely drained of life. His face had darkened, his cheeks had hollowed, and he had lost the characteristic gleam in his eyes. Alice was appalled to see that he looked ten or fifteen years older than he really was. What troubled her most was that Gregory had now lost his voice and could only communicate with a faint croak. It was almost as if he were dying slowly in front of her.

'Would you like another cup of tea?' she asked him.

'No, thank you.'

'What about something to eat?'

Tomkins shook his head.

'You hardly had any breakfast, Gregory.'

'I'm not hungry.'

'You haven't had a proper meal for days.'

'Leave me be, Alice,' he said.

'You must eat something.'

'I've lost my appetite.'

They were in the drawing room, seated opposite each other in armchairs. Eyes fixed on the ceiling above him, Tomkins seemed to be in another world. Alice studied him with growing fear. He was barely alive.

'Don't give up hope,' she pleaded. 'It's so unlike you, Gregory.'

'I've never been in such despair before.'

'You seem to forget that Inspector Colbeck and his detectives are working hard for your benefit. They'll find your silver cathedral somehow.'

'But they won't find Michael Langston alive,' mumbled her husband. 'Nobody can do that. He's gone forever – thanks to me.'

'You're not to blame,' she argued.

'Then why can't I get him out of my mind?'

'Stop punishing yourself.'

'I deserve the pain, Alice. It will be with me for the rest of my life.'

'Instead of thinking about yourself,' she said gently, 'you should be helping the detectives find what was stolen.'

'How on earth can I do that?' he bleated. 'I barely have enough strength to get up in the morning. I'm a silversmith – or, at least, I was. I'm not a detective.'

'But you may have information that you could pass on to Scotland Yard. Think hard, Gregory. Without realising it, you must know the person who gave away details of when your model was being sent to Lincoln by train. You discussed it with your partners beforehand.'

'That's true. We agreed that nobody else would know the day and time.'

'Yet someone else did know and he passed on the information – possibly by accident – to a criminal. A name is locked away in your memory. Think hard. Who of the people working alongside you is likely to have passed on the information?'

'I don't know, Alice.'

'Superintendent Tallis has gone to enormous trouble on your behalf. He's sent his best detective to Lincoln to find out the truth of what happened. Inspector Colbeck needs your help. Please give him a name. Was there an apprentice working alongside you who could not resist boasting about what you were doing?'

He shrugged his shoulders. 'I can't remember.'

'Try harder,' she urged.

'I try not to think at all about what happened because it brings back memories of Michael Langston. I have nightmares about his wife and family. I wake up wishing that I had never started work on that cathedral.'

'Don't say that. It was your crowning achievement.'

'Yes, and it's now in the hands of unspeakable rogues who were ready to kill to get their hands on it. They won't have a clue how much love, devotion and true artistry went into the making of it. That's what hurts me the most – my work is in the hands of vandals.'

'How did it get there?' she demanded.

'I've no idea.'

'Yes, you do. You know all the people that you employ. One of them must have found out details of when your work was being taken to Lincoln. Or was it someone who simply let the truth slip out when he'd had a drink or two? Rack your brains, Gregory. It's vital that we can give the detectives a name. It's the starting point they need.'

He looked at her blankly. 'I'm sorry but I can't help them.'

When Colbeck called on the chief constable, he was given an enthusiastic welcome. Richard Beard pumped his hand then waved him to a seat. When they heard a dozen horses cantering past in the street outside, they exchanged a wry smile.

'Your job would have been so much easier,' said Beard, 'if you were not here during the Horse Fair.'

'We had no idea how big an event it was,' admitted Colbeck.

'It gets bigger and more international each year. Walk through the streets and you'll hear a mixture of different languages. It's confusing for my constables on duty. How can you arrest a man if he doesn't speak a word of English?'

'Whatever language they speak, they understand the significance of a pair of handcuffs. Anyway,' said Colbeck, 'I've come to take you up on your offer of help.'

'How many men do you need?

'As many as you can spare but not until midnight the night after tomorrow.'

'Is that when you're hoping to get the gift back?'

'Yes, it's the date and time given to us by the people who stole it. They have been dealing directly with the Dean. In their latest communication, they tell us when the event will happen but not exactly where.'

'The sooner you know where, the sooner you can make preparations.'

'We'll have to think on our feet when the venue is declared. The one thing we do know is that they'll be coming on horses. They want for the money to be in saddlebags.'

Beard grinned. 'I'd have thought we already had too many horses in Lincoln.'

'How many of the gang there'll be, we can only guess. I'm inclined to think that one or more of them are farmers,' said Colbeck, 'but their leader hails from London and is clearly educated.'

'My men are usually exhausted at the end of the day but I daresay that I can let you have nine or ten on the night in question.'

'Excellent.'

'Where would you like them to be placed?'

'I'd prefer to take your advice on that score. You know the city – I don't. Where are the key points for entering and leaving Lincoln?'

'I can give you a list off the top of my head.'

'Nine or ten constables will be a great help.'

'There'll be an extra man at your disposal, Inspector.'

'That's good news. Who is he?'

'Me, of course,' said Beard, tapping his own chest. 'You don't think I'd miss a chance like this, do you?'

Jeremy Keane was strolling around the farm with his cousin. The compound of smells made him pull a face.

'How do you put up with this stink, Pat?'

'What stink?'

'The one you're so used to that you don't even smell it any more. During our walk, I spotted horse manure, sheep shit, chicken shit, cow shit and dog shit. I could never work in conditions like these.'

'You learn to love it, Jerry.'

'When I came here as a lad, I didn't smell a thing. I was too busy seeing all the animals and playing games with you. As soon as I arrived this time, the stench hit me.'

'It's nowhere near the stink you've got in London,' said Farr. 'The city always smells as if all the drains are blocked.'

'I thought you were keen to live there.'

'I was but now I want to move to Lincoln and live in comfort.'

'What are Silas's plans?'

'Don't worry about him. He and his wife will move off the farm and begin a new life in London. With money in his pocket he'll be able to dress properly. He used to make money as a wrestler, you know. That's where those muscles come from.'

'He's strong and dependable – that's all that matters.'

'I'll miss him when we split up.'

'All good things come to an end, Pat.'

'Silas could work from dawn to dusk without complaint.'

'He'll have time for a long rest now.'

'Not him, Jerry. He's going to London so that he can watch wrestling matches whenever he fancies. It's in his blood.'

'He should spend some of his money on getting an education.'

'Who needs brains when you can afford to pay for everything?'

'That's a fair point,' said Keane with a smile. 'All he has to do is follow my orders when we get to Lincoln, and he'll end up as a rich man.'

Madeleine Colbeck was so worried about her friend that she persuaded Lydia Quayle to go with her into central London. They went to a succession of agencies that provided reliable domestic servants. Lydia was grateful to her friend for suggesting the idea.

'Some of Robert's magic has rubbed off on you,' she said. 'I'd never have thought of doing this.'

'You were so upset at the thought that one of your former servants might be about to rob you that I felt action is needed. Let's find out if Kitty Piper still lives in London.'

'If she does, I feel sorry for anybody who employs her.'

'I thought she was good at her job when you first hired her.'

'Kitty could be very obliging when she wanted to be,' said Lydia. 'It was only after she left that I realised how unsatisfactory she had been.'

'Well, so far there's been no trace of her. The agencies we called on had never heard of her. She could always have changed her name, of course.'

'Kitty would know the best way to do that.'

'What do you mean?'

'She'd get married. Being a wife would be better than working as a servant.'

'You said earlier that she had a lot of attention from men.'

'Kitty knew how to arouse their interest,' recalled Lydia. 'Unfortunately, Martha didn't, so she'll be a spinster for the rest of her life.'

Martha kept the kitchen scrupulously clean. As soon as breakfast was over, she washed the dishes, wiped all the surfaces then used a mop on the floor. When she stepped out of the kitchen, she left it gleaming. Pamela was coming downstairs with a brush and pan. They fell into conversation.

'Do you think they'll find her?' she asked. 'Kitty Piper, I mean.'

'If they don't,' replied Martha, 'it won't be for want of trying.

Mrs Colbeck is very determined. I could see it in her face. They'll track Kitty down somehow.'

'What if it wasn't her who sneaked in here?'

'Who else could it have been?'

'A burglar who somehow found a way in when nobody was looking.'

'Kitty had a key to the front door.'

'That doesn't mean she'd use it, Martha. If she's working for someone else, she might not be allowed time to go wherever she wants.'

'She'd find time somehow.'

'Was she that cunning?'

'Oh, yes,' said the cook. 'There's something I haven't told you about Kitty. I didn't dare mention it to Miss Quayle at the time because I couldn't prove it.'

'Go on.'

Martha lowered her voice. 'I think Kitty invited a man here.'

'Did you see him?'

'No, I didn't. I'd gone to market on my own that afternoon and Miss Quayle was visiting someone. Kitty had been on her own – at least, that was what I thought.'

'How did you guess?' wondered Pamela.

'She couldn't stop smiling. Something had obviously happened while I was out of the house. She swore that nobody had called but I could see that she was lying. I'm certain that she let a man into the house.'

'How could you know that?'

'Kitty had a sort of glow about her.'

'Did you report her to Miss Quayle?'

'No, I didn't, because I couldn't be certain.'

'When was this, Martha?'

'A couple of years ago, I suppose. Kitty could see that I knew her guilty secret and she was quite brazen about it. She'd always attracted men and enjoyed their attention. I began to wonder how many times she'd let one of them in when she was alone in the house. That's why I was glad when she left,' said Martha. 'You were so different. I could trust you completely.' She spoke through gritted teeth. 'Kitty Piper was a slut.'

Colbeck was alone with Dean Courtney at the cathedral. The Dean was anxious.

'I've spoken with the chief constable,' said Colbeck, 'and he will provide us a handful of officers on the night in question.'

'That's heartening.'

'He will also be here to support us himself. He is as determined as we are to recover the gift from Gregory Tomkins and put it where it belongs in the cathedral.'

'I can't wait for that to happen,' said the Dean. 'I just wish that we weren't at the beck and call of these cruel men. They make all the decisions.'

'We have to tolerate that situation, Dean Courtney.'

'I can't wait to see them caught and punished.'

'It will happen in due course, I assure you.'

'We have every faith in you and your detectives, Inspector. It was good to meet Superintendent Tallis as well. I'm sorry that he had to leave so abruptly.'

'He wishes to lead the investigation in London,' said Colbeck. 'That is where the crime was planned. Vital information somehow fell into the hands of the man who planned the theft of the miniature cathedral.'

'Will the superintendent be able to unmask him?'

'Hopefully, he will – but the man is no longer in London. He's hiding somewhere close to us, issuing demands about how much money he wants. With luck, we will come face to face with him very soon.'

When he arrived at the house, Edward Tallis was told that the silversmith was fast asleep. Alice Tomkins's face lit up with hope.

'Have you made an arrest yet, Superintendent?' she asked.

'I'm afraid not, Mrs Tomkins, but my detectives have gathered a lot of relevant information. The cathedral has agreed to exchange a large amount of money with the men who stole it. Inspector Colbeck is confident of arresting the criminals when they hand over your husband's gift to the cathedral.'

'Will it be in good condition? That's what Gregory keeps asking.'

'I sincerely hope so.'

'If you'll excuse me, I'll go upstairs and wake him up.'

'There's no need, Alice,' said a croaking voice. 'I'm coming downstairs now.'

They waited as the old man came slowly down the steps, then entered the drawing room. Tallis was shocked to see evidence of physical decline in the man. His body was bent double, and he could barely move, but it was his face that told the story of his misery. Tallis had difficulty recognising him. He moved quickly forward to help Tomkins into an armchair, then he sat opposite the man.

'Have you brought good news?' asked Tomkins.

'We have made advances, sir. I have just returned from Lincoln to tell you what they are. Before I do so, however, I need help from you.'

'What can I possibly do?'

'Go back to the moment when you and your partners decided on the exact date and time when your gift would be transferred to Lincoln.'

'It seems such a long time ago,' said Tomkins.

'Concentrate, Gregory,' urged his wife. 'It's important.'

'It's vital that we identify the person who passed on the information to a man intent on having your gift stolen by his associates in Peterborough,' said Tallis. 'Who was present when the decision was taken?'

Tomkins gave a hopeless shrug. 'I can't remember.'

'Yes, you can,' said his wife. 'Mr Peat would have been there and Mr Hatherly. Were you alone in the room with your partners?'

'I may have been.'

'Was anyone else there?' asked Tallis.

'I can't remember.'

'What room were you in? Can you remember that?'

'It was the room where I work,' said Tomkins. 'It's on the first floor.'

'Was the door closed?' said Tallis.

'I think so.'

'Might someone have overheard you?'

'We tried to keep the details secret,' remembered Tomkins. 'That's what I agreed with my partners. Nobody else knew when my gift would be sent to Lincoln.'

'Then how did it come to be stolen?'

'Michael Langston was shot dead!' said the old man, trying to get up from the chair. 'And it's all my fault.'

'Sit back down again,' advised Alice, easing him back into

the chair. 'It's not your fault, Gregory.' She turned to Tallis. 'Is it, Superintendent?'

'No, it isn't,' he agreed. 'You should be applauded for what you did, Mr Tomkins. Presenting that gift to the cathedral was an act of Christian charity on your part. I have met the Bishop and the Dean. They told me that they think you are a latter-day saint. They sang your praises.'

Tears began to run down the silversmith's face. His wife moved forward to wipe them away with a handkerchief. She put a defensive arm around her husband.

'That's all that Gregory can tell you, Superintendent,' she said. 'It's no good firing questions at him. You'd be better off talking to his partners.'

'I'll go to their premises immediately,' said Tallis. 'I'm sorry to put pressure on your husband but the questions had to be asked.'

Alice nodded. 'I understand. But my husband doesn't have the answers you need. All that he talks about,' she explained, 'is the murder of Michael Langston. He thinks that it was his fault. Please prove to him that it was not.'

Madeleine Colbeck and Lydia Quayle had returned to the latter's house after a disappointing search. The were alone together in the drawing room. Lydia was despondent.

'There was no trace of her,' she sighed.

'That might be a good sign,' argued her friend. 'Kitty Piper may no longer be using that surname because she has married. She may not even be in domestic service now. Since we could find no trace of her, she might have moved out of London altogether.'

'She's still here. I feel it.'

'That doesn't mean she let herself into the house.'

'Perhaps not, Madeleine, but she must be a suspect. It's the kind of thing that Kitty would do. There was a wicked side to her.'

'Then why didn't you dismiss her earlier on?'

'I wish that I had, believe me. I had to warn her more than once about her behaviour. When it came to her chores, she was very efficient, but I could never trust her. Martha had doubts about her as well. I blame myself for not getting rid of the woman. Once she'd gone,' said Lydia, 'the atmosphere in the house improved at once.'

'That's partly because of Pamela. She's a godsend.'

'And she gets on well with Martha. That's so important. Martha tolerated Kitty but they never really became friends.' After having a sip of her tea, Lydia sat back in her chair. 'So where is she now?'

'My guess is that she's in service elsewhere.'

'Then why did we find no sign of her?'

'If she is as devious as you say, she could have changed her name. If she went through an agency,' suggested Madeleine, 'Kitty could have pretended to be someone else entirely.'

'She'd have needed to show proof of her identity.'

'According to you, she is guileful. She could have used false documents.'

'That never occurred to me.'

'You don't live with a detective inspector. Because I do, I've learnt to have suspicions about people until I really get to know them. My advice,' Madeleine went on, 'is to forget all about Kitty. There's no clear evidence that she used her key to let herself into the house. It's pure guesswork.'

'You're right,' said Lydia penitently. 'I've jumped to the wrong conclusion. Kitty has probably forgotten all about the time she was under my roof. I daresay that she's working for someone else now.'

'Under a different name.'

'What do I do, Madeleine?'

'Abandon the search for her. Kitty has moved on. She's leading a different sort of life now and does not wish to be found. That's why our search was a waste of time.'

'What if she was the person who broke into my house?' asked Lydia.

'That was simply a guess. London is full of burglars. According to Robert, they spend their time searching for premises they can get into easily. One of them got in here, Lydia, and you heard him leave. Having changed the lock on the front door, you should feel completely safe now.'

'I should,' agreed her friend, 'but somehow I don't.'

Although he was feeling weary, Edward Tallis continued his search. He went to the premises of Peat, Hatherly and Tomkins and told the two senior partners what had happened during his visit to Lincoln.

'This is where it all started,' he said. 'I came back to London to take a more active part in the investigation.'

'That's reassuring to hear,' said Oliver Peat.

'I began with a visit to Gregory Tomkins. Unfortunately, he was unable to shed much light on what happened. He's in a complete daze,' Tallis told them. 'That's why I came here.'

'We're glad to see you, Superintendent,' said John Hatherly, the eldest of the three partners, a short, stout man with a gleaming bald head. 'How can we help?'

'Information about how and when the silver cathedral was being taken to Lincoln somehow got into the wrong hands. That can only have happened if the details were leaked – by accident, probably – by someone employed by you.'

'All of our employees are above suspicion,' insisted Hatherly.

'Very few of them,' added Peat, 'knew the precise time of the train.'

'How many apprentices do you have working here?' asked Tallis.

'Three,' replied Hatherly. 'They are entirely trustworthy.'

'I would like to meet each one of them, if I may.'

'That can be arranged, Superintendent.'

'Thank you, Mr Hatherly.'

'One of them has been ill,' said Peat, 'and has been on sick leave for a few days. We expect him back soon.'

'Is he a silversmith?' asked Tallis.

'No, he is training to produce fine jewellery. It's an art that takes years to master.'

'What about the other apprentices?'

'Donald Bush wishes to specialise with gold,' said Hatherly, 'but Edgar prefers to work with silver. His full name is Edgar Venables.'

'Then I'll start with him,' decided Tallis.

During their time in Lincoln, the detectives had got to know the city well. Most of the main streets were occupied by horse dealers, but there were back-roads and lanes that allowed them to inspect the outer edges of the city. Colbeck and Leeming were seated in a cab that took them around the perimeter of Lincoln. They both made mental notes of what they saw.

'It's a beautiful place to live,' observed Colbeck.

'There's too many horses for my liking,' grumbled Leeming.

'Try to ignore them, Victor.'

'How can I? They've taken over the city.'

'The chief constable feels that the men we're after will enter from the south. He's going to position some of his men there.'

'I fancy that the thieves will come in from a different direction just to confuse us. Whoever is leading the gang is shrewd and cunning.'

'Then I'll enjoying putting handcuffs on him,' said Colbeck. 'He belongs behind bars until his execution. You'll be the first to meet him.'

'I wish that I didn't have to wear that cassock.'

'It's a good disguise and it suits you.'

Leeming shuddered. 'I'm glad that my wife is not going to see me in it.'

'Estelle would be very impressed. You look so convincing.'

'I'm a detective not a member of the clergy,' protested Leeming.

'It's all in a good cause. You'll get close to the man who planned the theft of that silver cathedral. Once you hand over the saddlebags filled with money you may be able to seize him.'

'If I'm supposed to be a priest, perhaps I should bless him instead.'

'There'll be no time for that,' said Colbeck, smiling. 'Be warned. My guess is that he'll put up a fight.'

'What about the others?'

'One of them will have brought the wooden box and be standing by. The other two will be lurking in the shadows to slow down any pursuit of them.'

'That makes four of them in all.'

'There may be more than that,' decided Colbeck. 'There certainly won't be a lesser number. And I still believe that one of them had army training. He's turned his back on Queen and country now.'

'Do you still think they're hiding on a farm somewhere?' asked Leeming.

'No, I don't. Instinct tells me that they're here in Lincoln, doing exactly what we are doing and examining all the possibilities. They'll devise a plan that gives them complete security.' Colbeck smiled. 'It will never occur to them that – by dint of a careful search – we may have found out what that plan is.'

Having conducted their search and made their decision, Jeremy Keane and his cousin headed for the Carpenter's Arms, a sizeable inn situated at the southern tip of the city. Keane had taken the trouble to wear clothing that made him look more like a farmer than a man employed in the jewellery trade. Patrick Farr was in his usual garb with a gun tucked away inside his coat. After a drink or two, they went outside to escape the jollity inside the inn. Keane was happy.

'Not long to go now, Pat,' he said. 'How do you feel?'

'I'm nervous,' confessed his cousin.

'Why? We've broken the law many times together.'

'That was when we were still lads, doing it for fun. It's on a very different scale now. The stakes are so much higher.'

'It's the very thing that excites me,' said Keane. 'We're not stealing apples from the market now. We've got a chance to make a whole new future for ourselves. And the same goes for Silas and Tim. Once we've got that money in our hands, we can follow our dreams.'

'They'll keep looking for us.'

'Keeping ahead of them will be easy when we're rich.'

'I'm still worrying about Inspector Colbeck. He's famous for catching people who commit crimes on the railway.'

'Forget about him. He doesn't have a clue who we are or where we are.'

'He'll keep on chasing us, Jerry.'

'Then we'll have great fun dodging him every time. Have faith in me, Pat. My plan is foolproof. By the time Colbeck and his men realise what happened to them in two nights' time, we'll be galloping off into the night with enough money to live in luxury.'

CHAPTER TWELVE

The next day, Edward Tallis had been given the use of a room in which he could interview the apprentices. On the mantelpiece was a collection of items made by the three young men. All of them showed great promise but none was good enough to be offered for sale. They were simply indicators of how much the apprentices had improved. Tallis was still admiring their work when there was a tentative knock on the door.

'Come in!' snapped the superintendent.

The door opened slowly, and Edgar Venables came into the room. Now in his late teens, he was tall, skinny and pale-faced. He had clearly been told that he was being interviewed by a senior detective from Scotland Yard. Tallis could see how apprehensive he was. He deliberately kept the young man standing.

'Edgar Venables?' he asked.

'Yes, sir,' replied the apprentice.

'Have you been told why I wish to talk to you?'

'Yes, sir. Mr Peat explained it to me.'

'Do you like working here?'

'I like it very much.'

'Why did you choose to specialise in silver items?'

'It was because I wanted to follow in Mr Tomkins's footsteps,' explained the other. 'He's been so helpful to me. It's a pleasure to be in the same place as him.'

'Did you know what he was working on?'

'I heard rumours, sir.'

'But you weren't told the full details?'

'No, Superintendent. Whenever I'm here, I devote all my time to whatever it is that I'm making. It's a job that needs great concentration. Mr Tomkins taught me that.'

'Did he ever mention Lincoln Cathedral to you?'

'No, sir.'

'What about the other apprentices? Surely, one of them must have mentioned that Mr Tomkins was making a silver model of the cathedral.'

'I work in a room on my own, sir. I don't spend much time with Donald or Sam. They're both older than me. Now and then, they go off to a pub for a drink. I'm too scared to join them. They tease me about that.'

Tallis had heard enough. Venables had clearly not been the person who passed on details of when the silver cathedral was travelling to its new home. He was patently honest and deeply grateful to be taken on by the firm as an apprentice. The truth was painful. Superintendent Tallis would have to look elsewhere.

'That's all, Edgar,' he said dismissively. 'I won't need to speak to you again.'

Sighing with relief, Venables hurried out of the room.

Lydia Quayle went into the kitchen and found Martha peeling potatoes.

'I'm sorry to interrupt you,' said Lydia.

Martha wiped her hands on a tea towel. 'Did you manage to trace Kitty Piper?'

'I'm afraid that we didn't.'

'Then she must have moved out of London altogether.'

'It's more than likely.'

'Unless she changed her name,' suggested Martha. 'It's the sort of thing she'd do.'

'We found out nothing at all about the woman. Knowing Kitty, she's probably forgotten all about her time here. She did, after all, leave under a cloud.'

'Life here is so much better since she left.'

'I agree with you, Martha, and so does Mrs Colbeck. Whenever Kitty answered the door to her, she never gave her a real welcome. Why was that?'

'I can think of one reason.'

'Can you?'

'Yes, Miss Quayle. When she worked here, Kitty was always jealous of some of the ladies who called at the house. Mrs Colbeck was one of them. She was always so smart. Kitty used to make remarks about her clothing and wish that she was able wear dresses like that.' Martha sniffed. 'I told her it was none of her business.'

'How did she react?'

'She gave me a glare.'

'I hope you told her off for doing that,' said Lydia. 'You were senior to her and have been with me since I first moved in here. Kitty had no place to make comments about any guests who came into the house.'

'That's exactly what I told her – in no uncertain terms.'

'I put up with Kitty for far too long.'

'She did work hard,' recalled Martha. 'I'll say that for her.'

'But you were glad when she left, weren't you?'

'Yes, I was, and I was so pleased when you employed Pamela in her stead. She's better than Kitty in every way.'

'I agree,' said Lydia. 'And so does Mrs Colbeck. She thinks that I'd be sensible forgetting all about someone who worked here in the past.'

Alan Hinton and Eric Boyce had not expected to be sent back to Peterborough again, but they found themselves travelling there by train. They were relieved to be escaping the ear-splitting noise and pungent odours of the Horse Fair. The journey there in an empty compartment gave them the opportunity to discuss the case that had brought them to that part of the country. Both hoped that a successful conclusion would be achieved. Once they reached their destination, they parted company.

Boyce went off to speak to the stationmaster to see if any more information about the incident days earlier had come in as a response to the notices on display seeking information about it. Hinton, meanwhile, made his way to the police station. He found Sergeant Wilkes on duty behind the desk.

'Have you made any arrests?' asked the sergeant, raising an eyebrow.

'No, but we hope to do so very soon.'

'Why have you come back?'

'I have a letter to deliver to the chief constable,' said Hinton.

Wilkes grinned. 'Have you never heard of the postal service?'

'Inspector Colbeck wanted it delivered by hand. That way, I can get an instant response.'

'Then I'd better take you to the chief constable's office.'

Wilkes led him down a corridor and knocked on a door. In response to a yell from inside the office, he opened the door and ushered Hinton inside before closing the door behind him and returning to his desk.

Marcus Napier looked up from the report he was reading.

'Ah,' he said, recognising his visitor. 'You're back again. I hope you've brought news of your success.'

'That may be delayed slightly, sir,' explained Hinton, 'but we have high hopes of arresting the gang when they come to exchange what they stole for money.'

'How much money?'

'None at all, we hope. What I came for was help from you. Inspector Colbeck,' said Hinton, offering an envelope, 'asked me to hand you this.'

'Thank you.' Napier opened the letter and read its contents. He looked up.

'The inspector has a very distinctive hand,' he observed. 'I really do hope that I get to meet him before you leave this part of the country.'

'I'll pass on that message, sir.'

Napier read the letter again and gave a nod of approval. 'He has made an excellent decision. We will help all we can.'

'Thank you, sir. The inspector blames himself for not thinking of it earlier. The telegraph sent to a member of the gang at

Peterborough station was intended for a man named Percy Gull. Inspector Colbeck decided that it was an alias.'

'In his position, I'd have done the same.'

'He's had second thoughts. He wonders if that name was on the telegraph because it meant something to the man who sent it and to the one who received it. In other words, Percy Gull is a real person.'

'It's possible, I suppose. Why did they choose to use it?'

'It concealed the name of the recipient. It wasn't plucked out of the air. The man who received the telegraph knew it well and – according to the inspector – he was the person who shot the private detective.'

'Colbeck is asking me to find Percy Gull, is he? How on earth do I do that?'

'If he lives in the county, there must be a record of him.'

'Do you know how many people live here?' asked Napier. 'It would take ages to track down this person.'

'Not if he owns a farm, sir.'

'What do you mean?'

'The inspector believes that the man who was waiting for that telegraph was a farmer. The chances are that Percy Gull is – or was – also a farmer. If he owned a farm, he'd surely be entitled to a vote. Don't you have access to election registers?'

'Yes, but it would take us ages to plough through them.'

'This is a murder case,' Hinton reminded him.

'Even so . . .'

'Don't farmers belong to some sort of association? A lot of trades in London encourage their members to join one. Then there are churches, of course. Couldn't you find him by asking all churches if they had a Percy Gull in their congregation?'

'If Gull is linked to the men you're searching for, he's unlikely to be a churchgoer. People who fear God don't usually have friends who are ready to shoot someone so that they can steal a precious item from a train.'

'That's a fair comment, sir.'

'I'm glad you realise it,' said Napier.

'Percy Gull must be found, however. His name is a vital clue.'

'Not necessarily – he may not even be alive.'

'It makes no difference. If we can connect him to the man who sent the telegraph and the one who received it, we can identify them in turn.'

'I believe that you're right,' agreed Napier, thinking it through. 'Tell Inspector Colbeck that I'll institute a search for Percy Gull immediately. And you can tell him something else as well. In choosing you to deliver his letter, he chose well. You've been a convincing advocate, Detective Constable Hinton.'

Hinton beamed. 'Thank you, sir.'

'On your way out, tell Sergeant Wilkes that I said so.'

Caleb Andrews was starting to become restless. Even though he felt much better, he was not allowed to play with his granddaughter. He voiced his grievance.

'Stop treating me as if I'd deliberately infect the girl,' he protested.

'We have to follow doctor's orders, Father,' she said.

'I feel as fit as a fiddle.'

'Then why is your face still so pale?'

'It's because I've been kept indoors against my will.'

Madeleine laughed. 'That's a ridiculous thing to say.'

'I know who's behind this – it's that doctor you set on me.'

'He's helping to make you better.'

'I am better,' insisted Andrews. 'I don't need him coming here every day to glance at me then charge you for bringing him here.'

'That's unfair, Father. Every penny it has cost has been worth it.'

'If you let me go home, you won't have to pay anything.'

'I need to keep an eye on my father.'

'That makes two of you. The doctor says the same thing, but he barely looks at me. If I ask him when I can play with my granddaughter, he tells me that I must be patient. Helena Rose is dying to see her grandfather. Stop depriving her of that pleasure.'

'She understands that you're poorly.'

'I'm better now, Maddy!' shouted Andrews.

'Don't yell!'

'It's the only way I can get any attention!'

Before he could continue his argument, however, he felt a warning tickle at the back of his throat and began to cough. Once he had started, he could not stop. He kept patting his chest, but it had no effect. Madeleine was sympathetic but firm.

'Thank goodness the doctor is coming here later on.'

Tallis was still in the room when the second of the apprentices turned up. Donald Bush was a tall, strapping, ebullient young man in a suit. He had far greater confidence than Edgar Venables and began with a polite apology.

'I'm sorry to keep you waiting, Superintendent. I was out of the shop on an errand. How may I help you, sir?'

'You can sit down, for a start.'

'Thank you,' said Bush, lowering himself onto a chair. 'I believe that you've spoken to Edgar.'

'That's right. I'll put the same question to you. How much

did you know about the project on which Mr Tomkins was working?'

'I knew it was something very dear to him but that's about all.'

'You never discussed it with him?'

'We never had time alone together,' said Bush. 'Once we're here, we're far too busy to speak to anyone else.'

'What about after you've finished your day's work?'

'I'm just eager to get home.'

'Venables told me that you and another apprentice sometimes go to a pub.'

'That's right, sir. The Red Fox is very close. At the end of a long day, a friend and I need something to cheer us up a bit because our work is very demanding. We're bent over a table for hours on end.'

'And is it the same for the other apprentice?'

'His name is Sam Fielding and he's been off work for a couple of days. Sam is good fun to be with. We get on well – and we both like a pint of beer.'

'I think that Venables envies your visit to the pub.'

'Edgar is too young to join us,' said Bush. 'Not that we'd want him there. He's got nothing of interest to say.'

'Is that why you tease him?'

'We just have some fun at his expense, that's all.'

'I take it that you know what happened to the model on which Mr Tomkins was working.'

Bush nodded.

'How did you react to it?'

'Well, I was very sorry for Gregory. We never actually saw what he was working on, but we knew that he was putting his heart and soul into the work. He always does that. It's the reason he became so famous.'

'Did you ever talk about him to strangers in the pub?'

'No, Superintendent,' replied Bush. 'Me and Sam have this agreement. When we go to the pub, we never say a word to anyone about our work. If we're set free at the end of the day, all we want is a drink and a chat.'

'Has anyone approached you at the pub and asked about Gregory Tomkins?'

'Never!'

'Are you quite sure?'

'All we're interested in is that first pint. We're always parched.'

'What sort of person is Sam Fielding?'

'He works hard but knows how to enjoy himself when he's got free time.'

'Has he ever been in trouble with the police?'

'No!' cried Bush, laughing. 'He's the most law-abiding person I know. He also sings in the choir at church. Sam doesn't like it, but he's got no choice.'

'Why not?'

'His father is the vicar.'

Having had dinner at the Colbeck house earlier in the week, Lydia Quayle responded by inviting her friend to have luncheon together. Before the meal, she and Madeleine were enjoying a glass of sherry in the drawing room. It was not long before they were talking about the mysterious intruder.

'I had a word with Martha earlier,' said Lydia. 'According to her, Kitty had a streak of evil in her.'

'Do you believe that?' asked Madeleine.

'Yes and no. Kitty could be outspoken at times, but I learnt to take no notice. We all have tantrums.'

'Sneaking back into your house is more than having a tantrum.'

'I'm not certain that Kitty did slip in here unseen.'

'Unseen,' said Madeleine, 'but not unheard. You were clearly aware that someone had been in the house and that she let herself out.'

'It could have been a man.'

'Either way, it was very distressing for you.'

Lydia shrugged. 'We might never know the truth.'

'But it's vital that you do, Lydia – if only to put your mind at rest.'

'Martha thinks that she got in here, and we must remember that she spent far more time with Kitty than I ever did. Martha believes that the woman just wanted to give me a scare.'

'But why? You treated her well when she was here.'

'For some reason, Kitty was unsettled.'

'Your cook should have told her to behave herself and get on with her work. And Kitty should have remembered that she was only a domestic servant.'

'She had ambitions to lead a more interesting life. I could see it in her face. She resented me yet, at the same time, she envied me. Whenever I put a new dress on, Kitty would stare at it in wonder. She was almost writhing with jealousy.'

'I'm surprised that you put up with her for so long.'

'I suppose that, deep down, I felt sorry for the girl.'

'You did her a great favour by employing her.'

'She did show hints of gratitude from time to time,' recalled Lydia. 'How sincere they were, I don't know.' She leant forward in her chair. 'Do you think that I should report her to the police?'

'No, I don't,' said Madeleine firmly. 'All that you're doing is relying on guesswork. You can't expect the police to look favourably on that. There are too many real crimes to keep them busy. Also, it may well be that Kitty was not the person who let herself into your house at all. It was somebody totally different.'

'It's possible, I suppose.'

'I'm telling you what Robert would tell you. Gather firm evidence before you even think of involving the police. I'm saying this to you for your own sake, Lydia. Wait until you have real evidence of who your intruder was.'

'You're right, Madeleine. I've been jumping to conclusions without any real facts to back them up. Oh,' she went on, heaving a sigh, 'I do wish that Alan was here to help me. He'd tell me exactly what I should do.'

Alan Hinton was seated in a room at the cathedral with Eric Boyce, delivering his report to Colbeck of their brief visit to Peterborough. The inspector listened carefully. When he had heard all the evidence, he gave a satisfied nod.

'I knew that it was worth sending you there,' he said.

'The chief constable was delighted to be involved in the investigation. He promised to set a search for Percy Gull in motion.'

'Well, I hope that he does it very soon. It's vital information. What else did Napier say to you?'

'That I was to tell you that I presented the argument for a search with real skill.'

'I'd expect no less of you, Alan,' said Colbeck. He turned to Boyce. 'Did you manage to garner anything from the stationmaster?'

'Yes, I did,' said Boyce. 'Because there's a substantial reward on offer, a lot of people have come forward, claiming that they saw a man leaving the guard's van with a heavy box. He had someone with him. The two of them headed for the exit.'

'How reliable were these witnesses?'

'The stationmaster reckoned that two-thirds of them had invented their stories in the hopes of making money. But there were genuine witnesses as well. One of them was waiting at the cab rank when the two men came out with the box. When it had been lifted onto a cart, the men jumped on beside it and the driver snapped his reins. One of the witnesses – a woman, actually – was able to give a rough description of the men. It occurred to her at the time that they were up to no good.'

'She confirmed what we've already been told,' said Colbeck. 'Thank you, Eric. It's good to have someone else's version. We'll have an opportunity to meet the two men in question very soon. Hopefully, they will have brought that wooden box with them.'

Jeremy Keane watched as the first panel was prised open by his cousin. It was not long before Patrick Farr was able to remove all the packing around the silver cathedral. With an effort, he lifted the object out and put it on the carpet in the living room. Farr only gave it a cursory glance, but Keane was captivated once again.

'It's truly amazing,' he said. 'I don't know of anyone in the trade who could produce a work as detailed and accurate as this.'

'The silversmith was born and brought up in Lincoln. Before he moved to London, he used to see the cathedral every day. When I first looked at this version of it, I was flabbergasted.'

'Since I work in the jewellery trade, I see work of the finest silversmiths in the capital. This outshines any of them, Pat.'

'Only if you go to church.'

'What do you mean?'

'Well, when me and Silas first got it out of the box, we were astonished. It's so big and detailed and shiny. But I wouldn't want to go on staring at it because it reminds me that I haven't been inside a church for years, let alone a cathedral.'

'Would you prefer a collection of farm animals in silver?' teased Keane.

'No,' said Farr with a laugh. 'I've spent a lifetime looking at cows and sheep and pigs. I'd want to look at something different.'

'Such as?'

'Whatever it is, it wouldn't be in silver. To be honest, I find this version of the cathedral too . . . well, I just can't look at it for long.'

'Whereas I could study it all day,' said Keane, eyes moving slowly over every detail. 'The man who made this is not a silversmith – he's a genius. It's such a striking work that I'm reluctant to part with it.'

'Don't say that, Jerry,' protested his cousin. 'We took a lot of risks to get our hands on it. I shot dead the man who was guarding it, remember. I just want to use it to get a lot of money from the cathedral.'

'We'll do that very soon, Pat.'

'As long as it's in our hands, I don't feel safe.'

'Why not?'

'This famous detective is searching for it.'

'Forget about him,' said Keane with a derisive laugh. 'Inspector Colbeck doesn't have a clue who we are or where we're hiding. And when he meets us, we'll be wearing masks, so he won't even see our faces.'

'I was pleased to hear that.'

'Everything has been planned carefully.'

'You always were the brainy member of the family.'

'I've finally got a chance to prove it,' said his cousin, grinning. 'I know when to keep my ears open and I know how to make people talk when there's enough beer in them. Those apprentices have probably forgotten that they mentioned details to me of when this silver masterpiece was being sent to Lincoln.'

'They must have been shocked when they learnt it had been stolen.'

'The news will have shaken the daylights out of them. One day soon, they may realise that they made the theft possible by talking to a stranger in the Red Fox.'

'Won't they realise that you were that stranger?'

'No, Pat. They don't know me from Adam. Besides, they're not stupid.'

'I don't follow.'

'Put yourself in their position. Because they passed on information that led to someone being shot dead and a priceless piece of silverware being stolen, they'll have red faces. Those drunken idiots made the crimes possible. Can you imagine them going to the police?' asked Keane. 'Of course not! They'd lose their jobs for a start and nobody in the jewellery trade would ever employ them.'

'They'll have to keep their gobs shut.'

'Exactly!'

'You're amazing, Jerry. You helped us commit a perfect crime.'

'Wait until we have the ransom money in our hands the night after tomorrow,' said Keane. 'That's when you'll realise how brainy I am.'

* * *

Edward Tallis was too impatient to wait for the third apprentice to return to work. When he had got Samuel Fielding's address from his employers, he took a cab to the young man's home. He soon found himself being let into a vicarage by a servant. Jane Fielding came into the hall to welcome the visitor. A short, thin, nervous woman in her fifties, she was taken aback when told why Tallis had come.

'You want to speak to Samuel?' she said in alarm.

'If I may, Mrs Fielding. I've already interviewed the other apprentices at the shop where they work. I was told that your son was unwell.'

'Actually, he's much better now. My husband is busy at the church, but I will join you, if you wish.'

'That won't be necessary,' said Tallis. 'I'd prefer to speak to Sam on his own.'

'Oh, I see.'

Mrs Fielding took him into the drawing room and introduced him to her son. At the news that a senior detective from Scotland Yard needed to interview him, the apprentice was badly shaken. Fielding was a tall, handsome young man with dark hair and thick dark eyebrows. He was seated in a chair beside the fireplace. After talking nervously for a minute or two, his mother left the room and closed the door after her.

Tallis sat down opposite the apprentice and studied him carefully.

'How are you now, Sam?' he asked.

'I feel much better,' replied the other. 'Why do you want to speak to me?'

'Let me ask the questions, please.'

'Yes, of course.'

'I've already spoken to Donald Bush and Edgar Venables. I was told you were unwell, but I felt that I had to see you immediately. Can you understand why?'

'No, I can't, Superintendent,' said Fielding, shifting in his chair.

'It's to do with the theft of something made by Gregory Tomkins for Lincoln Cathedral. The private detective taking it to Lincoln was shot dead.'

Fielding swallowed hard. 'Yes, I . . . heard about that.'

'The crimes were only possible because the people who committed them had vital information about the exact time when the train was due to arrive at Peterborough station. The only people in possession of that information worked for Peat, Hatherly and Tomkins. You were one of them, Sam.'

'It's true, but I had no idea at what time the train left King's Cross, or when it reached Peterborough.'

'You must have picked up gossip at the premises.'

'I haven't been there for days, Superintendent.'

'Gregory Tomkins is justifiably famous for his talent as a silversmith. You must be glad that you work under the same roof.'

'I feel honoured. We all do.'

'That's exactly what Edgar Venables said. He also told me that you and Bush sometimes go to a nearby pub for a drink.'

'It's only now and then, Superintendent,' said Fielding quickly. 'My father is a vicar. He disapproves of strong drink. That's why I only have one glass at the Red Fox.'

'You've been deceiving your father, have you?'

'I don't see it that way. I just feel that I'm old enough to make my own decisions.'

'There's a note of rebellion in your voice.'

'I love my father,' insisted the other, 'and I obey his strictures. If you spoke to Donald, he'd have told you that I sing in the church choir – even though I hate doing so.'

'That's to your credit, Sam.'

'As for my work, I'm grateful for the chance to learn my trade in one of the best firms in London. It's a wonderful preparation. I would never do anything to upset my employers. I'd swear that on the Bible.'

'Given your father's profession, I daresay that you know the Bible well.'

'I do, Superintendent.'

'Well, let's imagine that you've got your hand on it right now,' said Tallis, watching him carefully. 'Would you swear that you had no idea of the time when Mr Tomkins's silver cathedral was leaving London?'

'I would,' replied Fielding, thrusting out his jaw.

'And are you sure that – when you go with Donald Bush to the Red Fox – that you only ever have one glass of beer?'

'That's correct.'

'After a long day at work, it must be nice to be in a convivial atmosphere in a pub. Other regular visitors there must know where you and Bush work. I daresay that they ask what is going on at the premises of Peat, Hatherly and Tomkins.'

'Occasionally, they do,' said Fielding guardedly.

'You probably can't help boasting about the famous Gregory Tomkins.'

'His name does come into the conversation occasionally, but most of the time we just have a chat about whatever is in the news. Honestly, it's all very harmless.'

'Bush tried to give me the same impression,' said Tallis, 'but I don't know how reliable a memory he has of drinking and chatting in a bar. When you return to work, I'd suggest that you speak to him seriously about what exactly the pair of you said during your last visit to the pub. Can you do that, please?'

'Yes,' replied Fielding, face impassive. 'I can and will do that.'

CHAPTER THIRTEEN

It was late that afternoon when Martha and Pamela finished their shopping and started to walk back to the house. Pamela was curious.

'How long have you worked for Miss Quayle?' she asked.

'Ever since she bought the house and moved into it.'

'The two of you get on very well.'

'That's because we both make the effort to do so,' said Martha. 'It's not always the case. When I worked for Mr Sanderson, a retired lawyer, he used to criticise me every five minutes because he was so finicky. His wife apologised for his behaviour, but she couldn't change it. In the end, I left their house.'

'That was brave of you. It's not easy to find a good employer.'

'Miss Quayle is very good. Well, you've found that out for yourself.'

'It's true,' said Pamela. 'There are times when she treats me as if I'm a member of the family. And she's such a beautiful woman. I can't understand why she doesn't have men taking an interest in her.'

'She does have one close male friend.'

'Is that the detective who comes here from time to time?'

'Yes, it is – Detective Constable Hinton.'

'I wish that someone as handsome as that would take an interest in me.'

'When we're out together, lots of men stare at you, Pamela.'

'Yes, but most of them are married. I can always tell.' She turned to her companion. 'Do you really think that Miss Quayle heard someone leaving the house by the front door?'

'Of course I do – don't you?'

'I'm not sure. I wonder if she imagined it.'

'It was no mistake, Pamela. There was an intruder and it was obviously Kitty. It's the sort of thing she'd do.'

'Why on earth should the woman come back here?'

'There's one obvious answer – curiosity. Perhaps she just wants to see if the house is still the same. I thought that Kitty somehow got in there to steal something – yet nothing is missing.'

'Does she have any other reason to come back?'

'I hope not. I hate seeing Miss Quayle so upset.'

'So do I, Martha. I just wish there was something I could do to help her.'

'You're already doing it and so am I. We must both get on with our jobs and give Miss Quayle the support she needs. As for this person she heard sneaking out of the house,' said Martha, 'we must keep our eyes peeled. If he – or she – can get into the property somehow, then this intruder must be caught and stopped.'

'How can we help?'

'It's quite simple – keep your eyes open and ears pricked.'

Bishop Jackson was finding that the wait was starting to interfere with his sleep. Alone with the Dean, he confided that he was feeling increasingly nervous. The Dean tried to reassure him that his fears would soon be shown to be groundless.

'Inspector Colbeck assures me that these men will be arrested.'

'Then why do I have difficulty believing it?' asked the Bishop. 'The amount of money demanded is frightening. When I spoke to the bank manager, he was shocked that we were taking out so much.'

'Bank managers are always nervous of large withdrawals. Face the facts. If we don't accept the ultimatum sent by these appalling men, we'll never see Gregory Tomkins's wonderful gift to us. That would be a tragedy.'

'I agree, Alexander.'

'Put your trust in Inspector Colbeck and his men. If they assure us that the gang will be arrested, then I believe them.'

'I try my best to do so but my doubts linger.'

'Please try to banish them. The detectives have been working hard to gather fresh evidence. Colbeck tells me that his men contacted Marcus Napier in Cambridgeshire, and that a promising new line of enquiry is being explored.'

'Well, I hope it produces results very quickly.' The Bishop raised both palms. 'I'm sorry to be so nervous and fearful. It's the thought of drawing the money out of the bank tomorrow. What if we hand it over and get nothing in return?'

'The men who stole Tomkins's gift are not stupid. If they don't sell it to us, it will have no value. Who else would buy it from them?'

'No other cathedral would touch it.'

'Exactly,' said the Dean. 'That is why they want a quick sale so that they can pocket a large amount of money. What they don't know is that we have Scotland Yard detectives, supported by officers from our own constabulary, waiting for them. You should be reassured, Bishop.'

'I know,' said the other. 'But I still have the gravest doubts. I have prayed daily for deliverance from this appalling situation in which we find ourselves. To no avail, alas,' he confessed. 'I'm frightened, Alexander. I sense danger – and I fear that we are about to lose a terrifying amount of money.'

Edward Tallis waited until the Red Fox opened that evening then he went into the public house. The bar was large, well-appointed and filled with small tables. Tallis was pleased to see that very few customers were there. It meant that he could have a private conversation with the owner, Tobias Hall, a fleshy, middle-aged man of average height who stood behind the bar. Hall had sharp instincts. One glance at his visitor was enough for him. He beckoned Tallis to him and spoke quietly.

'You'll find nothing untoward here,' he said with a smile. 'We keep strictly to the rules imposed on us.'

'You know who I am?' asked Tallis in surprise.

'No, sir, but I can see what you are. Only a policeman could have your bearing.'

'It's very unflattering to be identified as a mere constable. For your information, I am Superintendent Tallis from Scotland Yard, and I would like a quiet word with you.'

Hall was impressed by his rank. 'Welcome to the Red Fox, sir. Since it's your first visit, I'm happy to offer you a free drink.'

'No, thank you, Mr . . .'

'Hall . . . Tobias Hall. I'm the proprietor. How may I help you?'

'I want to ask about two of your customers. They're young men who work in the jewellery trade and sometimes pop in here at the end of their working day.'

'I think I know who you mean, Superintendent.'

'Their names are Donald Bush and Samuel Fielding.'

'That's right. They're apprentices at Peat, Hatherly and Tomkins. We see them quite often, but they rarely stay long. On their wage they need to watch the pennies.'

'Understandably,' said Tallis.

'Are they in trouble with the law?'

'Not at all, not at all. Bush struck me as a law-abiding person and Fielding, as you may know, is the son of a vicar. However, I'm less interested in them than in someone they may have met in here.'

'And who might that be, sir?' asked Hall.

'I'm hoping that you may be able to tell me. I believe that they met and talked to another man recently and, in all probability, were happy to let him buy them a drink.'

'I can't remember all the customers who come in here,' said Hall. 'I only serve in here when we open. My bartenders take over then and I have a rest.'

'How full does this place get of an evening?'

'Ordinarily, it's quite busy. I'd say we have upwards of forty in here, sometimes as many as fifty or more. I don't know the names of all the regulars, but I always remember what their favourite tipple is.'

'Bush and Fielding prefer your bitter.'

'After a hard day's work, they usually drink the first pint very quickly.'

'When the place starts to fill up, then,' noted Tallis, 'the two of them will be in a very relaxed mood.'

Hall grinned. 'No law against that, is there?'

'Can they hold their drink?'

'I've never had to throw them out of here, if that's what you mean.'

'When do your bartenders take over?' asked Tallis.

'They'll be here in the next half an hour. Why do you ask?'

'I'd like to have a word with them. And since that means waiting, I'll be happy to take you up on that kind offer of a free drink.'

Hall grinned at him. 'What will it be, sir?'

Robert Colbeck and Victor Leeming were also in a public house but theirs was in Lincoln. They had managed to grab the last empty table in the King's Arms, a large inn filled with people staying in the city for the Horse Fair. Over a restorative drink, they were able to review the situation.

'What have we learnt today, Victor?' asked Colbeck.

'That time goes very quickly here. In less than thirty hours, we'll be hiding near the cathedral as we wait for our targets to arrive.'

'Go back to what Hinton and Boyce told us.'

'They've recruited the chief constable of Cambridgeshire.'

'It's something I should have done earlier,' admitted Colbeck. 'When I heard that one of our suspects received a telegraph from London, I thought that the name Percy Gull was an alias. How wrong could I be?'

'You did realise your mistake in time, sir.'

'I'm just praying that I haven't left it too late. If we can identify and find Percy Gull, we are taking a giant step forward in this investigation.'

'I thought we did that when the superintendent decided to go back to London. It means that we now have a free hand again.'

'I admit that I was relieved to see him go.'

'So was I. He casts a long shadow.'

'I was very worried about him.'

'He always terrifies me. Though, in fairness,' remembered Leeming, 'he was much quieter this time. He didn't throw his weight around in the usual way.'

'That's what worried me. At first, he seemed to have mellowed but it soon became clear that he has slowed down – mentally and physically. Tallis has suddenly become aware of his age. There are things he can no longer do.'

'Yes, he did look weary from time to time.'

'I was glad when he responded to the impulse to get involved but it turned out to be a huge mistake on my part. He has simply not been of any real use to us.'

'He never is.'

'That's unfair. When an investigation really interests him, he can be very helpful. The problem that used to arise was that he always insisted on being in charge. The superintendent can't handle responsibility any more. That's a great loss.'

'Not to me,' murmured Leeming.

Lydia Quayle was seated in the drawing room, trying to read a book, but her mind kept wandering from the text. Unable to maintain concentration, she put the novel aside and rose to her feet. Once again, she was in the grip of the fear that an intruder had got into the house. As she sought for ways to clear her mind, she remembered what Dolly Pearson, her former nanny, had once told her. The woman had died many years ago but most of her advice was still valid, in Lydia's opinion. When one's mind was fixed on a particular problem or an individual person, there was a simple way to get rid of them from one's brain. Fresh air clears the mind. That was Dolly Pearson's cure for any problem. A long walk would refresh Lydia and allow her brain to think of something entirely different. She could hear the old woman's voice repeating the advice in her ear and wagging her finger as she did so.

Lydia responded at once, standing up, walking into the hall, putting on her coat and hat, then opening the door to step out into the fading light. As she inhaled deeply, there was an instant reward. She felt better. Starting to walk, she loved the feeling of the gentle breeze on her face, and she lengthened her stride. When neighbours walked past her on the other side of the road, she gave them a cheerful wave and received the same gesture from them. Lydia then began to think about the way she had made so many friends in the neighbourhood. She always felt safe walking around the streets. It meant that she often talked to one of the many dog-walkers, taking their pet for its daily stroll.

The fresh air did indeed clear her mind, and it stimulated her body as well. It allowed her to think of all the things that she needed to do on the following day. Lydia felt better than she had done so for weeks. Fond thoughts of Dolly Pearson came flooding into her mind. Her nanny had taught her so much and shielded her from so many setbacks and disappointments. The woman had practised what she preached, taking the children out regularly on long, bracing walks that filled their lungs and lifted their spirits.

Strolling along, Lydia went through a whole album of treasured memories.

It was only when she realised how far she had come that she turned to make her way back. The breeze had stiffened now and, because it was at her back, it seemed to be easing her along. All her anxieties had somehow been blown away. Lydia was filled with a sense of joy. When she considered her life, she had so much about which to be thankful. She scolded herself for being trapped by an obsession.

Then she turned in to the road in which she lived, and everything suddenly changed. Standing opposite her house was a woman, pointing out something to the man beside her. He was nodding, as if receiving instructions. Then they linked arms and marched briskly away. Mouth agape, Lydia came to a sudden halt.

She had recognised the woman. It was Kitty Piper.

By the time that the two bartenders had taken over at the Red Fox, the superintendent had finished his free drink and ordered a second one. He was seated in a corner as the pub slowly filled up. Since the place was so close to the jewellery quarter, it was not surprising that more than a few people employed there drifted into the bar. They were in small groups and took it in turns to buy rounds. Though he watched carefully, Tallis failed to see anyone lurking there to catch conversations about what they were working on at their various places of employment. Donald Bush came in alone but settled down quickly with some colleagues who were already here. What was clear was that, once released from an arduous job at their respective shops, they needed something to take their minds off it. One group broke into laughter as someone told a joke.

When he had the opportunity, Tallis spoke to both bartenders in turn, asking if they'd served a relative stranger in recent days, someone who came into the bar, attached himself to two apprentices from Peat, Hatherly and Tomkins. Neither bartender could help him. Since they had been unusually busy on the nights in question, they had had no time to monitor the behaviour of their customers.

'We always get a few scroungers in,' one of the bartenders told him. 'They join a group, tell a joke or two, and gradually work their way in. When it's someone else's turn to buy a round, they get included.'

'But the moment it's their turn to pay,' said Tallis, 'they've slipped quietly out of the pub. It was ever thus. The world is full of payers and scroungers. The person I'm after is someone ready to spend money to buy a token friendship. He knows how well beer loosens tongues. Unwary drinkers don't realise that they've lowered their guard.' Tallis hardened his voice. 'That's when their new "friend" can probe for information.'

Madeleine Colbeck was surprised when a troubled Lydia Quayle turned up on her doorstep that evening. Seeing her friend's evident anxiety, she took her into the drawing room and sat beside her.

'I'm sorry to turn up out of the blue,' apologised Lydia.

'Something has obviously upset you,' said Madeleine. 'What is it?'

'Earlier on, I went for a walk. I had some thinking to do.'

'Fresh air clears the mind – isn't that what your nanny taught you?'

'Yes, it is, Madeleine. And she was quite right. After a brisk stroll, my mind cleared, and I was able to think properly at last.' She took a deep breath. 'Then I saw the pair of them.'

'Who are you talking about?'

'Kitty Piper and a man friend.'

'Where were they?'

'Close to my house,' said Lydia. 'They were on the pavement opposite, and Kitty was pointing. She seemed to be giving instructions to the man.'

'That must have alarmed you.'

'It did. It brought me to a sudden halt.'

'Did they see you?'

'No, their attention was fixed on the house. After a minute or so, they walked off in the opposite direction.'

'How far away from them were you?'

Lydia shrugged. 'I suppose that it was twenty or thirty yards.'

'Are you quite sure that it was Kitty?'

'Oh, yes,' replied Lydia.

'But it's a long time since you've seen her.'

'It doesn't matter. I'd recognise Kitty anywhere. I'm certain that it was her.'

'What about the man?'

'He was older than her and well-dressed. He kept nodding as if he was hearing instructions. I was mortified,' confessed Lydia. 'All I could do was to stand there and stare. Then they walked off in the opposite direction.' She grasped her friend's arm. 'I was so shaken, Madeleine. My immediate thought was that Kitty was telling the man how to get into the house.'

'That's nonsense – you had the lock on the front door changed.'

'I know.'

'And what reason would she have to help someone get in illegally?'

'All I could think was that she was taking revenge. The more I dwell on it,' said Lydia, 'the more convinced I am that the person I heard leaving my house so quietly the other day must have been Kitty.'

'Don't jump to conclusions,' advised Madeleine.

'She's determined to wreak some sort of havoc.'

'Kitty has no cause to do so.'

'Then why was she standing outside my house and pointing?'

'The answer might be that she was just indicating the place where she once worked. Describe the man to me, please.'

'He was much older, very well-dressed, a proper gentleman.'

'What happened when they moved away?'

'He offered his arm and Kitty took it. They walked off together.'

'Then that's the answer,' suggested Madeleine. 'Kitty has found herself a man to look after her. Did it never occur to you that he might be her lover, or even her husband?'

'No, it didn't.'

'If she has moved up in the world, Kitty might have wanted to look at the house where she had once worked as a maidservant. It was a way of reminding her how much her life had improved.'

'Then why did her visit seem so sinister to me?'

'We tried to trace her by visiting agencies. I'm wondering if the person you saw earlier today was not Kitty but someone remarkably like her.'

'It was her, Madeleine. I'd swear it.'

'But you were twenty or thirty yards away.'

'It makes no difference. She lived with me for years. I recognised her posture and her gestures. I'd swear that it was Kitty Piper.'

'Calm down,' said Madeleine, taking her friend's hand. 'You've clearly had a nasty shock and I'm so glad that you came here to tell me what happened.' She took a deep breath. 'Let's go through it once again, shall we? You'd been for a walk to clear your mind.'

'And that's what happened,' said Lydia. 'On my way back, I felt wonderful. Then I turned in to my road and saw the pair of them. It brought me to a sudden halt. I wasn't just shocked, Madeleine. When I saw Kitty standing there,' she said, 'I was absolutely horrified.'

Lincoln by night was a noisy place. The sound of horses still dominated but there was laughter and celebration in the many public houses. With so many visitors to the city, the brothels were in demand. Drunken clients queued for service outside them and laughed coarsely at crude jokes. As they walked around the streets, Colbeck and Leeming heard revelry in a variety of languages. The sergeant complained.

'It's almost as bad as London at night,' he said.

'People are here to celebrate,' argued Colbeck. 'They're entitled to their fun.'

'Well, I hope it won't be this loud tomorrow night.'

'There certainly won't be so many people in the streets, Victor. Let's see what it's like nearer the cathedral. That's where we'll be the night after tomorrow.'

'Yes,' said Leeming, stepping over the body of a sleeping beggar. 'We need to work out where exactly they decide to hand over the stolen cathedral.'

'They'll want to feel the money in their hands before they do that.'

'What if they try to cheat us?'

'Then they'll live to regret it. You must not hand over those saddlebags until you've seen Gregory Tomkins's work safely in the hands of the Dean.'

'He's a brave man to face such devils in the darkness.'

'I reckon that there'll only be four of them. That means we'll outnumber them.'

'They'll realise it,' warned Leeming, 'and find a way to make things awkward for us. I fear the worst.'

'Preparation is everything, Victor. That's why I wanted to check all the possible locations for the exchange. My guess is that one or more of them will be here in the darkness tonight, finding out where best to stage everything and how to escape with the money afterwards.'

'Can the cathedral afford the amount demanded?'

'Probably not,' replied Colbeck, 'but my advice was to agree to their demand. It may be the only way to lure them out of hiding.'

Leeming was uneasy. 'I still don't like the idea of wearing a cassock.'

'It will be largely invisible in the darkness.'

'I'll feel such a fraud, posing as a clergyman.'

'You'll be a hero, Victor. Now let's walk up to the cathedral itself and check every possible place where they might choose to hide.'

'Lead the way, sir,' said Leeming. 'I'm right behind you.'

They had camped a few miles outside the city. Having found a place off the beaten track, they had built a fire and sat around it. Jeremy Keane was still dressed as a farmer and looked indistinguishable from his three companions. His cousin, Patrick Farr, had cooked a meal on the fire and they were washing it down with copious amounts of beer. Keane looked around the faces of his companions.

'Can you all remember the plan?' he asked.

'Yes,' replied Farr. 'You drummed it into our heads, Jerry.'

'We can't go through it too many times.'

'There's only one problem,' said Redshaw.

'What is it, Tim?'

'Well, you're assuming that everything will go our way. What if there's an emergency? I mean, supposing we find ourselves up against dozens of policemen?'

'We won't,' promised Keane. 'The police are fully employed looking after the masses of people who came here for the Horse Fair. There'll be nobody left to keep their eyes peeled for us.'

'Listen to Jerry,' advised Farr. 'He's thought of everything.'

'Yes,' agreed Weaver. 'He even got a woman friend to make these masks for us.'

'That's because nobody must recognise us,' said Keane. 'Darkness will be our friend, but the masks will be an extra form of disguise.'

'Silas ought to keep his mask on all the time,' said Farr, sniggering. 'It makes him look almost human.'

Not knowing whether to complain or throw a punch, Weaver settled for a grin.

'I like this,' he said.

'Like what?' asked Redshaw.

'Sitting round a fire with friends. It feels good.'

'It will feel much better when we're sitting in armchairs in big houses,' promised Keane. 'All our problems will disappear then – if we keep to the rules. Agreed?'

All three of them nodded in unison.

When the cab took her back to the house, Lydia Quayle paid the driver then used a key to let herself into the building. She had turned down Madeleine's invitation to stay for dinner, feeling that she had already taken up too much of her friend's time. Besides, she was eager to get back to a place she felt needed to be defended. Madeleine might have voiced doubts that the woman Lydia saw opposite her house was, in fact, a servant who had worked there in the past. In Lydia's opinion, there was not the merest shadow of doubt. The person she had seen earlier on the opposite side of the road was Kitty Piper, and the woman had been pointing out the house to the man beside her.

Once inside her own abode, Lydia felt a sense of reassurance. She was behind locked doors and therefore immune from danger. She tried hard to dismiss the memory of Kitty Piper, but the woman would not be dislodged. Lydia turned for help once again to her ever-reliable former nanny. How would Dolly Pearson cope with the situation? It was a foolish question to ask because the woman had remained a nanny throughout her life and therefore had limited experience of the wider world. Dolly Pearson had never employed someone like Kitty Piper, nor had she had such an ambivalent relationship with another human being. For once, the long-dead nanny was of no practical use. It meant that Lydia had to deal with her problems herself. Hoping that Madeleine would support her to the hilt, she instead found the latter unwilling to accept that the person seen by her friend was indeed Kitty Piper. Madeleine had been kind, attentive and ready to help, but she clearly believed that the person seen by her friend could not possibly have been the former domestic servant.

It was a severe blow to Lydia. At a time when she most needed support, it was simply not available. She was on her own.

When he arrived at the cathedral on the following morning, Robert Colbeck learnt that he had an unexpected visitor. It was Marcus

Napier, the chief constable of a neighbouring county. The latter had risen early so that he could get to Lincoln by train. Offered the use of the Dean's office, the two men gladly accepted it. They shook hands warmly and appraised each other.

'It's good to meet you,' said Colbeck. 'Apart from anything else, it gives me an opportunity to thank you for your offer of help.'

'I've long admired your exploits on the railways, Inspector, and it's a pleasure to be able to play a small part in your latest investigation. Thank you for your letter.'

'Dare I hope that you've tracked down the man we're after?'

'I'm afraid not,' said Napier. 'We found a Percy Gull, but he died over twenty years ago and could not possibly have been the man you're after.'

'Why is that?'

'He was a blind man from Stamford, who eked out a living by playing tunes on a small flute in the town square. If the weather was bad, of course, he would stay at his lodging with his dog. Gull had a miserable life, relying on food from his few friends.'

'He is obviously not the Percy Gull we need to find.'

'My men will not give up the search,' promised Napier, 'but I have only been able to spare a few of them.'

'I'm grateful that you took the trouble to do so,' said Colbeck.

'I couldn't miss the opportunity to play a small part in your latest investigation. News of your many successes have served as an inspiration to me.'

'That's very gratifying.'

'How certain are you that Gull is a native of my county?'

'I'm not certain at all, to be honest. All I know is that the telegraph sent from King's Cross station to Peterborough had Gull's name on it. I assumed that the man was still alive,' confessed

Colbeck, 'but perhaps he was not. At all events, I've tackled the problem from the other end, so to speak.'

'I don't follow,' said Napier.

'If the telegraph was sent from King's Cross station, the person who despatched it may remember the man who sent it to Peterborough.'

'That's highly unlikely. People who work in telegraph stations must send hundreds of messages a day. You can't expect them to remember the contents of every telegraph they despatched.'

'In this case, I'm confident someone did remember the message.'

'Why?'

'Because it was so unusual.'

'In what way?'

'It consisted of two words – "guard's van".'

Napier was taken aback. 'Is that all?'

'It was enough to set two serious crimes in motion – the theft of a silver model of this very cathedral and the death of the private detective guarding it.'

'I remember the newspaper account of the man's murder. Talking of which,' said Napier, 'did you not think of harnessing the power of the press? If you asked for information about the whereabouts of Percy Gull, you would certainly have got quicker answers than the ones my officers could find.'

'I did consider using the press,' Colbeck told him 'Two considerations held me back. If Percy Gull was indeed the killer, he would have been warned that we were on his tail. It's more than likely that he'd make a run for it. In other words, we'd have scared him off. I'd hate to have done that.'

'What was the second consideration?'

'We've had unhappy experiences with newspaper editors in the past. Some have been very helpful, but the majority often have reporters who harass us and who try to solve the crime themselves. The last thing we need are well-intentioned rivals from the press. They get in the way and often delay the success of an investigation.'

'That's true,' sighed Napier.

'Without telling any reporters, I have switched the search to London. The man who despatched that unusual telegraph will certainly have remembered it. How many customers send a message consisting of only two words?'

'I'd certainly remember the person who did.'

'First thing this morning,' explained Colbeck, 'I made use of the telegraph system myself. Even as we speak, Superintendent Tallis of Scotland Yard may be questioning the person at King's Cross who sent that fatal telegraph to Peterborough Railway Station.'

Edward Tallis stepped down from the cab that had taken him to King's Cross and paid the driver. He then strode into the building and headed for the telegraph station. The man behind the counter was a short, moon-faced individual with a large moustache. Tallis had to wait in a small queue before he was served.

'Can I help you, sir?' asked the man, manufacturing a smile.

'I hope so,' said Tallis. 'Have you been on duty here throughout the week?'

'Yes, I have.'

'Then you may be able to help me. I'm Superintendent Tallis from Scotland Yard and I'm searching for a vital piece of information.'

'I hope that I will be able to provide it, sir,' said the man.

'Does the name Percy Gull mean anything to you?'

'Yes, it does but I can't remember why at the moment.'

'Think back a few days. Someone came in here to send a telegraph to Peterborough Railway Station. It consisted of two words – "guard's van".'

'Oh, yes,' said the other, snapping his fingers. 'I recall the customer now.'

'Describe him, please,' said Tallis, taking out his notebook.

'Why?'

'Just do as you're told. Or would you prefer to have this conversation in Scotland Yard?'

'No, I wouldn't,' cried the man in alarm. 'I can't leave my job.'

'Then tell me what I need to hear,' ordered Tallis, 'and bear this in mind. You could be helping us to capture some dangerous criminals. Every detail is of value to us. Now then,' he added, pencil poised, 'describe the man who sent that unusual telegraph to Peterborough.'

Lydia Quayle was in a quandary. Desperate for assistance and support from her closest friend, she had been given neither. Madeleine Colbeck had not only failed to give her the unquestioning help that she needed, Lydia began to have doubts about the whole incident. Had she really seen her former servant, Kitty Piper, on the opposite side of the road? Or was it a case of mistaken identity? And even if it had been Kitty, could the young woman really be advising her male companion how best to get into the property to steal items from it?

Madeleine's objections had sown doubts in Lydia's mind. Had she really seen Kitty Piper or someone who looked very much like her? Who was the man with her? He had been well-dressed and respectable, yet Lydia had immediately identified him as a potential burglar. Why, in any case, would Kitty wish to steal from her former employer? The two of them had enjoyed a reasonably good relationship. When Kitty was offered employment elsewhere, Lydia had given her an excellent reference. Yet she was now convinced that the young woman had returned with a male friend to look at the possibilities of breaking into the house.

What evil urge had made someone like Kitty Piper wish to steal from a woman she had cause to thank for treating her so well? It was a question that Madeleine had put to her and Lydia could find no answer. A dangerous gap had suddenly opened between the two friends, and it caused Lydia great pain. She was forced to question her memory of the event and wonder if she had made a dreadful mistake. What if the woman on the opposite side of the road had not been Kitty Piper at all, but someone who looked very much like her? It was a strong possibility. Yet it eliminated another memory that haunted Lydia.

Someone unknown had been in the house and had left it as silently as possible.

Lydia still shuddered at the thought that a stranger could somehow have got into the property and moved about at will. Had it been Kitty Piper on that occasion? The servant would have known when and how to gain entry and might even have had a key to let herself in and out. The fact remained that Lydia had been deeply upset by the incident. When she had told her friend about it, Madeleine had been sympathetic and supportive. Why could she not respond in the same way to Lydia's account of the two people seen on the opposite side of the road, apparently studying her house?

A rift had occurred between them and Lydia had no idea

how to close it. Instead of turning once more to Madeleine, she decided, she would keep her anxieties to herself. It might be the best way to deal with them.

When he went to the Red Fox, the place was closed. It was only when he hammered on the door that he got some attention. Tobias Hall unlocked the front door and saw Edward Tallis standing there.

'We're not open yet, Superintendent,' he warned.

'I haven't come for a drink.'

'Then why are you here?'

'I want to show you something. May I come in?'

After giving him a grudging welcome, Hall stepped back to admit him. Tallis stepped in and waited until the door had been locked behind him. Folding his arms, the proprietor looked at him sternly. 'We told you everything we could.'

'I've gathered more detail about the man we're after,' said Tallis. 'He sent a telegraph from King's Cross to his henchmen in Peterborough. When I spoke to the man who transmitted the message, he remembered the person who had sent it because it was so short.'

Hall shrugged. 'What has this to do with me?'

'The man in question got the information he needed right here in your pub.'

'How do you know that?'

'Call it professional instinct,' said Tallis. 'He must have overheard the two apprentices from Peat, Hatherly and Tomkins discussing the time when the silver cathedral was being sent to Lincoln.'

'That's just guesswork,' protested Hall.

'Hear me out, sir. The description I have of the person I believe was within earshot of the two friends was as follows. He was dark-haired, of medium height, in his early forties, well-dressed and – according to my source – he had a knowing grin. Do you remember anyone fitting that description who was in here recently?'

'I can think of two or three people it might have been.'

'Do they all work in the jewellery trade?'

'No, they don't. Only one of them does that. He comes in here now and then.'

'Is he usually with friends?'

'No, he's on his own as a rule, but he usually chats to people in the same line of work. And he obviously has more money than they do because he often buys a round of drinks.'

'What's his name?'

'I'm not sure. Jimmy? Johnny? Something like that.'

'Would one of your bartenders know?'

'Probably. I'll ask them when they come on duty.'

'There's no need to do that,' said Tallis. 'I'll ask them myself. I'll be back when they start work this evening.'

After taking his leave, he left the Red Fox and walked jauntily along. He had the satisfying feeling that he was about to make an important contribution to the ongoing investigation. His spirits lifted as he realised that his instincts were still as sound as ever. Perhaps he was not ready for retirement, after all.

CHAPTER FOURTEEN

Caleb Andrews felt markedly better that morning. After an uninterrupted night's sleep, he had awakened refreshed and alert. When he met his daughter, he announced his decision.

'I think it's time for me to go home, Maddy.'

'You're very welcome to stay,' she said.

'I know and I'm very thankful for the way you've looked after me.'

'Helena Rose loved having you here.'

'It's a pity I was unable to see her properly,' he said, 'but I have things to do at home. First, of course, I must thank Mrs Dyer, my next-door neighbour, for raising the alarm. If she hadn't taken the trouble to come here and tell you how ill I sounded, I might have got worse and worse.'

'Don't even think about it, Father. It was lovely to have you here where I could keep a close eye on you and make sure that you took the tablets prescribed by the doctor.'

Andrews grimaced. 'They tasted horrible!'

'They worked. That's all that mattered.'

He studied her through narrowed eyes. 'What are you going to do about Lydia?'

'Help her in any way I can.'

'She turned up on your doorstep in a terrible state,' he recalled. 'I only had a glimpse of her, but I could see that she was worried about something. Did you manage to calm her down?'

'I did my best,' said Madeleine, pursing her lips. 'But Lydia was still unsettled when she went back home. She needs reassurance, that's all. I'm going to call on her later this morning.'

'You've been such a good friend to her, Maddy.'

'It's the reason she felt able to ask for help. As for friends,' she went on, 'you draw strength from them as well. It's the reason you want to leave here, isn't it?'

'What do you mean?'

'Don't look so innocent. Tonight is the night when you meet your friends at Euston station for a drink and a chat about old times working on the railway.'

'I'd hate to miss seeing them. If I don't turn up, they'll worry about me.'

'Put their minds at rest by going along this evening.'

'I will, I promise. It will be a real tonic for them.'

'I'm only interested in the fact that it will be a real tonic for you.'

'Thank you, Maddy,' he said, reaching out to take her hand. 'I'm so grateful that you brought me here. Being with you and my granddaughter did far more for me than that doctor ever did. He just gave me orders – you didn't.'

'You're always welcome here, Father,' she said, embracing him.

'There's only been one disappointment.'

She frowned. 'Disappointment?'

'Yes,' he told her. 'Robert hasn't asked for my opinion about this latest case of his. I could have been helpful. I could have told him that the Great Northern Railway doesn't look after its passengers properly. That's why someone was shot dead in broad daylight. The railway company is to blame.'

Madeleine burst out laughing.

He was offended. 'What's so funny?'

'You are, Father. I'm so glad that you're back to your old self . . .'

Edward Tallis was confused. When he'd got back to Scotland Yard, he'd felt so weary that he'd drifted off to sleep for a few minutes. Coming suddenly awake, he chided himself for such a lapse of concentration. Then he glanced down at his desk. Standing in the middle of it was the notepad in which he had jotted down the description he had taken from the man at the telegraph station of the person who had sent the brief instruction about the guard's van. Tallis had immediately passed on those details to Colbeck in a telegraph. In other words, he consoled himself, he had done his duty.

When he looked down at his desk again, however, he noticed a pile of folders. They contained details of all the other crimes with which he was dealing. By giving preference to one case, he had neglected the others. Had that been a wise decision? At the time, it had seemed so. In retrospect, however, he had serious doubts. As he looked back, he saw that his sudden visit to Lincoln had been of limited use to the investigation. More to the point, it had taxed his strength and exposed him to an agonising train journey back to London.

Tallis was shaken. His body still ached but it was his mind that troubled him more. The truth was cruel but had to be faced. He had not only made a series of mistakes, he had also lost the iron determination that helped him do his job so efficiently. Old age had finally crept up on him. His judgement had begun to falter. Strict towards those of lesser rank, he needed to be equally strict with himself. Was he able to do his job as effectively as he had always done so before? Or was it time to step aside and be replaced by someone younger, fitter and more alert?

Before he could answer the questions, he drifted off gently to sleep again.

Back in Lincoln, it was time to visit the bank. No chances were taken. When the Dean and the Bishop went off to collect the money, Robert Colbeck went with them. Leeming and Hinton were also in attendance. On the route to the bank, there were uniformed members of the local constabulary on duty. When they entered, Colbeck, the Bishop and the Dean went straight to the manager's office, and saw the saddlebags on his desk.

The manager rose at once from the seat behind his desk. Philip Henderson was an unusually tall man with flecks of grey in his neatly barbered hair. His face was lined with anxiety and his eyes were pools of deep concern. There was a brief exchange of niceties between them.

'I'm glad to meet you, Inspector,' said Henderson.

'And I am glad to meet you, sir.'

'I won't pretend that I am enjoying this moment,' said the

manager, picking up the saddlebags. 'The amount you requested is all here, Dean Courtney.' He handed the bags over to him. 'Count it, if you wish.'

'That won't be necessary, Mr Henderson,' said the Dean.

'We hope to return the money to you in due course,' added Colbeck.

'It grieves me that you are taking such chances with it,' said Henderson.

'Have faith in us, please.'

'I will pray for your success, Inspector Colbeck.'

'If I'm honest, we may need more than prayer.'

'They feel so heavy,' said the Dean, indicating the saddlebags.

'I hope that they come back to us equally heavy,' said Henderson with a wan smile.

'They will,' promised Colbeck.

'Then I wish you well, gentlemen.'

After shaking hands with him in turn, they left the office.

When she got to the house, Madeleine was told that her friend was in the garden. She therefore let herself out there so that she could talk to Lydia Quayle in the open air. As she sat beside her on the bench, she gave a smile of approval.

'I see that you're obeying the wise words of Nanny Pearson,' she said.

'Fresh air stimulates me, Madeleine.'

'That depends on how cold it is.' She studied her friend. 'How do you feel today?'

'To be honest, I feel very tired.'

'Did you have a bad night?'

'I hardly slept a wink.'

'Oh dear!' said Madeleine. 'I'm so sorry. Is it preying on your mind?'

'I'm afraid so. I kept getting up to peer through the curtains in case they were still there on the other side of the road.'

'That was silly. You wouldn't have been able to see them in the darkness.'

'I know but it didn't stop me doing it.'

'What can I do to help?'

'You're already doing it, Madeleine. Simply by being here, you've made me feel better. It's so good to know that someone cares about me.'

'Of course I do. We're friends. That means I feel your pain.'

'It's more like fear at the moment,' confessed Lydia. 'I feel under threat because I think that someone is planning to break into my house.'

'You don't know that for certain.'

'Why else did Kitty and that man stare at the place for so long?'

'It must have revived a lot of memories for Kitty.'

'Bad memories.'

'Not necessarily,' argued Madeleine. 'There must be good memories as well. When you first employed Kitty, I remember you telling me how bright and hard-working she was. And she got on reasonably well with Martha.'

'Yes, that was a real bonus.'

'Have you told your cook what you saw yesterday?'

'Of course,' said Lydia. 'If the house is under threat, Martha needs to be warned so that she can be on guard.'

'Did she believe that Kitty would do such a thing?'

'Yes, she did. Martha never liked Kitty. She made the effort to get on with the girl but they were never real friends.'

'What possible motive would Kitty have?'

'I think there was a deep-seated dislike of me, Madeleine. We got on famously at first then her manner changed slightly. I noticed a faint resentment in her manner. It was as if she saw how comfortable a life I was leading and wondered why she was a mere domestic servant with only a small room to call her own.'

'A small room that you actually owned.'

'Exactly. It rankled.'

Madeleine remained silent and gazed at the flowers that looked so beautiful in the bright sunshine. Her friend had a house with a lovely garden. Lydia should be able to live there without any fear of her security.

'All I can offer you is support,' said Madeleine. 'You need professional advice.'

'I know.'

'Unfortunately, the best person to give it is in Lincoln with Robert.'

'Yes,' said Lydia. 'That's unfortunate. I did wish that I could turn to Alan. Have you any idea how long this latest case will take?'

'No, I don't, I'm afraid. It's too full of complications.'

'That's a pity!'

'If you want advice, you'll have to turn to me.'

'And I'm so happy to do so, Madeleine. I can't tell you how wonderful it was to be able to call on you yesterday evening and get a sympathetic hearing. I didn't agree with all that you said, but I felt so much better from having poured out my woes.'

'I still think those woes might be imaginary.'

'Why else was Kitty there with that man?'

'He was a friend,' Madeleine reminded her. 'She linked arms with him.'

'That was after she'd shown him the house and explained how he'd get in.'

'Did you actually hear her giving him instructions?'

'No,' conceded Lydia, 'I was too far away.'

'Why didn't Kitty see you? She must have been aware of someone watching her.'

'She wasn't, I promise you. She never once glanced in my direction.'

'There you are, then,' concluded Madeleine. 'She was so preoccupied with her friend that nobody else mattered.'

Lydia laughed.

'What's so funny?'

'You talk like a burglar.'

'I was only trying to think like one.'

'Well, I'm so glad that you did so, Madeleine. I feel as if a great weight has been lifted off me. Your advice, as usual, is sound. Kitty is not really telling someone how to get into my house and what to steal. Your earlier suggestion was right. Now that she has gone up in the world, she wanted to look back on her old life in domestic service.'

'Why didn't you believe me when I told you just that?'

'I really don't know,' said Lydia, searching for an answer. 'I've been so upset by the experience.'

Back at the cathedral, Colbeck had been counting the money stuffed in neat piles into the saddlebags. It was all there. Dean Courtney sighed with relief.

'I can't tell you how stressful that visit to the bank was,' he admitted.

'You were perfectly safe,' Colbeck assured him.

'I was afraid that someone would pounce on us as we left the bank and disappear with the saddlebags before we knew what was happening.'

'I can see that you've never been a policeman.'

'What do you mean?'

'If you had been, you'd have developed a sense of danger. That's what I did when I was in uniform. It saved me from attack on more than one occasion.'

'I was hoping that the Bishop's and my vestments would act as a deterrent.'

'The men we're dealing with have no respect for your status, I'm afraid,' said Colbeck. 'If they had even the smallest Christian impulses, they would never have dreamt of stealing a silver model of Lincoln Cathedral.'

'They're complete heathens!'

'Then we will have to tell them in the most forthright way.'

'Our loss has caused great pain, Inspector, but there is someone for whom the situation is even more shattering.'

'Gregory Tomkins?'

'It should have been his crowning achievement,' said the Dean. 'Instead of that, the theft of his final work as a silversmith might make him die of utter despair.'

Ignoring the advice of his wife, Tomkins had travelled that morning to the premises where he had spent so many happy years. He was given a delighted welcome by his partners and by the rest of the staff. Asking to be left alone, he went up to his work room on the first floor. As he stepped into it, he felt a surge of pleasure. It was the place where his most brilliant creations had come into existence. There was something about silver that fascinated him, and he had never been happier than when he was fashioning it into wondrous shapes to delight the eye. He did so in a world of his own. On his desk was the original design for the model of Lincoln Cathedral. As he stared at it, he remembered how he had felt inspired to be bringing the building to dramatic life in silver. Tomkins also recalled that during those long months of intense dedication, he had kept himself going by singing the words of hymns he had sung with the congregation of his beloved cathedral. It was as if he were attending a service day after day.

The work of which he was most proud had now lost its lustre. Did he have the strength to bring it to life once more? Even as he asked the question, he knew the answer. Because the cathedral had taken so many long months of his time, energy and genius as a silversmith, it had left him utterly exhausted. He had neither the strength nor the ability to recreate it. What worried him most was the fear that he would never see the earlier version again. It was in the hands of vile thieves who had killed a man so that they could steal it. They would show it no respect.

Tomkins sat back in his chair and closed his eyes. He had given up all hope of ever seeing the gift on which he had laboured so long and with such love. The result had been a triumph. He had produced a work of art. But he now felt certain that it had gone forever.

Pamela had finished her cleaning duties for the morning and drifted into the kitchen for a chat with Martha. The older woman was washing the crockery used during breakfast.

'What's wrong with Miss Quayle?' asked Pamela.

'She's worried about something.'

'Do you know what it is?'

'Yes,' replied Martha. 'She believes that she saw Kitty Piper yesterday.'

'Where?'

'More or less opposite the house.'

'What on earth was the woman doing there?'

'According to Miss Quayle, she was pointing to the house and talking to a man. After a while, they went off arm in arm.'

'I noticed that she was very upset after her walk.'

'She was afraid that Kitty was instructing the man on how he could get in here.'

Pamela shivered. 'I don't like the sound of that.'

'That may not be the truth. It was what Miss Quayle thought was happening.'

'Do you think Kitty is capable of such a thing?'

'Yes. I do.'

'Why didn't Miss Quayle mention it to me?' asked Pamela.

'It was because she didn't want to alarm you. But I feel that you ought to know. If we are under threat of a burglary you should be prepared.'

'Do you think it's a serious threat?'

'Frankly, it's possible.'

'Then why is she so nervous about it?'

'Kitty left here under a cloud. She was bound to blame Miss Quayle.'

'That doesn't mean she'd want this house burgled,' said Pamela. 'Anyway, the lock on the front door was changed so we should all feel secure. I know that I do.'

'My feeling is that Miss Quayle made a mistake.'

'What makes you say that?'

'She'd been for a long walk and got back when light was starting to fall. When she saw a woman who looked like Kitty, I think she must have jumped to the wrong conclusion. It wasn't her,' decided Martha.

'Then why was Miss Quayle so sure that it was?'

'It's because Kitty has been on her mind lately. I take the blame for that.'

'Why?'

'Well, I was the person who first mentioned Kitty's name when Miss Quayle heard someone sneaking out of the house. It was a mistake. Kitty had her faults but she was not a criminal.'

'Then who did?'

'I don't know, Pamela. But it's caused Miss Quayle a lot of anxiety. It's so unfair. She was living so happily here with the two of us. Suddenly, she's become very nervous and keeps glancing over her shoulder. That walk she took yesterday ended in disaster,' said Martha. 'She was so certain that she'd seen Kitty that she went off to tell Mrs Colbeck what had happened.' She lowered her voice. 'We must be very kind to her. Miss Quayle is going through a difficult time. She needs all the support we can give her.'

Colbeck was alone with the Dean in the cathedral. Only yards away from them was a large safe containing the money collected from the bank. Dean Courtney kept shooting nervous glances at it.

'I think that we should have a change of plan,' decided Colbeck.

'What do you mean?'

'So far we have been following their orders to the letter. It's time that we shifted the burden of proof to them.'

'How can we do that, Inspector?'

'We should insist on a guarantee that they really do have the silver cathedral.'

'But we have evidence that they stole it from the train at Peterborough Railway Station. More than one person saw the box in which it was kept being carried out to a waiting cart.'

'That's true,' conceded Colbeck. 'But these men have absolutely no scruples. What is to stop them replacing Mr Tomkins's masterpiece with something of similar weight? You would be paying an enormous amount of money for an object that is utterly worthless.'

'God forbid!'

'How did they contact you?'

'A demand was slipped under the door of this cathedral,' said the Dean. 'My reply to it was handed over at a place appointed by them. I stood alone in a lane not far from here and someone snatched the message from me and vanished.'

'Write another letter and take it to the same place.'

'What if nobody turns up?'

'Oh, someone will,' insisted Colbeck. 'They'll have that spot monitored throughout the day. We're up against an invisible enemy, Dean Courtney. They are watching every move you make.'

'I followed their orders, Inspector. As you know, the money they demanded was taken from the bank earlier this morning.'

'Yes and, as I pointed out, you would have been under surveillance. They know that you danced to their tune. That's why it's time for you to put pressure on them for a change. Insist on visible proof that they do have the stolen object.'

'What shall I say exactly?'

'If you wish, I'll dictate the message to you. Take it to the place you mentioned and wait until someone snatches the missive from you. All that we need to do then is to wait. Their reply will be delivered here somehow.'

'What if they refuse our demand?'

'Then they are left with a beautiful object that has suddenly lost its value. Who else would buy it from them?' asked Colbeck. 'They will be confused by our change of tactics. I don't believe that they expect you to fight back.'

'It will give me great satisfaction to do so, Inspector,' said the Dean, gritting his teeth. 'All of a sudden, I feel that we can put them at a disadvantage. Please help me to write our demand and I will take it to the place where I can hand it over.'

'At the very least, it will sow confusion.'

'Your advice is sound. I am deeply grateful for it.'

'Let's hope that it does what it's designed to do. And remember,' Colbeck went on, 'that we are dealing with men who have no respect whatsoever for religion. It's time to show them that Lincoln Cathedral can fight back.'

When the bartenders arrived at The Red Fox, they found Superintendent Tallis awaiting them. He took one of them aside.

'The last time I was here,' said Tallis, 'you told me the names of the two young men who worked at Peat, Hatherly and Tomkins.'

'That's right, sir,' agreed the man.

'Please remind me what their names were?'

'Donald Bush and Sam Fielding.'

'Have you see them talking to anyone in particular recently?'

'They've chatted to a number of customers, Superintendent.'

'Let me describe one of them,' said Tallis. 'He's short, slim and well-dressed. I'm told that he's in his early forties. Oh, yes, and he's very agitated. He twitches a lot. Does that description of him ring a bell?'

'Yes, it does,' said the barman.

'What's his name?'

'It's Jerry something. And he seems to know everybody in the jewellery trade. He works somewhere not far away. He's very popular. Lots of people seem to know him.'

'Is he in the habit of buying people drinks?'

'Now that you mention it, he is. I fancy that he earns more than most of the people who come in here.'

'Who does he work for?'

'I don't know. I think he deals with more than one jewellery shop.'

'Has he been in here in the last few days?'

'Oddly enough, he hasn't,' said the barman.

'Is that unusual?'

'Yes, it is. Jerry is one of our regulars.'

'Thank you very much. You've been very helpful.'

'I'm always glad to help the police. What can I get you to drink, sir?'

'Nothing,' said Tallis, firmly. 'I need to make a few calls elsewhere in the area.' He headed for the door. 'Please excuse me.'

When she called at the house later that day, Madeleine heard two bolts being drawn back before the door was opened by Pamela. The maid smiled at her.

'Good morning, Mrs Colbeck,' she said.

'There only used to be one bolt on the door,' observed Madeleine.

'When the locksmith changed the lock, he advised an additional bolt. He also put an extra one on the door to the garden.'

'In matters of security, we can never be too careful.'

'I agree,' said Pamela, standing back to admit the visitor. 'Miss

Quayle is in the drawing room. I'm sure she'll be delighted to see you again.'

'Thank you, Pamela.'

Walking past her, Madeleine tapped on the door of the drawing room and opened it. Delighted to see her, Lydia Quayle put aside the book she had been reading and got to her feet to give her a welcoming hug.

'I was hoping you would come, Madeleine,' she said.

'Why? Has there been a development?'

'No, but I still believe that we're in danger here.'

'With a second bolt on your front door you should have no worries.'

'Then why did I have such a sleepless night?'

'Might it be that your imagination got the better of you?'

'I suppose so,' conceded Lydia. 'But do please take a seat. Chatting to you on my feet makes me feel it's terribly formal.' They sat opposite each other. 'Have you had any news from Robert?'

'Yes, his letter came first thing this morning. He thinks that the end is in sight.'

'That's heartening news.'

'It is and it isn't,' said Madeleine. 'There was no hint of Robert coming back home yet – and the same goes for Alan, of course.'

'He does love working on cases with your husband.'

'The feeling between them is mutual. Robert finds Alan so willing and reliable.'

'They both seem so far away at the moment,' complained Lydia.

'At least they have solved one problem.'

'What was it?'

'Superintendent Tallis has returned to London, apparently.

They thought he would take change of the investigation, but he was happy for Robert to remain in control.'

'That's completely out of character. He usually insists on given the orders.'

'Perhaps he is mellowing now that he's getting older. Anyway,' said Madeleine, 'I came to talk about the experience you had. Are you still convinced that you saw Kitty Piper on the opposite side of the road?'

'I am – and I'm not.'

'It's unlike you to be so uncertain, Lydia.'

'I know and it's worrying me.'

'Yesterday, you'd have bet money on the fact that you saw Kitty so close.'

'By the time I went to bed I began to have doubts.'

'Did you tell your servants about what happened?'

'I told Martha because she knew Kitty. They'd worked beside each other for some time. In her opinion, the person I saw was unlikely to be Kitty. If she was instructing a man to break in here she'd have done so in the dark – not in daylight.'

'Light was fading when you got back here.'

'That's true.'

'But the two people you saw were clearly visible. As for Pamela, I daresay that Martha told her about the incident. It was only fair to warn her of the danger.'

'But there was no danger,' argued Madeleine.

'There was in my mind.'

'How do you feel now?'

'I suppose that I feel a sense of relief. Nothing happened in the night, so my fears were groundless. But it did rain heavily at one point. I could hear it drumming on the roof. It may be that Kitty's friend did plan to get in here, but that the weather conditions made him change his mind.'

'Assuming that this man is a potential burglar . . .'

'He is.' Her face fell. 'At least, he seemed so yesterday.'

'What could he possibly be after?'

'There are valuable items in here and in the dining room.'

'Do you honestly believe that Kitty would turn to crime?' asked Madeleine.

'Yes,' replied her friend. 'I do.'

'Then she must have changed completely. What I remember about Kitty is that she was always interested in what I was wearing. I could see the envy in her eyes. But she was always polite and obedient.'

'People can change, Madeleine.'

'That's true. Even so . . .'

'I can see that we must agree to differ,' said Lydia. 'When I saw Kitty on the opposite side of the road, pointing something out to the man beside her, I had this awful feeling in the pit of my stomach. My house was in danger.'

'Yet nothing at all happened in the night.'

'I blame that on the rain.'

'Then you're right,' said Madeleine firmly. 'We must agree to differ. I'd hate anything to come between us, Lydia. Let's leave it at that, shall we?'

'I agree. Let's talk about something completely different.'

'Such as?'

'My father, for instance. Since he's feeling better, he'll be going home today. But he volunteered to take Helena Rose for a walk before he left. She was thrilled. They're probably still out in the fresh air.'

'Then he's obviously shaken off his cold,' said Lydia. 'I envy him. I wish I could shake off my fears quite so easily. But there's no doctor who can cure this sense of being at the mercy of someone waiting to break into my house. I'm a victim, Madeleine,' she cried. 'I feel so helpless.'

Victor Leeming and Alan Hinton were on patrol. As they walked down a narrow lane, a man came running towards them. In his hands were the reins of the three horses trotting behind him. The detectives had to flatten themselves against the walls so that the animals could pass. There was no apology from the man leading them.

'I've seen enough horses to last me a lifetime,' complained Leeming.

'They've taken over the city.'

'You won't believe it, Alan, but there was a time when I liked the idea of being a cab driver. It's regular work, you get to meet lots of customers, and there's always the chance that some of them will give you a tip.'

'You'd have made a good cab driver,' said Hinton. 'You know how to get on with strangers and I've never met anyone with such a detailed knowledge of London.'

'There's only one problem.'

'What is it?'

'I don't like horses,' said Leeming. 'Since we've been here, I've learnt to hate them. They can be so dangerous.'

'A cab driver has only one horse to worry about.'

'Yes, but the animal needs to be harnessed every day and given food and water. Then, of course, you need to stable him for the night. Also, the cab driver is out in all weathers. If there's heavy snow on the ground, he won't make a penny. I prefer my job. At least we get a regular income.'

'We have to earn it the hard way sometimes.'

'That's true.' Leeming turned to his companion. 'What do you think about this change of plan the inspector told us about?'

'I think it's a wise move, Victor.'

'And so do I. The men we're after are hardened criminals. Until now, we've been at the mercy of their demands. It's time we stood up to them.'

'I agree, but I'm not sure that the superintendent would agree with the plan.'

'Luckily, he's not making the decisions in this case.'

'He worries me,' said Hinton.

'Why?'

'It's because he seems to have lost his old fire.'

'Thank goodness for that!' said Leeming.

'To be honest, I was glad that he went back to London. He was in the way when he was here. There were times when he seemed so confused.'

'I know the feeling,' said Leeming.

'There was a point when I wondered if he was ill . . .'

Given a new sense of purpose, Edward Tallis responded immediately. He walked to the jewellery quarter and went into a succession of shops. There was no immediate success. Whenever he mentioned the Christian name that he had been given, all that he got in return was a shake of the head. Undaunted, he pressed on and eventually he had some success. Walking into another shop, he told the manager whom he was then asked if the firm employed – or knew of someone who did – a person with the Christian name of Jerry. The manager curled a lip.

'Do you mean Jeremy Keane?' he asked.

'Possibly,' replied Tallis. 'Did you ever employ him?'

'No, but I know people who did. They lived to regret it.'

'Why might that be, sir?'

'Jeremy Keane – or Jerry, as he liked to be called – is one of those cunning people who work in the jewellery trade simply to make money. He offers managers deals that will make them certain profits, and sometimes they succeed. Most of the time, however, the only profit made goes into the pocket of Jeremy Keane.'

'Are you telling me that he is a confidence trickster?'

'That's too kind a word for him,' said the manager. 'In fairness, he does have some knowledge of the trade, but he has no respect for those of us who work in it. We are simply targets for him. I sent him packing as soon as I looked at him because I smelt a rat.'

'Do you know where he lives?'

'I don't know, and I don't wish to know. May I ask why you are interested in this fellow, Superintendent?'

'First,' suggested Tallis, 'let me give you a description of this individual so that we can be certain that we're talking about the same man.'

'That's a wise precaution.'

Tallis repeated the details he had been given by the man in charge of the telegraph station at King's Cross. Before he had finished, he was interrupted.

'That's a perfect description of Jerry Keane,' confirmed the manager. 'The only thing you missed out is that he's a loathsome deal-maker with no consideration for anyone unlucky enough to be targeted by him.'

'Thank you, sir,' said Tallis. 'You've been more than helpful.'

When he left the shop there was a spring in his step. Tallis had the feeling that he was making progress at last. It was time to send a telegraph.

It was Tim Redshaw's turn to be on guard. He was lounging against a wall in a lane not far from the cathedral. For a man of action like him, it was a boring assignment. Hours had passed and nothing had happened. His only consolation was that he would soon be relieved by Patrick Farr. For the moment, however, he had to remain where he was and think about the substantial amount of money that he would get in due course.

He was jerked out of his reverie by the sudden appearance of the Dean. The latter came bustling towards him, face impassive. Redshaw stepped out so that he could be seen. Dean Courtney walked straight up to him and offered him a letter. Snatching it from the man's grasp, Redshaw turned on his heel and marched swiftly away downhill. He stopped when he reached the inn where his friends were waiting.

'Here he is at last,' said Keane, sitting up.

'I've got a message for you,' said Redshaw, handing it over.

Taking it from him, Keane opened the letter and read it. He winced.

'What's the trouble, Jerry?' asked Farr.

'They're demanding proof that we've got the silver cathedral,' said Keane.

'They'll have that when we hand it over.'

'They don't trust us, Pat. We know that they drew the money out of the bank because we watched them go in and come out again with the saddlebags I ordered. This letter from the Dean says that it's time to be certain that what they get in return for the money is that so-called work of art made by Gregory Tomkins.'

'What do we do, Jerry?' asked Redshaw.

'Shut up, Tim,' snapped the other. 'I need to do some thinking.'

CHAPTER FIFTEEN

Robert Colbeck was glad to hear that the Dean had handed over the message to a member of the gang who had stolen the miniature cathedral. The inspector believed that it would prompt the thieves into action. Meanwhile, he had a pleasant surprise. Earlier on, he had sent Alan Hinton on an errand. The latter had gone to the telegraph station to see if there were any messages there for Colbeck. He was given one that had just arrived. After hurrying back to the cathedral, Hinton handed the telegraph over. When he read the message, Colbeck was visibly thrilled.

'Is it good news, Inspector?' asked Hinton.

'It's the best news possible, Alan. We have good reason to congratulate Superintendent Tallis. While working on our behalf in London, he has identified the name of the man who is leading the gang we are hunting.'

'How on earth did he do that?'

'I look forward to discovering how. This telegraph has given us the weapon that we needed – and all because the superintendent has devoted himself to the case. He even promises us another gift.'

'What is it?'

'He has switched his search to Percy Gull. We found no sign of him here. Could it be that Gull lives in London? If he does so, the superintendent will smoke him out.'

'That's wonderful news, sir. When he came to Lincoln, he seemed to be tired and unable to devote himself to the case. Superintendent Tallis has now confounded us all. What has happened to him?'

'He feels that he owed us some assistance. Unable to give it here, he went back to London and unearthed valuable evidence. I can't wait to pass on this intelligence to Dean Courtney. He will be thrilled.'

Having achieved what he believed was significant progress in the case, Edward Tallis turned his attention to another problem. Who was Percy Gull and why had his name been on the telegraph sent by Jeremy Keane to someone waiting at the railway station in Peterborough? To find out the truth, Tallis needed help. He therefore gathered a small team of detectives and gave them their instructions.

'Find this man,' he demanded. 'There must be a good reason why his name was used on a telegraph. A search for Gull has been made in Peterborough and beyond, but it failed to find the man we are after. My guess is that they were looking in the wrong place. Instinct tells me that Gull is more likely to live in London. We need to find him.'

'How do we do that, sir?' asked one of the detectives.

'By a combination of hard work and imagination,' said Tallis. 'If this man is here, there must be a written record of him somewhere. For example, he may be entitled to vote. He may own a house. He may have a bank account somewhere. Put your heads together and find this man. It's vital that you do so.'

'Can I make a suggestion, sir?' asked another man.

'Make as many as you like,' urged Tallis.

'Might this person have been arrested in the past?'

'It's more than likely, so that's another avenue to explore. Check police records. Leave no stone unturned. Percy Gull is the link between Jeremy Keane, the leader of the gang we are after, and someone who lives near Peterborough. Get out there and find Gull. He is somehow involved in this dreadful crime.'

As the detectives left his office, Tallis reached for a cigar and lit it. As he exhaled a first cloud of smoke, he began to feel genuine hope that he could make another major advance in the case. In Lincoln, he had been out of his depth. By returning to Scotland Yard, he was on familiar ground. Tallis felt a surge of optimism.

They had been keeping out of each other's way for days now. Donald Bush and Samuel Fielding had been having the same fears and doing their best to ignore them. It was Fielding who finally broke the silence. During a break at work, they spoke to each other at last. They did so with a sense of fear.

'Mr Tomkins is back again today,' said Fielding.

'Yes, I noticed that. He looks worse than ever.'

'I wonder if we might be responsible for what happened.'

'I don't think so,' snapped Bush. 'Whatever gave you that idea?'

'I keep thinking of that man we met at the Red Fox.'

'Which man?'

'The one called Jerry. You must remember him. He bought us drinks.'

Bush was repentant. 'We had too much beer that evening.'

'I know that. My father could smell it on my breath. He was very angry. It was the reason I haven't been back to the Red Fox.'

'I've kept away myself.'

'Did we tell Jerry something that was supposed to be secret?'

'I don't think so,' said Bush.

'We'd been warned against doing so, Donald.'

'To be honest, I can't remember what we said to that man.'

'He kept asking us when the silver cathedral was going to Lincoln.'

'We didn't know the precise time.'

'We knew it was on the following day.'

'I don't recall telling him that, Sam. Do you?'

'No – but, then, I'd drunk far too much.'

'So had I,' admitted Bush.

'Do you think we should tell anyone?'

'No, I don't.'

'But Jerry could have used that information to—'

'Shut up!' demanded Bush, grabbing his jacket. 'We had nothing to do with the theft of that silver cathedral. Forget that we were even in the Red Fox that evening. We told the inspector what happened, and we must stick to that same story. Do you understand?'

'Yes,' murmured Fielding.

'Don't ever mention it again. Agreed?'

Fielding gave a reluctant nod.

* * *

Colbeck was still with the Dean when the message was delivered to the latter. It had been slipped under the main door of the cathedral and picked up by a member of the clergy. Holding it in his hands, the Dean seemed nervous. He suddenly offered it to Colbeck.

'You open it, Inspector,' he said.

'It was you who wrote that letter to them.'

'Yes, but you dictated it.'

'That's true,' agreed Colbeck.

He took the letter from the Dean and opened it. Colbeck read the message, and his eyebrows lifted in surprise.

'What do they say?' asked the Dean.

'They agree to provide the proof we demanded, but they need extra time to do so. They suggest that we move the time of the exchange to midnight tomorrow.'

'May I see their exact words?'

'Of course,' said Colbeck, handing him the letter.

Dean Courtney read the message. 'Why do they ask for an extra day?'

'They have their reasons. We should be pleased by their response. It shows that we've exercised a degree of control at last. Hitherto, they have simply issued orders. By making a demand of our own we've changed the balance of power.'

'How will they give us the proof that we asked?'

'They will devise a way, Dean Courtney. If they're clever enough to steal the silver cathedral, they'll know how to convince us that it is in their possession.'

'Where exactly are they at the moment?'

'One of them at least is in the city, keeping us under surveillance. When we visited the bank, we must have been seen coming out with the saddlebags. In short, we were doing exactly what we were told.'

'Do they have the stolen model with them?'

'I'm sure that they do. It's hidden away somewhere.'

'Who sent this latest letter?'

'Jeremy Keane. Thanks to Superintendent Tallis, we now have his name. That gives us a huge advantage.'

'We are eternally grateful to the superintendent.'

'His time in London has not been wasted,' said Colbeck. 'Having identified one person we need to arrest, he will now be searching for another.'

'And who might that be?'

'Percy Gull.'

'Does the fellow live in London?'

'It's a possibility, Dean Courtney. If he is there, he will certainly be traced. Superintendent Tallis is a tireless bloodhound. When he picks up a scent, he invariably finds his man.'

There were times in the past when Madeleine Colbeck had been directly involved in a case. Unknown to his superiors, her husband had used her to go to places only accessible to women. It had been a valuable move on Colbeck's part, gaining him evidence he would not otherwise have seen. Since the birth of their daughter, however, Madeleine was no longer able to help him. She was too busy looking after the child and pursuing her own career as an artist. Her detective work, however, had not been forgotten. It was the reason she had taken Lydia out of the latter's house and across the road.

'Show me where they were standing,' she said.

'It was somewhere near here,' said Lydia, taking up a position.

'And where were you? Point to the place.'

'It was well over twenty yards away, Madeleine.'

'Over here?' asked her friend, moving into position.

'A bit further back.'

Madeleine stepped back into position then asked Lydia to stand at the same angle as the two people she had witnessed after her walk. To her surprise, Lydia turned away from her. All that Madeleine could see was the side of her face.

'Did you never manage to see the whole of her face?' asked Madeleine.

'No,' confessed Lydia.

'Then how can you be so sure that it was Kitty?'

'It looked so much like her.'

'But you're too far away to be certain. In fading light, you could easily have been mistaken. Face the direction that she did.' Lydia did so and Madeleine nodded. 'I know you well enough to recognise you anywhere, but I can't be a hundred per cent certain that it is you. It's someone very much like you, Lydia, but I could be mistaken.'

'Why are you trying to prove that I was wrong?' asked her friend.

'Because I want to get rid of the fear that the incident gave you.'

'Seeing Kitty came as a real shock.'

'If it really was her . . .'

'I'm certain of it.'

'Are you?' asked Madeleine. 'And there's another problem. Because you only looked at the woman, you ignored the man. You couldn't give me any details about him beyond the fact that he was much older than . . . the woman he was with.'

'I told you that he was well-dressed.'

'If the woman really was Kitty, she was no longer in domestic service.'

'Yes, I know. She and the man seemed very close.'

'And the woman was pointing at your house?'

'Yes, Madeleine. It simply had to be Kitty. I'd seen her gesture like that before.'

'If she had designs on your house, she could have stolen whatever she wanted when she was living with you. Why leave it so long?'

'Perhaps the man talked her into it. When she explained how well-furnished the house was, he might have been interested in selecting items to steal.'

'There's one problem, Lydia.'

'What is it?'

'Why has Kitty come back? It's ages since she stopped working for you. Surely, she would be living an entirely different life now.'

Lydia shrugged helplessly. She had no answer.

Patrick Farr had been left guarding the box containing the silver cathedral. It was inside the tent where he and his friends had slept. They had chosen the field because it was a long way from the farmhouse itself. Nobody had come to chase them off. Feeling lonely, Farr was delighted when he saw his cousin riding towards him. The sight of Jeremy Keane stilled his fears. He got to his feet and held the horse's bridle while Keane dismounted.

'What's happened, Jerry?'

'We had a letter from the Dean. He wants information.'

'What sort of information?'

'The cathedral won't part with a single penny until they're certain that we have the gift offered by Gregory Tomkins.'

'But that's impossible,' cried Farr. 'We can't show it to them.'

'Yes, we can,' said his cousin, removing the saddlebag from

the horse. 'I knew that the fair would have what I wanted. They're selling these things to children, but I think that they'll suit us as well.'

Opening the saddlebag, he put in a hand and brought out a bundle of items.

Farr was astounded. 'What on earth are they for, Jerry?'

While he had trust in his officers, Edward Tallis did not expect any of them to return with news about the whereabouts of Percy Gull. Yet that is what happened. Detective Constable Higgs was a rotund man with a rather bewildered look on his face, but he had clearly been busy.

'I found Percy Gull for you, Superintendent,' he declared.

Tallis was delighted. 'He's here in London?'

'He'll always be here, sir.'

'What do you mean?'

'He's buried in the cemetery where he used to work as a gravedigger,' said Higgs. 'He's been there for the last five years.'

'If he died five years ago, he can't be the man we're after.'

'Yes, I know. But I wanted to prove that I'd tracked down someone with the same name.' He took out his notebook and flipped the pages before stopping at the one he needed. 'Here we are,' he said. 'Percy Edward Gull was born in Whitechapel in 1817. He worked in a factory at first and then—'

'Stop!' howled Tallis. 'I want to hear about the real man, not someone who happens to have the same name.'

'It does prove that I've been busy, sir.'

'Your efforts are noted, Higgs. Now get back out there and continue searching.'

'Yes, of course.'

'And make sure that the next Percy Gull you find is actually alive.'

'He will be, I assure you.'

As Higgs let himself out of the room, Tallis heaved a sigh. He had needed a great deal of luck to track down Jeremy Keane. He was still congratulating himself on his success. Had his good fortune now deserted him? It looked likely. There was no time to smoke a celebratory cigar this time.

When he came out of the room where he had been working on his latest project, Samuel Fielding saw Gregory Tomkins coming down the staircase. The old man looked frailer than ever. Fielding moved forward.

'Good day to you, sir,' he said, politely.

'Hello, Sam,' muttered the other.

'I'm so sorry about what happened.'

'It's broken my heart, lad.'

'I remember you letting us see it before it was almost finished. It was dazzling. Your work really belonged in a cathedral.'

'It may not get there, alas. I will never see it again.'

'Take heart, sir. I will pray that it comes back somehow.'

'But in what state will it be?' asked Tomkins. 'The people who stole it are savages. They have no idea of its significance. I fear that it will be badly damaged.'

'You could always repair it, sir.'

'Not with these hands,' said the silversmith, holding out both palms. 'Working on that cathedral drained the last of my talent. It will never come back.'

'I don't believe that, Mr Tomkins.'

The old man peered at him. 'Your father is a clergyman, isn't he?'

'Yes, he's vicar of St Mark's.'

'Please ask him to pray for me. I need all the help I can get.'

After touching Fielding's shoulder, he shuffled on past him.

Having finished their latest round of jobs, Martha and Pamela were in the kitchen, enjoying a cup of tea together. The older woman was concerned.

'I'm worried about Miss Quayle,' she said.

'So am I, Martha.'

'She seems so distracted. As a rule, she is always happiest when Mrs Colbeck has called. This time, however, she was really upset.'

'Do you know why?'

'Kitty is at the root of it somehow.'

'It's almost as if she's haunting Miss Quayle.'

'I think that she should count her blessings.'

'What do you mean?'

'Kitty's long gone and you're here in her place. You work much harder than she ever did. More to the point, you obviously respect Miss Quayle.'

'I do, Martha. She's a kind employer.'

'I've never met a kinder one. She's been a real friend to me. Her only problem is that she worries too much. Earlier today, she was still talking about the time when she heard a stranger leaving the house.'

'It must have frightened her.'

'I agree, Pamela, but she should have shrugged it off by now.'

'Does she still believe that it might have been Kitty?'

Martha nodded. 'I'm certain of it.'

'But she left a long time ago. What reason could Kitty have to come back?'

'Kitty had a nasty streak to her.'

'What do you mean?'

'Perhaps she nursed a grievance against Miss Quayle. I don't know why. She was always treated well when she worked here. But Kitty was a strange woman and likely to do strange things.'

'Sneaking into someone else's property is a bit more than strange.'

'I'd believe anything of her, Pamela.'

'But why would she have come here? Nothing was stolen.'

'I think that Miss Quayle was right. After a lapse of time, Kitty has come back with a man she wants to burgle the house. How she met such a person, I don't know. But she was seen looking at the property and giving instructions.'

'Did Miss Quayle hear these instructions?'

'She was too far away. Since then,' said Martha, 'she's been as nervous as a kitten. It's a warning to both of us. Lock the door of your bedroom tonight. That's what I'm going to do. We must take no chances.'

Bishop Jackson and Dean Courtney were alone together in the vault where the safe was kept. The Bishop kept staring at it with misgivings.

'I'm not happy about this, Alexander,' he confessed.

'Why is that?'

'There's a king's ransom locked in that safe.'

'It will help to buy us Gregory Tomkins's precious gift to the cathedral.'

'But it was offered to us by the silversmith with no mention of money.'

'That was before it was stolen,' said the Dean. 'It suddenly went up in value.'

'The thought of parting with that amount of money terrifies me.'

'The inspector assures me that we will not lose a penny.'

'That assurance fails to calm my fears,' confessed the Bishop. 'At midnight tomorrow, I have a horrible feeling that we will be parting with the money and getting nothing in return.'

'The delay in handing over the money works in our favour. Inspector Colbeck has told me that the thieves are no longer anonymous criminals. By dint of making exhaustive enquiries, Superintendent Tallis has managed to identify the leader of the gang.'

'That's wonderful news.'

'He is based in London, it seems, but he is now here in Lincolnshire.'

'Can't the fellow be arrested by our police?'

'They've no idea where he is, Bishop. Also, we only have a brief description of the suspect. He works in the jewellery quarter in the capital. Evidently, he discovered when the gift was being transported here and contacted friends near Peterborough. In the telegraph sent to alert his associates, he appended the name of Percy Gull.'

'Is he also a member of the gang?'

'We won't know that until he has been arrested.'

'Is there a search for this fellow?'

'Yes, Bishop,' said the Dean. 'It is being led by Superintendent Tallis. He has a team of detectives searching London even as we speak.'

'Then why don't I feel optimistic?'

'You are still worrying about the money drawn from the bank earlier.'

'That's true,' conceded the Bishop, 'and it's wrong of me. When the silver cathedral was stolen, a man's life was also cruelly snatched away. No amount of money can restore him to his wife and family. I should bear the murder of Michael Langston in mind,' he added. 'If the money in that safe could bring him back to life, I would gladly sacrifice every penny of it.'

Returning to work had been both salutary and depressing for Gregory Tomkins. Being back among his colleagues had given him a reassuring sense of belonging but there was a downside as well. Though he could enjoy looking at designs for items he had created in the past, he had to accept that he had no future as a silversmith. His hands had lost their magic, and he no longer possessed the concentration needed to work long hours. Then there was his failing eyesight. He could still pass on words of advice to the apprentices but that was his only useful function when he went to work. Tomkins began to feel excessively weary that afternoon and, on the advice of his partners, he went back home to rest.

His wife, Alice, was glad that he had accepted his limitations. After welcoming her husband back home, she handed him a letter that had arrived in his absence. Tomkins sat down before opening it. When he read the missive, he saw that it contained details of the funeral of Michael Langston, the private detective who had taken the silversmith's model to Lincoln and been killed in the process. He handed the letter to his wife. She read it with dismay.

'You can't possibly go,' she announced.

'I must go, Alice. It would be shameful if I were not there.'

'You're not well enough to travel. Besides, you hardly knew the man.'

'As soon as I shook hands with him, I sensed how courageous he was. To get my work to the cathedral, he put his life at stake.'

'Send his wife an apology for being unable to go. Explain that you've been ill since that terrible incident in Peterborough.'

'Michael Langston deserves my thanks. The best way of giving it to him is to attend his funeral and honour his passing.'

'The train journey would be too much for you.'

'I could sleep all the way.'

'And what sort of state would you be in when you arrived? No, it's unthinkable. Your health must come first. We must send our apologies for being absent.'

'You can send your apologies, my love, because you had no direct connection with the man. I did and I liked him enormously. Going to his funeral is the least I can do.'

After taking a deep breath, she folded her arms and stamped a foot. 'Put yourself first for once, Gregory.'

'Michael Langston needs me to be there.'

'He's dead. He won't have a clue who is there.'

'Perhaps not,' he said, eyes glowing with determination, 'but that won't stop me going to Lincoln. It's my duty, Alice. Nothing you can say will change my mind. I must pay my respects to Michael Langston – and that's that.'

Patrick Farr was standing outside the tent as a sentry. He had no idea what Jeremy Keane was doing inside the tent and wondered why his cousin was taking such a long time. It seemed the best part of half an hour before Keane finally emerged with a piece of paper in his hand.

'I've got it right at last,' he said, holding up the paper. 'I had a lot of false starts, but I eventually got what I wanted.'

'And what was that, Jerry?'

'It's proof that we have Gregory Tomkins's work.'

Farr stared in amazement at the paper. On it was the signature of the silversmith on an elaborate scroll. Keane had somehow copied it.

'That's why I bought that paper earlier on,' explained Keane. 'It's very thin. By holding it against the signature on the cathedral, I used a pencil to scribble over it. I'm sorry that I was so long. I kept making mistakes. This version is the fourth one and it will help us to convince the Bishop and the Dean that we have Gregory Tomkins's model of the cathedral.'

Farr gaped. 'Is that all it takes to convince them?' he asked.

'No,' replied his cousin. 'There's more work to be done now. It's the reason I bought a much larger sheet of paper. I'm going to draw the whole thing.'

'Can you do that, Jerry?'

'I don't know, but I'll have a good try. The silversmith's work is a direct copy of the cathedral. I'll simply copy the silversmith's cathedral. I'll make some rough sketches then come back here to see which is the best.'

Farr was impressed. 'I didn't know you were an artist, Jerry.'

'I'm a man with hidden depths,' boasted his cousin.

'I'd never have thought of scribbling on a piece of paper to get Tomkins's name.'

'That's why you need me, Pat. I like solving problems.'

'What about the really big problem?'

'Big problem?'

'Yes,' said Farr. 'When we hand over the model we'll get a huge fortune in exchange. They're not going to let us walk away with it. They'll probably have policemen hidden everywhere.'

'I've thought about that.'

'What are we going to do?'

Keane grinned. 'Wait and see.'

* * *

It was late afternoon when Lydia went into her kitchen. Martha was in the process of making a cake. She stood back from the table and used a cloth to wipe the flour off her hands. Lydia looked around.

'I wanted a word with Pamela,' she said.

'She had a headache, Miss Quayle, so I suggested she went for a walk. She won't be long. Is it anything important?'

'I have a guest dining with me this evening.'

'Yes, I know. It's Mrs Colbeck.'

'I wanted to give Pamela some instructions, that's all.'

'I'll tell her the moment she comes back.' Martha lowered her voice. 'That business yesterday evening has upset her. Pamela was so worried that a man might break into the house somehow. She not only locked her door, she put a chair up against it as well. Pamela hardly got a wink of sleep.'

'I'm sorry to hear that. What about you, Martha?'

'I slept like a log. I always do after a long day at work.'

'That's reassuring to hear. You're so wonderfully reliable. Nothing seems to upset you – not even the threat of a burglar getting in here.'

'I'll say this for Kitty, she was so grateful to work here. Apart from anything else, she was so grateful to you for taking her on. Kitty had never been in a house as lovely as this.'

'I was sorry to see her go, Martha.'

'It was her decision. She did write to me soon after she moved to another house. She said that she had settled in very well and was happy with the move.'

'Their gain was our loss,' said Lydia sadly. 'Anyway, I'm sorry to interrupt you when you're making a cake. I know that it takes concentration.'

'I don't believe that it was her, Miss Quayle.'

'Who are you talking about?'

'Kitty Piper, of course. She was a good girl at heart. I think you must have seen someone who looked a bit like her, and decided she was giving advice to a man about getting in here.'

'That's what it looked like,' said Lydia.

'But you never got close enough to see her properly.'

'That's true, but I was close enough to see her gestures.'

'Did you actually hear her voice?'

'No,' admitted Lydia. 'I was not near enough. She and the man spoke very quietly to each other. They were obviously friends.'

'Might I ask you a question?' said Martha softly.

'Of course.'

'If you were so certain that it was Kitty, why didn't you challenge her?'

'I wish that I'd done just that, Martha, but I was so shocked. Before I could get the words out of my mouth, Kitty and her friend had walked away – arm in arm.'

'If you had challenged them it might have been embarrassing for you. They'd have turned to face you, and you'd have realised they were complete strangers.'

'It was definitely Kitty,' insisted Lydia.

'Don't you have any doubts at all?'

'There are one or two lurking at the back of my mind.'

'I saw you standing on the spot where you claim you saw them. Mrs Colbeck was with you. She was shaking her head.'

'Why won't anyone believe me!' shouted Lydia. 'I saw two people standing opposite this house and I sensed danger.'

'Then we must take precautions, Miss Quayle. I'm sorry that

I didn't accept your word. It was wrong of me,' said Martha. 'I promise you that it will not happen again.'

Without a word, Lydia turned on her heel and strode out of the kitchen.

When he sent his team of detectives out into the city, Edward Tallis had been filled with hope and optimism. As the hours slipped past, his hope slowly withered, and his optimism began to fray at the edges. He was forced to accept that it was a very difficult assignment. With very little information to help them, his officers were searching for a man in one of the largest cities in the world. How could they possibly locate the suspect when he was one of well over a million inhabitants living in the nation's capital? There was an additional problem. The figures that appeared in the latest census were misleading. They did not include the masses of foreigners who had sneaked into the country and who were living illegally in its capital. Their names and nationalities were not recorded anywhere. For the most part, they lived in appalling slums and eked out a living in a variety of ways. Respect for the law was a concept that meant nothing to them.

As his detectives began to come back to Scotland Yard, they told the same tale. There was no sign of a man by the name of Percy Gull. The general view was that the individual was not even in London. Tallis was dismayed. Having found out the name of the leader of the gang, he had assumed that it would be relatively easy to track down a man by the name of Percy Gull, who was somehow linked to him. Clearly, it was not. If such a person did live in London, he was hidden away somewhere in the teeming multitude. Tallis began to fear that he might never find the individual.

* * *

Robert Colbeck faced a similar problem, although on a much smaller scale. He and his officers were searching for a gang who were in – or close to – Lincoln. Because the Horse Fair was now at its height, the city was filled with strangers, many of them from foreign countries. When Colbeck had gone to the bank to collect the money demanded, he was conscious of being watched. The men who had Gregory Tomkins's silver cathedral in their possession were taking no chances. They wanted to make sure that their orders were being followed.

Walking through the city with Victor Leeming, Colbeck looked down every alley. All that he and the sergeant saw were victims of excessive celebration, men who had drunk so much so quickly that they were now propped up against walls or stretched out on the ground. Leeming was reminded of his early days as a uniformed constable.

'It's just like old times,' he said. 'I lost count of the number of drunks I found. The lucky ones stumbled home to their wives with the usual excuses. The others eventually woke up to find that their pockets had been emptied. I remember one man who was naked from the waist down. He was so drunk that he didn't realise that thieves had stolen his trousers while he was fast asleep.'

'There will always be people who drink too much, Victor.'

'What about the men we're after?'

'I fancy that they may have camped just outside the city, taking it in turns to keep the cathedral under scrutiny. Jeremy Keane, their leader, will make sure that they don't get caught up in the general excitement. They're not here to buy or sell horses. They're here to collect a huge fortune.'

Leeming was outraged. 'They're robbing a cathedral. That's disgusting.'

'They have no qualms about their crimes,' said Colbeck. 'Theft and murder mean nothing to them. I hate to admit it, but Jeremy Keane's organisation has so far been excellent. He has anticipated every possible danger.'

'Will he anticipate the number of policemen who'll be on duty when the exchange takes place?'

'I'm sure that he'll expect us to set a trap. I daresay that he's trying to work out a way to make an escape. Don't underestimate him, Victor. He's a clever man.'

Edward Tallis was close to accepting that the search was a complete failure. The team of detectives included some of the most promising men under his command. Surely, their combined efforts would bring a satisfying result. Sadly, they had not. As he sat in his office at Scotland Yard, the superintendent was beginning to lose heart. One person by the name of Percy Gull had been identified but the man had been dead for five years. At the end of his working day, Tallis had to face the uncomfortable truth. The man they sought would never be found.

When he heard a knock on his door, he vented his frustration.

'Come in!' he yelled.

The door opened slowly, and a nervous head came round it.

'Is this a bad time to speak to you, sir?' asked a detective.

'It depends on what you've got to say.'

'I just wanted to give my report.'

'If it's another admission of failure, I don't want to hear it. What's your name?'

'Detective Constable Green, sir.'

Tallis took a moment to study the newcomer. He was a tall, fair-haired, moderately smart individual with a look of fear in his eyes. The superintendent realised that it was the detective who had suggested that the man they sought might have a criminal record.

'Well? asked Tallis. 'What did you find?'

'I tracked down a man named Percy Gull. It may not be the man we're after, but I wanted you to know that I'd found someone with the right name.'

'Please don't tell me that he's been dead for five years.'

'He's very much alive, Superintendent.'

'Did you speak to him?'

'I couldn't get permission to do so.'

'Why?'

'Percy Gull is in Pentonville Prison,' said the detective, 'and he's likely to stay there for some time.'

'What was his offence?'

'Fraud. They wouldn't let me interview the prisoner, but your rank would be enough to get you into the prison. I should warn you that I've no idea if this is the man we're after, but his name is Percy Gull.'

'Well done!' said Tallis, getting to his feet. 'Good news at last.'

CHAPTER SIXTEEN

When they returned to their tent in a field outside the city, Silas Weaver and Tim Redshaw found Patrick Farr sitting on the grass.

'Where's your cousin?' asked Redshaw.

'He's inside the tent,' replied Farr, 'but he's not to be disturbed.'

'Why is that?' asked Weaver with a grin. 'Has he got a woman in there?'

'Jerry is working,' said Farr. 'Leave him be.'

'What's he working on?'

'You'll soon see, Silas.'

'Your cousin has got brains,' said Weaver. 'He thinks of everything.'

'That's why he's never been arrested.'

'Why do we have to wait another day?' complained Redshaw.

'I hoped that by midnight tonight, I'd be a rich man.'

'You'll have to wait another twenty-four hours, Tim.'

'I want to get away from this place. The longer we stay, the more chance we have of being arrested. There are policemen everywhere.'

'But they don't know who we are or why we're here.'

'I'd still like to be somewhere else – a long, long way away.'

'Be patient,' advised Farr. 'Think of how you're going to spend the money when you finally get it.'

Sitting on the grass, they fell into a discussion of what they were going to do once they had ridden away from Lincoln as wealthy men. Farr reminded them that they had to be patient and follow his cousin's advice. If they did anything too sudden, they risked giving themselves away. The three of them were still discussing their futures when Jeremy Keane came out of the tent.

'Who've you got in there?' asked Weaver.

'I had work to do,' replied Keane, 'and it took a lot of time.'

'Why was that?'

'Because it's the proof that they demanded. Before they hand over the money, they wanted to be sure that they got the cathedral we stole. I've already copied the silversmith's name. To convince them that we really have the item I've been working on rough drawings of it. That's why I bought so much paper.'

'Show them what you've done, Jerry,' said Farr.

'I will,' said Keane.

He disappeared into the tent to collect various items. When he came out, he had an armful of papers. The first one he showed them bore the name of the silversmith. They were duly impressed. The other drawings were of parts of the cathedral. When he laid them out on the grass, they formed a complete picture of the stolen model. All three of his companions goggled in wonder.

'You're a genius, Jerry,' said Farr. 'Who taught you to draw like that?'

'It took me several attempts and I'm almost satisfied,' replied Keane. 'Once I am, I'll slip these under the main door of the cathedral. It's the visible proof they insisted on seeing. Then – at midnight tomorrow – we can collect our money and ride out of here towards a golden future.'

'You're amazing, Jerry,' said his cousin. 'Percy would be proud of you.'

Edward Tallis had been driven in a cab past Pentonville Prison many times, but he had never had cause to visit the place. Now that he did have a legitimate reason to enter the premises, he had sent a letter by hand to the governor, asking for permission to talk to one of the prisoners. Tallis got an immediate answer, delivered on the day that his request was made. Tearing open the letter, he was delighted to find an invitation to visit the prison whenever he wished. He set off at once.

When the cab dropped him off outside the building, he was conscious of being viewed by unwelcoming eyes. He reached the gate and rang the bell. One of the guards came out to challenge him. Tallis therefore showed him the invitation from the governor, and the man's attitude changed completely. He opened a door to admit the visitor and conducted him to the governor's office. After knocking on the door, the guard opened it and led Tallis into the room.

The governor was on his feet at once. He came around his desk to pump the hand of his newcomer.

'It's good to meet you, Superintendent,' he said, effusively. 'We don't often have such a distinguished Scotland Yard officer on the premises. You're most welcome.'

'Thank you, Governor.'

As the two men exchanged niceties, Tallis had the opportunity to take a good look at the governor. He was a big, solid man with a prominent nose and a fringe beard turning grey. What struck the visitor most about Angus Murray was that the man had the air of a country parson. Tallis was offered a seat and Murray sat opposite him.

'You've not been here before, then?' asked the governor.

'I've not had a good reason to do so,' said Tallis. 'Suddenly, Percy Gull is that very good reason to do so.'

'As soon as I saw the name, I knew exactly which prisoner it was.'

'Why?'

'Percy Gull stands out because of his age. He is over seventy years old. Most of our prisoners are aged between fifteen and twenty-five. Many of them will be transported to Australia. While they are here, we try to turn them into decent human beings. Each of them has an individual cell. It's a place of work during the day and a place of rest at night – not that they get much rest.'

'What do you mean?'

'Cast your mind back to your own youth, Superintendent. Can you recall that wonderful sense of zest you must have had? Imagine how upset you'd have been to have it snatched away from you.' Murray smiled. 'It's another reason why Gull sticks out here. He's completely at ease.'

'I look forward to meeting him.'

'He'll be here at any moment. I gave orders that, as soon as you arrived, the prisoner was to be brought to my office.'

'I understand that that the crime that put him here is fraud.'

'Oh, that's only one of the crimes that earnt him time behind bars.

'What sort of man is he, Governor?'

'Out of the ordinary.'

It was good to have time alone with the family. As she, her father and her daughter walked through the park, Madeleine Colbeck reflected that she always felt so happy when she was outdoors. There was something empowering about spring. Not only did it delight the eye with all manner of new growth, there were new creatures to watch, identify and, in some cases, even chase. Helena Rose needed no encouragement to do that. When a squirrel popped up directly in her path, she ran excitedly towards it. The animal headed swiftly for the nearest tree, shinning up it at speed until it was well out of reach. Helena Rose stood there with hands on her hips.

'I only wanted to get closer,' she complained.

'Squirrels are nice to watch,' said her grandfather, 'but you mustn't get too close. When all is said and done, they're wild animals and have sharp claws.'

'But they're so cuddly, Grandpa.'

'They just don't want to be cuddled.'

'Dogs and cats are different,' added her mother. 'They're domesticated. That means they can live at home with us. They're nice to have around.'

'Yes,' added her father. 'Look at me. Because I live alone, I like to have a cat under the same roof as me. Patch is my friend. It means that I'm never alone. Mind you,' he added with a wry chuckle, 'it also means that I need to feed him, and clean his bowls and so on. I never complain because Patch means so much to me.'

Madeleine suppressed a smile. She could remember all the times when her father had raged against the cat because the animal was such a nuisance to him.

'There's another squirrel,' cried Helena Rose excitedly. 'Can we chase him?'

'We'll never catch him,' warned Andrews. 'He can dart up any tree that he chooses and laugh at us. Whatever game we try to play with him, he wins.'

'It's time to head back home,' decided Madeleine. 'I'm hungry . . .'

When the prisoner was brought into the governor's office by a guard, he was kept standing. Percy Gull was tall, haggard and in his early seventies. He wore the same prison garb as the others detained in Pentonville. When he was introduced to Edward Tallis, he showed more than a flicker of interest.

'Why did you send for me, Superintendent?' he asked politely.

'I need information,' said Tallis.

'What about?'

'Murder and robbery on a train.'

'Well, I'm innocent of both. I've been safely locked up in here.'

'Do you know someone called Patrick Farr?'

'No, I don't.'

'And do you know a man named Jeremy Keane.'

Gull shrugged. 'Who are these people?'

'I think that they're friends of yours,' said Tallis. 'Keane works in London. On the day when a precious item was lifted into the guard's van, he sent a telegraph from King's Cross to Farr, who was waiting at Peterborough station. It told Farr where on the train he would find the box they were after.'

'I wasn't involved in any way,' said Gull firmly, 'because I was locked up here. Your visit has been a waste of time, Superintendent.'

'There's something I haven't mentioned,' said Tallis. 'The name on the telegraph that set the crime in motion was Percy Gull. How do you explain that, Percy?'

'I was nowhere near King's Cross at the time. Ask the governor.'

'I'd prefer to ask you. When I mentioned two names to you, I saw more than a flicker of interest in your eyes. You know these individuals, don't you?'

'No, I don't.'

'Then how is it that they know you?'

Gull smiled. 'It's a question I can't answer. Why not put it to them?'

Outwardly, Tallis was calm and controlled. Inside, however, he was quivering with anger. During his long career in the police force, he had built up a huge reputation for dealing with villains of every kind. In this strange, watchful old man, however, he sensed that he had finally met his match.

Having got up at the crack of dawn, they realised how close they were to the time of the exchange. Lincoln was still filled with the stink of the Horse Fair and business was as brisk as ever. Robert Colbeck had breakfast with Victor Leeming at Riseholme Hall. While the inspector was boosted by the fact that they had a chance to confront the men they were after at last, the sergeant was strangely depressed.

'The soup is not that bad, is it?' asked Colbeck.

'No, no,' said Leeming, who had been stirring his bowl with his spoon.

'Then why did you only have one sip?'

'I don't know, sir. My mind was somewhere else.'

'And where was that?'

'To be honest,' said Leeming, 'I'm not sure. I just have this feeling that our luck has run out.'

'It's not like you to have cold feet,' said Colbeck.

'I'm just bracing myself for disappointment, sir. Yes, we've made progress since we've been here, but the best information we've had all came from the superintendent.'

'That's not a complaint, surely.'

'It is and it isn't, sir. Frankly, when he was here, he got in our way.'

'Yet he made no attempt to throw his weight around.'

'That's true . . . though I always felt he had his eye on us.'

'Superintendent Tallis is the leader of our team,' Colbeck reminded him. 'Think of the information he's gleaned for us since he went back to London.'

'It's been amazing, sir.'

'This case has touched his heart somehow.'

'He's certainly driven to do what he can to help us solve it.' Leeming shrugged. 'I suppose that's what I find difficult to handle.'

'We need from help from anyone who can supply it.'

'But why does it have to be from the superintendent?' said Leeming. 'Since he went back home, he's sent us useful information every day. What about all the other cases he's in charge of? Why can't he work harder on them?'

'Tallis goes where he feels he's needed the most,' explained Colbeck.

'Yes,' moaned Leeming. 'And that means us.'

'Aren't you grateful for all the information he's dug up?'

'Yes, of course . . .'

'I'm grateful for every nugget of evidence that he's managed to find.'

'And so am I, sir. In a way, that is . . .'

Colbeck put his spoon in the empty bowl and studied Leeming carefully. 'What's troubling you, Victor?'

'Nothing, sir . . .'

'You're upset at a deep level. Why is that?'

Leeming wrestled with his thoughts for minutes before he spoke.

'Well,' he said at length, 'it's this case. First, he puts us in charge of it then he turns up out of the blue to take over.'

'Now be fair,' warned Colbeck. 'He insisted that I was the senior officer.'

'He was always there, looking over our shoulders. When he finally moved to London, I felt that we could control the case at last.'

'And that's what we've been doing.'

'No, it isn't. Be honest. The only useful pieces of information have come from London, from the superintendent. He's been beavering away like mad. It's almost as if he's determined to solve this crime on his own.'

Bishop Jackson was alone in his office with the Dean. They had just been going through details of the cathedral's finances. The Bishop looked down at the account book with mixed feelings.

'If we hand over that money to these villains,' he said, 'we will be in a much more precarious position than we deserve.'

'Don't talk as if this gang gets exactly what they want,' advised the Dean. 'I put my faith in the inspector. He's handled situations like this before.'

'Then why am I so alarmed?'

'You do have a tendency to fear the worst, Bishop.'

'My duty is to protect this cathedral.'

'It's one that I share with you.'

'In the circumstances, I am bound to feel a ripple of danger. Bringing all that money back here from the bank was agonising for me.'

'It's now locked up securely in our safe.'

'Yes, but it will have to be brought out at midnight and offered to these desperate men.'

'Try not to worry about it, Bishop. When the time comes, we are in the hands of Inspector Colbeck and his officers. They will know exactly what to do.'

'I'm glad that you have such confidence in them.'

'Don't you?'

'I did at first,' said the Bishop. 'Then they were joined by Superintendent Tallis, and my hopes soared. I felt that he would make a difference. But he disappeared without any explanation and I'm still wondering why.'

'He left to pursue evidence in London,' explained the Dean.

'We need him here.'

'Information he has gathered in the capital has been an enormous help to the case. Inspector Colbeck assured me of that. Just because the superintendent is not here in person,' stressed the Dean, 'it doesn't mean he has forgotten all about us.'

* * *

As he lay in his bed that night, Edward Tallis was able to remember his conversation with Percy Gull word for word. Tallis was so used to browbeating suspects that he expected instant success. In the case of Gull, however, he had come up against a man who could parry his questions with ease. It was unsettling.

'You've been in trouble with the police before,' noted Tallis.

'They were silly mistakes on my part,' said Gull with a smile. 'I learnt my lesson and kept my nose clean.'

'Then how did you end up in here?'

'That was a case of bad luck, Superintendent.'

'You took advantage of a neighbour who trusted you and you robbed him.'

'I borrowed the money, that's all,' said Gull. 'I'd have paid him back in due course.'

'The governor showed me your record. This is the third time you've been sent to prison.'

'The third and, I promise you, the very last. I'm too old to survive conditions like these. Once I'm released, I'll lead a blameless life.'

'How much help will you get from your relative?'

Gull's wizened face was blank. 'I've no idea who you're taking about.'

'I'm talking about Jeremy Keane and Patrick Farr. My guess is that you are related to them in some way. Why else should they use your name in a telegraph?'

'Ask them.'

'One of them works in the jewellery trade, and the other owns a small farm. I believe that the pair of them are part of a gang who shot dead a private detective and stole a silver model of Lincoln Cathedral.'

'There must be some mistake.'

'Don't you dare to lie to me,' hissed Tallis. 'I tracked Keane down and I also tracked you down. The pair of you are beneath contempt.'

'Then why are you bothering me?' asked Gull, spreading his arms. 'I had nothing to do with the crime.'

'Yes, you did. It has your name scribbled all over it.'

'I'm far too old to break the law, Superintendent.'

'And I'm far too experienced to believe the nonsense you've been spouting,' warned Tallis. 'Let's start again, shall we? And try to be honest this time.' He stared into the prisoner's eyes. 'What is your connection with Jeremy Keane?'

While his cousin worked away inside the tent, Patrick Farr sat on guard outside. To his relief, nobody came. Tucked away in a corner, they were invisible. It seemed an age before Keane finally emerged. He showed his cousin the drawings he'd made. Now that he had made significant changes, they looked even better.

'They're amazing, Jerry,' said Farr.

'The real cause for amazement is Gregory Tomkins's artistry. It's brilliant. It was an honour to copy some of its elements.'

'Do you think your drawings will persuade the Bishop and the Dean?'

'I'm sure that they will, Pat. Don't forget that they will have seen the original design for the cathedral. They can measure my version against that.'

'Does that mean they'll hand over the money?'

'They dare not refuse.'

'I can't wait for midnight to arrive.'

'Neither can I,' said Keane. He examined his drawings again

then sighed. 'It's a pity that he won't be there to enjoy the moment.'

'I agree, Jerry. He taught us so much.'

'He deserves his share of the money. It's such a pity that he's not here to have it.'

'He will be very soon. In less than three months, he'll be a free man again.'

'And we'll all be very rich!'

Laughing happily, they hugged each other.

As soon as he received the summons, Robert Colbeck made his way to the Dean's office in the cathedral. Evidence that the silver cathedral was in the hands of the men who stole it was laid out on a table. Colbeck was impressed by the quality of the drawings and struck by the copy of the silversmith's signature.

'These appear to be genuine,' he said.

'I can vouch for them,' added the Dean. 'I had the good fortune to see Gregory Tomkins's work before it was sealed in a box. Michael Langston and I were duly impressed. It will be wonderful to have the gift back in our own hands.'

'I agree, Dean. Your interest is naturally centred on the silver cathedral. Mine, however, is fixed on the gang who stole it and who shot dead the man protecting it. I want every one of them caught and locked up behind bars.'

'I will pray that that is what happens, Inspector.'

'We may need more than prayer,' said Colbeck.

'Do you foresee problems?'

'When dealing with criminals, I always foresee problems and do my best to solve them in advance. My detectives are well trained and will respond to any eventuality. I have spoken to the chief constable and told him what I expect of his men.'

'They won't let us down, Inspector.'

'There is, of course, the small matter of tonight's weather,' said Colbeck. 'The forecast is in our favour. It will be breezy but dry.'

'I still feel very much on edge,' confessed the Dean. 'Handing over such a huge amount of money means that we are taking a dreadful risk. Bishop Jackson is rightly terrified that we may somehow lose it all.'

'That will not happen, I promise you.'

'How can you be certain of that?'

'We know who these men are,' said Colbeck. 'We have their names and their occupations. They have never done anything as difficult as the exchange planned for tonight. It means that they will start to feel immense pressure. It will tell on them.'

'It is already telling on me,' admitted the Dean, pursing his lips. 'I am sorry that the superintendent is no longer here. After all, it was he who identified the leader of the gang.'

'Superintendent Tallis has done far more than that, I promise you. It's because he is so profoundly moved by the silversmith's plight. He understands how Gregory Tomkins must feel at the fate of his work,' explained Colbeck. 'And he won't rest until this case is brought to a successful conclusion.'

'What can the superintendent do while stuck in London?'

Colbeck smiled. 'He will continue to supply us with vital information.'

On his second visit to the prison, Edward Tallis thanked the governor then asked for more information.

'I'm glad that you feel that your earlier visit was worthwhile,' said the governor.

'I do indeed.'

'Percy Gull is a hardened criminal.'

'That's what shocked me. He glories in his villainy.'

'For the younger prisoners in our hands, there is always the hope that some of them will benefit from their time spent here. They may repent of their sins and go on to live decent, honest lives.'

'That's not the case with Percy Gull.'

'Exactly. His whole life has been dedicated to crime. Nothing will ever change him – not even a spell in here. Gull is beyond redemption.'

'That was my feeling,' said Tallis. 'He refuses to denounce his past. There was never the slightest hint of remorse.'

'Did he admit to being related to members of the gang you mentioned?'

'Gull denied ever having heard their names.'

'Obviously, you were not misled.'

'I detected lying immediately, and that's what Gull tried to fob me off with. He did his best to find out why I was so interested in the people I mentioned while, at the same time, claiming that he had no idea who they were.'

'Do you feel that there was a family connection?'

'Yes, I did, Governor.'

'Then we may be able to find out who these people were. We have limited visiting times at Pentonville. Being shut off from their family and friends is all part of the punishment. When they've served the bulk of their sentence, we try to put them in touch with the outside world again.'

'How do you do that?'

'We let them receive letters from family members.'

Tallis became excited. 'Did you allow Percy Gull to do that?'

'I'm certain that I did,' replied Murray, reaching for a ledger on his desk. 'If the old man had letters at any point, the names of those who wrote them will be found in here . . .'

The superintendent smiled at the thought of interesting new evidence.

Madeleine Colbeck was glad of a moment alone with her father. While her daughter was playing happily upstairs with Nanny Hopkins, Madeleine took the opportunity to ask for his opinion.

'I'm worried about Lydia,' she confided.

'You've good reason to do so, Maddy.'

'She's become obsessed with this young woman who used to work with her.'

'Kitty Piper – I remember meeting her once or twice.'

'Did she strike you as being vengeful?'

'Not at all, Maddy,' he said. 'She was always quiet and polite whenever I went to the house. Lydia seemed to rely heavily on her.'

'That was my impression as well. Lydia was glad to see her go. She was never really happy with Kitty…'

'And she soon found a good replacement for her. Pamela is a dutiful servant.'

'Why is Kitty the person who seems to haunt Lydia?'

'Your guess is as good as mine, Maddy.'

'This latest business is causing her such grief. I just wish that I could do more to help her.'

'Your friendship is the best thing that ever happened to her,' said Andrews. 'And it works both ways. Each of you draws strength from the other.'

'Supposing that Lydia is right?'

'What do you mean?'

'Perhaps the person she saw the other evening really was Kitty.'

He shook his head. 'I don't believe that.'

'Why not?'

'If Kitty has found a man to look after her, the last place she'd take him to is the house where she used to work as a servant. Kitty would want to put that life behind her, surely. Not that my opinion counts,' admitted Andrews with a smile. 'I've never been able to understand the way that women behave. All I know is that Lydia is in some sort of trouble and that she needs your help.'

'I've made myself available to her whenever she chooses.'

'That's very kind of you, Maddy.'

'It's the least I can do.'

'Don't let her become a burden.'

'She's my best friend, Father. I just want to rescue her from this weird idea that Kitty has been hanging around her house with a man, giving him instructions how to burgle the place. Lydia just can't relax. She's on guard all the time.'

Even though she was alone in the house with her servants, Lydia was plagued by the thought that her property was in danger. Every so often, she would abandon whatever she was doing and go to the nearest window so that she could pull back the curtain and peep out. Nobody was ever there but she never accepted that. After peering out of the bedroom window, all she could see was the gathering gloom.

'I know that you're out there somewhere, Kitty,' she said to herself.

Alan Hinton and Eric Boyce had been taking it in turns to visit the telegraph office in Lincoln to see if there were any messages for Inspector Colbeck. None had so far come that day. It was only when Hinton had made the latest call that his effort had borne fruit. When he read the message from Superintendent Tallis, it took his breath away.

Percy Gull had been found at last.

When the time of the exchange finally came, Robert Colbeck and Victor Leeming were waiting in the cathedral in the Dean's office. Alexander Courtney was showing the first signs of mild panic.

'What if they don't come?' he asked.

'Oh, they'll be here,' promised Colbeck. 'And they'll be on time.'

'How do you know that?'

'I feel it in my bones, Dean Courtney. These men are organised. They leave nothing to chance. I guarantee that they'll be here on the stroke of midnight.'

'What if they fail to turn up?'

Colbeck was about to reply when there was a tap on the door. It opened to admit Alan Hinton. He was carrying a telegraph. Without a word, he handed it to Colbeck. The message caused the latter's eyebrows to lift in surprise.

'Bad news?' asked the Dean fearfully.

'On the contrary, Superintendent Tallis has done us a signal favour.'

'That makes a change,' muttered Leeming.

'He has not only found Percy Gull,' said Colbeck. 'He has visited the man in Pentonville Prison. Gull is firmly under lock and key there.'

'This is cheering news,' said the Dean.

'The superintendent has provided vital information yet again.'

'It may not help us to catch the gang,' said Leeming, 'but we now have a clearer idea of the sort of people they are.'

'We also know the names of two of them,' added Colbeck. 'Jeremy Keane and Patrick Farr wrote to him separately in prison. I believe that that makes them part of the same family. It also explains why Gull's name was used on that telegraph.'

'We've reason to thank the superintendent yet again,' said Leeming.

Colbeck turned to Hinton. 'Did you acknowledge receipt of his message?'

'Yes, Inspector,' said the other. 'I could see how valuable these details were. Superintendent Tallis deserves our thanks.'

'I was afraid that he'd abandoned the case,' confessed the Dean.

'On the contrary,' said Colbeck. 'Since he returned to London he has made it his priority to search for every detail. I sense that it is not only because this case is so important to him, I believe that the superintendent feels an obligation to the silversmith to rescue his gift to the cathedral.'

'We share that obligation,' said the Dean. 'I think that a prayer is in order.'

As they bowed their heads, he made a heartfelt appeal for help.

Patrick Farr and Silas Weaver had remained together because they were guarding the silver cathedral. Hidden away in its box, it had been carried into the city by Weaver. When they reached their chosen hiding place, they found that Jeremy Keane was waiting for them in a dark corner. He was in a buoyant mood.

'They seem to be behaving themselves,' he said.

'How do you know?' asked his cousin.

'Tim has searched the area around the cathedral. There's no sign of policemen hiding there.'

'What about those detectives from London?'

'They seem to have disappeared,' said Keane. 'We found no trace of them.'

'How long is it before we reach midnight?'

'There are hours to go yet.'

'What do we do until then, Jerry?'

'We bide our time and stick to our plan.'

'Will the cathedral do what you've told them to do?'

Keane grinned. 'They wouldn't dare to disobey.'

Madeleine Colbeck had been glad to accept the invitation to dinner at her friend's house. When the cab had dropped Madeleine off there, Lydia came out to welcome her with a warm hug. They went into the house together. Alone in the drawing room, Madeleine had a close look at her friend.

'How do you feel now?' she asked.

'I have mood swings,' replied Lydia. 'One minute, I'm convinced that the house is under threat from that man I saw with Kitty Piper. The next minute, I feel as if I'm making a mountain out of a molehill. Kitty would never dare to be party to a burglary.'

'That's my feeling as well.'

'As soon as I get into bed, however, the doubts return. I start to feel that my house is under threat, after all.'

'How do we get rid of that constant fear?'

'I wish that I knew.'

There was a tap on the door, then Pamela entered with two glasses of sherry on a tray. After handing one to each of the women, the servant bobbed then went out. The two friends clinked glasses before taking a first taste.

'I needed that,' said Lydia.

'Then I can tell you something else that will cheer you up,' said Madeleine. 'I had a letter from Robert earlier today. He is confident that arrests will be made very soon and that he and his team will be able to return to London.'

'That is good news.'

'There is, as always, a proviso that things may go awry. Robert never takes anything for granted. But, with luck, they may be on a train back here within days.'

'Was there any mention of . . . Alan?'

'He was commended for his sterling work.'

'I do worry about him when he is up against men prepared to kill.'

'It's in the nature of his work,' said Madeleine. 'I feel the same about Robert. Every time he is on a new case, I pray that he stays safe. Then I remember how well he looks after himself and his detectives.'

'Perhaps that's what I should be doing, instead of fearing that someone is going to burgle my house the moment my back is turned.'

'Do you still believe that you saw Kitty Piper pointing to the house?'

'I do and I don't, Madeleine. Every so often, I get this irrational fear about her. Then I remembered how glad I was to get rid of her. The idea that Kitty is planning to rob me seems ridiculous then.'

'It is ridiculous, Lydia. Put your trust in the woman. Kitty means no harm.'

'Then why did I see her standing on the pavement opposite?'

'Let's not have that argument again,' suggested Madeleine. 'Enjoy the taste of this wonderful sherry and tell me what you've been doing all day.'

* * *

When the clock chimed to mark eleven o'clock at night, they were all startled. Colbeck and Leeming were taken by surprise. Dean Courtney was jerked fully awake. He glanced at the saddlebags that had been brought from the safe and laid on a table.

'What are they doing now, I wonder,' he said.

'Waiting nervously, I daresay,' replied Leeming.

'I doubt if they have any nerves,' added Colbeck. 'If they're able to kill a man in cold blood and steal a precious gift to the cathedral, they won't be troubled by anything resembling remorse. At this moment, I believe, they will be checking that their orders have been obeyed and that we have nobody lurking near the cathedral waiting to stop and arrest them.'

'Will they be that careful, sir?' asked Leeming.

'I'm certain of it.'

'Do I still have to hand over the saddlebags to them?'

'It's an important duty and I know that you will discharge it well.'

'Then why is my heart beating nineteen to the dozen?'

'You've been in far more difficult situations than this,' Colbeck reminded him, 'and you've always come through them without injury.'

'That's true, sir,' said Leeming. 'The difference is that I've never been holding such a massive amount of money in my hands before. That changes everything.'

'Would you prefer it if I handed over the saddlebags?' volunteered the Dean.

'No,' said Colbeck firmly. 'Sergeant Leeming knows that it's his duty and he will perform it with his usual bravery.'

'That's a promise,' said Leeming, straightening his shoulders.

'Where are they at the moment?' asked the Dean.

'Waiting and watching,' replied Colbeck.

'The city gates have all been locked. How can they possibly escape?'

'I'm sure that they've given the matter great thought, Dean. Look at the way they responded when we asked for proof that they really do have the silver cathedral in their grasp. One of them provided the clear evidence we required.'

'How on earth did he do that?' wondered the Dean.

'I'll make a point of asking him when I arrest the man,' said Colbeck. 'And I'll also enjoy the pleasure of telling him that Percy Gull has been tracked down in Pentonville Prison.'

As a rule, Percy Gull would be asleep within minutes of the time when he was locked away in his cell for the night. The prison was a clamorous place. The sound of cell doors being opened or locked was constant. Gull had learnt to ignore the noise. But there was no rest for him that night. Too many questions were buzzing around in his brain. One of them had pride of place.

What had Jeremy Keane and Patrick Farr been up to?

As midnight approached, Keane and Farr had made their final patrol, checking that everything was in readiness. Weaver was hidden safely away near the cathedral with the box covered by a tarpaulin. Tim Redshaw had his orders and was standing by. The weather was mercifully dry. Most of the city was fast asleep but there were always sounds that pierced the gloom. Horses neighed constantly. Dogs and cats made their contribution. Carts and wagons creaked in the stiff breeze. And there were dozens of other random noises that made their contribution to the midnight hour.

Dominating them all was the sound of the cathedral clock,

booming out for the first of its twelve times. As each sound followed in sequence, the main door of the cathedral was slowly opened and two figures stepped out. One belonged to the Dean, resplendent in his vestments, and the other person was Victor Leeming. Clad in a cassock, he was carrying the saddlebags across his outstretched arms. Before the exchange could be made, however, there was a loud explosion from nearby and flames began to dance in the air.

Two mounted riders suddenly galloped onto the scene. One of them scooped up the saddlebags from Leeming's arms and left him flailing uselessly. The second rider had another horse in tow. Strapped to its back was the box containing the gift from Gregory Tomkins. After tossing the reins to Leeming, the rider set off after his friend and vanished into the darkness. There was more noise to come. A second explosion went off and large amount of hay was instantly turned into a wall of flames. Panic and confusion seized the whole city. While the detectives were still wondering how the suspects had escaped, all four members of the gang were galloping off on their horses into the darkness.

CHAPTER SEVENTEEN

It was several minutes before Victor Leeming and the Dean realised what had happened. Masked horsemen had stolen the saddlebags containing the money and left a silver model of the cathedral in return. Dean Courtney was utterly mortified. Not only had the detectives and the police been completely fooled, the cathedral had, during the brief exchange, lost a vast amount of money from its coffers. There had been no arrests. The whole city had been roused by the pandemonium. Dean Courtney was in despair.

'This is appalling, Inspector Colbeck,' he wailed. 'Do you know how much money was in those saddlebags?'

'It will be found, I promise you,' said Colbeck. 'Meanwhile, I'll take part in the chase. I daresay that Sergeant Leeming would be glad to join me.'

'I certainly would,' asserted Leeming. 'Someone snatched the money from me before I even knew that he was there.'

'Excuse us while we find some horses.'

'I hope that you find those saddlebags as well,' cried the Dean.

'We'll do our best, I promise you.'

Taking Leeming by the arm, Colbeck dragged him away in search of mounts. The police were quick to offer them horses, but pursuit was difficult. The four members of the gang knew exactly where they were going but anyone trying to chase them would soon be lost in a dark void. Still in his clerical robe, Leeming mounted one of the horses.

'Where on earth have they gone?' he wondered.

'They'll have left a trail of some sort,' said Colbeck, putting a foot in the stirrup and hoisting himself into the saddle. 'We'll pick it up somehow.'

Kicking their horses into action, they headed towards the southern gate to the city. A handful of mounted policemen were hard on their heels. It was a positive response to the outrage, but they knew that it was far too slow.

Somewhere in the darkness of Pentonville Prison, a lone figure suddenly sat up in his hammock. Still very much asleep, Percy Gull waved a skinny fist in triumph without realising what exactly had happened in Lincoln.

They rode for almost an hour before they dared to stop and hide. Resting their horses near a stream, they gave themselves the pleasure of counting the money at last. Every penny demanded was there. Jeremy Keane divided it up with care then handed it over to the members of his gang. The money felt crisp and tempting in their hands.

'This will change my life,' said Weaver, drooling.

'And mine,' added Farr, fondling his share.

'Spend it wisely,' warned Keane, 'and don't appear lavish.'

'When you divided it between us,' noted Redshaw, 'you put some money aside. Who was that for?'

'That belongs to Percy Gull,' replied Keane. 'He taught me everything.'

'I thought you said that he was in prison.'

'Not for much longer, Tim. He'll be released soon and deserves a proper welcome to the outside world.'

'I agree,' said Farr. 'Welcome home, Percy!'

'Welcome home!' sang all four of them.

Then each of them counted his own money and thought about the future.

Though they rode as hard as they could, the posse had little faith in catching the members of the gang. Having ridden for what seemed like an age, they reined in their horses.

'We haven't seen hide nor hair of them,' said Leeming gloomily.

'They planned their escape carefully,' admitted Colbeck. 'All that we've been doing is to chase shadows in the darkness.'

'Which way should we go now, sir?'

'Your guess is as good as mine, Sergeant.'

'The last signpost we saw was pointing towards Peterborough.'

'Then that's the route we'll take. We know that one of them has a farm in the county. Let's see if we can find it.'

'We'll follow you,' said Leeming.

'Then off we go,' decided Colbeck, kicking his horse into action. 'Be sure to keep together. We don't want to lose anyone.'

They moved off at a steady canter. To add to their troubles, it started to rain.

Back at the cathedral, both the Bishop and the Dean were in despair. They had recovered the silversmith's gift, but it came at a devastating price. Countless thousands of pounds had been stolen from them and the thieves had fled the city. Nothing the Dean could say was able to raise the Bishop's spirits.

'We've been tricked,' said Jackson, walking up and down.

'They'll be caught,' the Dean assured him. 'The police from both counties will be snapping at their heels.'

'We made no allowance for how clever they might be.'

'That was a mistake on our part, Bishop.'

'Inspector Colbeck must take some of the blame.'

'He's a brave man,' the Dean pointed out. 'The moment he realised what had happened, he grabbed a horse and led the chase after those villains. Sergeant Leeming is with him along with members of our constabulary.'

'They will never catch those villains.'

'Have more faith in the inspector,' advised Courtney.

'What a dreadful night this has been for us!' sighed the Bishop.

'Think of the compensations.'

'There are no compensations.'

'We have Gregory Tomkins's sublime model in our hands at last.'

'That's no consolation. It was offered to us as a gift, and it has cost us a fortune. I daren't face the bank manager again.'

'I'm sure that he will be sympathetic to the unexpected change of events.'

'He'll think that we were exposed as fools.'

'I still believe that we were right to trust Inspector Colbeck.'

'I wish that I could agree with you, Alexander,' said the Bishop, eyes flashing, 'but facts are facts. By employing detectives from Scotland Yard, we took several large steps towards bankruptcy.'

'My faith in Inspector Colbeck remains unchanged,' said the Dean firmly.

There was an ominous silence.

When the thieves reached Peterborough, they paused to rest their horses and to consider what to do next. As usual, Jeremy Keane had the answers.

'We split up and go our separate ways,' he advised. 'I'll ride back to the farm with Silas and my cousin. You make your way back home, Tim.'

'My wife will be relieved to see me,' said Redshaw.

'Don't tell her about the money just yet.'

'She knows nothing of what we've been up to.'

'Keep it that way.'

'What if the police come sniffing around my farm?' asked Farr.

'Then they'll find it working as usual,' said Keane. 'You and Silas will be going through your daily routine, and I will make myself scarce. Once we know that danger is past, we can think about our next move.'

'When are you going back to London, Jerry?' asked Redshaw.

'As soon as I feel that it's safe to do so.'

'You've organised everything perfectly.'

'Thanks, Tim.'

'I know one of the first things I'll do,' said Farr.

'What's that, Pat?'

'When I get to London, I'll somehow get word to Pentonville Prison.'

'Yes, Percy deserves to know what we've been up to,' said Keane.

'He should be proud of us,' added Farr.

'What's so special about Percy Gull?' asked Redshaw. 'The pair of you always talk so fondly of him.'

'He's our grandfather,' said Keane and Farr in unison. 'We love him.'

Still in his prison cell, Percy Gull came awake with a start. Something told him that he had reason to be proud of his grandsons. He swung happily to and fro in his hammock. There was a triumph to celebrate.

Victor Leeming was not the best of riders even when everything was in his favour. In difficult conditions, he had trouble keeping up with Colbeck. It was pitch dark, rain was pelting them, and they were unsure of their geography. In Leeming's opinion, the ride to Peterborough was akin to a continuous torment. He eased his mount alongside the one being ridden by Colbeck.

'How much further is there to go, Inspector?' he asked.

'Your guess is as good as mine,' replied Colbeck.

'The villains have the advantage. They know where we're going – we don't.'

'We've picked up clues about where they're heading.'

'But they must be miles ahead of us.'

'I don't care how long a distance it is, Victor. We must stick at it.'

'I feel so annoyed that they snatched the saddlebags off me.'

'That should make you even more determined to get them back.'

'How much have they stolen?'

'Far too much,' said Colbeck, 'but there's a hope of getting the money back. What we can't get back is Michael Langston, the detective guarding that silver model of the cathedral. He was shot dead at Peterborough Railway Station. The only way that we can bring his family solace is to arrest the man who killed him.'

'I'll volunteer for that task,' promised Leeming.

'The most likely killer is Patrick Farr. He has a farm somewhere in this county. He was also one of the men who wrote to Percy Gull in Pentonville.'

'Yes, it was the superintendent who found that out.'

'Since he went back to London, he's been our best source of information.'

'Then let's hope he stays there,' said Leeming under his breath. 'Why is everyone slowing down?' he added as the pace eased considerably.

'We need a rest and time to get our bearings.'

'I've ridden far enough for one day.'

'All of us are saddle-sore but we must press on. And we must find the farm that one of them owns. That's where they'll be heading.'

Once they had crossed the boundary into the adjoining county, Tim Redshaw took his leave of the trio. Heading for his home, he had pleasing memories of doing his best to confuse the detectives at the cathedral, and of being paid handsomely as a result. Exactly how he would make use of the money, Redshaw was uncertain, but he knew that it would buy him and his wife a far better life in a different part of the country.

His companions were sad to see him go. As the three of them rode abreast, Keane was the first to admit how valuable an asset Tim Redshaw had been.

'I was wrong about him,' he admitted. 'I'd hoped to cheat him out of some of the money, but he earnt every penny of it. His timing was perfect. He set off that explosion at midnight near the cathedral then set all that hay alight so that we could see our way out of Lincoln.'

'I knew that Tim wouldn't let us down,' said Farr.

'Yes,' said Weaver. 'It was good to have him on our side. Tim has got another virtue as well. He knows how to keep his mouth shut.'

'That's something we must all do,' insisted Keane. 'Nobody must boast about what we did. The time to beat our chests is when we're all living very different lives to the ones we have now. That might take months. Until then – keep your traps shut. Understood?'

'Understood,' chorused Weaver and Farr.

The chasing pack had pushed themselves hard. Having left the county of Lincolnshire, they felt that it was time to rest the horses, take refreshment and relieve themselves. Colbeck drifted across to the officer in charge of the mounted police.

'Are we sure that this is the way that they came?' he asked.

'Yes, Inspector,' replied the man. 'Everybody we've spotted along the way has said the same thing. Four horsemen have galloped past as if the hounds of Hell were barking at their heels.'

'Does that mean they're pushing their horses too hard?'

'It means that they're well ahead of us, sir.'

'Then let's get everyone back in the saddle,' ordered Colbeck. 'We need to chase them every inch of the way.'

* * *

After a disturbed night, Lydia Quayle had woken shortly after dawn. Getting out of bed, she wiped the sleep from her eyes and tottered across to the curtains. When she opened them, light flooded into the bedroom. It also lit up the scene in front of her. On the opposite side of the road, she believed that she could see a woman staring up at her house with intensity. For a second, Lydia thought that it was Kitty Piper. When she took a second look, however, she realised that it was not her former servant at all. It was a young woman, taking a dog for an early-morning walk.

Lydia's mind was playing tricks on her.

Edward Tallis was routinely early that morning. When he got to his office, he found a daily newspaper waiting for him alongside some correspondence. Disappointingly, there was no telegraph from Robert Colbeck, passing on good news from Lincoln.

'Damn you, Colbeck,' he chided. 'Let's have some action.'

When they eventually reached the farm, the posse found that the daily round was already under way. Colbeck led the short tour of the place, noting the activity in the milking shed and the feeding of some of the younger livestock. Everything seemed to be working as it would have done on any other day in the calendar. Colbeck spoke to the farmer.

'We've been chasing a group of men,' he explained. 'Four in number.'

'Well, they've not come anywhere near us,' replied Patrick Farr. 'What have they done wrong?'

'They stole money from Lincoln Cathedral.'

'That's shameful, Inspector. I hope that you catch them.'

Colbeck looked around. 'It's a nice little farm you have here.'

'It's a bit of a handful now that I'm older, but we manage somehow.'

'If you do catch sight of the four men . . .'

'Don't worry,' Farr assured him, 'we'll send word to the police at once. Where will you be?'

'Not too far away. I sense that our quarry is somewhere close.'

'I'll keep my eyes peeled, Inspector.'

'Please do that.'

After a final look around, Colbeck led his men away.

Age was no protection for a prisoner at Pentonville. Whether young or old, each one of them had to endure regular exercise in the yard in one of two concentric circles. The rope that they held was knotted at fifteen-foot intervals so that they never got close enough to fellow prisoners to have a conversation, let alone to develop a friendship. As they trudged around in circles, they were watched by prison warders.

One of them spotted a man with a broad smile on his face.

'Why is that old fool grinning?' asked one warder. 'This is a prison. There's nothing here to be happy about.'

'That's Gull,' replied his colleague. 'He thinks he's here to enjoy himself.'

Having visited several farms near Peterborough, they had to accept that they had not found the one they were after. Colbeck led the way back to the county town. Since they had met him before, Alan Hinton and Eric Boyce were sent to the police station to tell the chief constable that their chase had brought them there. Colbeck and Leeming, meanwhile, had returned to Peterborough Railway

Station. They renewed their acquaintance with Nathan Powell, the stationmaster.

'I had a feeling I'd see you back here,' he told them.

'We chased four men here from Lincoln,' explained Colbeck. 'One of them is likely to catch a train to London.'

'So are lots of other passengers, Inspector.'

'This man is very special.'

He gave Powell a description of Jeremy Keane. The stationmaster shook his head.

'I've seen nobody like that this morning,' he said. 'And if he'd ridden through a storm, he'd surely be bedraggled – rather like you, Inspector.'

'And me,' added Leeming.

'Do you have any spare uniforms?' asked Colbeck.

'There's one belonging to a guard we had to get rid of,' said Powell. 'He was even taller than you, Inspector. Would you like to try on his uniform?'

'Yes, please.'

'It's a bit grubby, I'm afraid.'

'I don't care about that.'

'But you pride yourself on your appearance, Inspector.'

Colbeck laughed. 'I daren't look at myself in a mirror at the moment.'

'Both of us got soaked,' explained Leeming.

'Come this way,' said Powell, heading for his office. 'Let's see if you can squeeze into Charlie's uniform.'

'What about me?' asked Leeming.

'You stay here, Victor,' said Colbeck. 'Keep your eyes peeled.'

'Who am I looking for?'

'Jeremy Keane. Remember the description we had of him.'

'He'll have gone to ground somewhere, surely?'

'With all that money in his pocket? I fancy that he'll want to get back to London as soon as possible. If he does,' said Colbeck, 'I'll be on his tail.'

It was a minor incident, but it nevertheless disturbed Lydia Quayle. As soon as she had finished her breakfast, she took a cab to the Colbeck residence. She was given a warm welcome by Madeleine.

'I wasn't expecting you so early, Lydia,' she said.

'Something odd happened. I need to tell you about it.'

'Then let's make ourselves comfortable, shall we?' She led the way to the drawing room, and they sat opposite each other. 'What seems to be the problem?'

'I saw Kitty Piper first thing this morning,' said Lydia.

'Where?'

'When I pulled back the bedroom curtains, she was standing on the pavement opposite.'

'Are you quite sure that it was her?'

'I was at first, Madeleine. Then I took a closer look at her. She was taller and older than Kitty and was taking her dog for a walk.'

'How did you feel when you realised that you'd made a mistake?'

'I was shocked,' said Lydia. 'It was almost as if I'd seen Kitty's ghost.'

'But this woman wasn't your former servant.'

'It took me minutes to realise that. I wonder if I should see a doctor and tell him that I'm being haunted by Kitty.'

'Let's talk this through first,' suggested Madeleine. 'When you went to bed last night, was Kitty on your mind?'

'She's always on my mind.'

'Have you talked with Martha about her?'

'Yes, of course.'

'Does she have the same obsession?'

'No, Martha was just pleased when Kitty left my employment.'

'Are you still leading your normal life?'

'I'm trying to, Madeleine, but I have this feeling of being watched all the time. It makes it impossible for me to concentrate.'

'That must be so irritating.'

'It's maddening. It means that, when I try to do something as simple as reading a novel, I just sit there and stare at the pages.'

Madeleine took a deep breath. 'Let's go back to the beginning of this problem you've been having,' she said. 'Do you still believe that it was Kitty you saw standing outside your house with a man?'

'I do and I don't,' replied Lydia.

'And what about that feeling you had that somebody had been inside your house and let themselves out very quietly?'

'That was Kitty as well. It must have been. I mean, who else could it have been? The more I think about it, the more certain I am that Kitty had been inside my home again.'

'What proof do you have, Lydia?'

'I have this feeling deep inside me,' said her friend. 'I'm being tormented.'

During the long ride through the night, Colbeck had been very much aware of the fact that he was not ideally dressed for a hunt. There had been more than one occasion when he had to grab the brim of his hat to prevent it being blown off. When he went into the stationmaster's office and looked in the mirror, he saw how dishevelled he really was. The uniform he was being offered was slightly too large for him, but he did not object. It had transformed him. Colbeck was no longer the dandy of Scotland Yard. He had turned into a guard on the Great Northern Railway. Nobody would give him a second look.

'It's amazing,' said Leeming, studying him. 'It's simply not you, sir.'

'Then the disguise is a good one.' He turned to Powell. 'Thank you very much for the loan of these clothes. I'd be grateful if you could keep what I was wearing in here.'

'It will be as safe as houses,' promised Powell.

'I hope that your father-in-law doesn't see you wearing that,' said Leeming. 'If he spotted you in a uniform belonging to a rival railway company, he'd go mad.'

'Then he's best kept in the dark,' decided Colbeck.

'What happens now?' asked Powell.

'We watch and wait. My feeling is that, sooner or later, the leader of the gang will head for London. I have an accurate description of him. Where he goes, I'll follow.'

'He'll be travelling first-class,' announced Leeming.

'How do you know that, Victor?'

'With all that money in his pocket, he can afford the most comfortable way to travel. I'd do the same in his position.'

When it was time for her to leave, Lydia Quayle embraced her friend warmly.

'Thank you so much, Madeleine,' she said effusively.

'All that I did was to listen.'

'Yes, but you did so patiently.'

'You needed to talk, Lydia. My job was to let the words flow.'

'There's nobody else in whom I can confide.'

'What about Alan?' teased Madeleine. 'I'm sure that Detective Constable Hinton would listen to anything you had to say.'

'You are far more impartial than he is.'

'But he's a trained detective. If you told him about your problem with Kitty Piper, I'm sure that Alan would give you some good advice.'

'Your advice was the best – try to ignore the woman completely.'

'Unfortunately,' said Madeleine, 'you can't do that. Whatever you do, Kitty keeps popping up in your mind and distracting you.'

'I should have tackled her when I had the chance.'

'That means you still believe you saw her on the opposite side of the road.'

'It looked so much like Kitty,' insisted Lydia.

'But she had no reason to be there. I'm wondering if she's just a figment of your imagination.'

'It was definitely her, Madeleine.'

'You said the same thing about that woman you saw early this morning.'

'That was a silly mistake on my part.'

'It's good that you're able to acknowledge that. What possible reason would Kitty have to come back here? I can't think of one. In my opinion, the best thing you can do it to forget that you ever knew the woman. Free your mind, Lydia.'

Her friend sighed. 'I wish that I could.'

As they waited at Peterborough Railway Station, they kept their eyes peeled. All that they had was a brief description of Jeremy Keane, but it was enough to pick him out of the crowd. Colbeck and Leeming stood well apart so that they could see newcomers arrive from a slightly different angle. When someone finally stepped onto the platform, they knew that their quarry had arrived.

The middle-aged man had a decisive strut that set him apart from everyone else. They recognised his overweening confidence.

'Why not arrest him here?' asked Leeming.

'I need to follow him to his lair in London,' said Colbeck. 'I want to catch him when he feels there's no hint of danger.'

'What about me?'

'There are horses to return to Lincoln. Don't even think of trying to ride them back there. Gather up Hinton and Boyce and the mounted police,' suggested Colbeck, 'and take the animals back in a stock wagon when one arrives. After that long chase, the animals deserve to travel by rail.'

'When will I hear from you, Inspector?'

'When I've changed out of this smelly uniform. By that stage, I may have an arrest to report. Jeremy Keane is the leader of the gang. When I've put handcuffs on him, we can think of rounding up the rest of them.'

'What about the money? That's what the Bishop will ask.'

Colbeck beamed confidently. 'I expect to get every single penny back.'

Dean Courtney and Bishop Jackson were still in a quandary. The events of a dreadful night had left the pair of them exhausted. As they sat in the Bishop's office, all that they could do was to lament what had happened.

'What a calamity!' moaned the Bishop.

'All is not yet lost,' argued the Dean.

'We had a vast amount of money stolen from under our noses, Alexander.'

'The thieves will be pursued until they are caught.'

'I appreciate your attempt to cheer me up, but I am beyond that stage. Imagine the letter I will have to write to Gregory Tomkins.'

'He should be pleased that his work has finally reached the cathedral.'

'Yes – but with horror in its wake!'

'There's no need to burden him with details.'

'If I don't tell him,' said the Bishop, 'the newspapers certainly will. He'll read of the daring escape by that gang who stole an indecent amount of money from us. Tomkins will blame himself for what was an act of kindness on his part.'

'Unfortunately, it led to murder and violation.'

'The silversmith is not in the best of health. The facts of what happened may be too much for him to bear. The only way we can celebrate his genius is by holding his funeral in the cathedral.'

'I think that we should concentrate our efforts on getting our money back.'

'Inspector Colbeck is already in pursuit of the gang responsible.'

'They know this part of the country well – Colbeck does not.'

'He is a very quick learner,' observed Bishop Jackson.

As soon as the train squealed to a halt in Peterborough, doors opened to let passengers get out and to allow their replacements to get in. Nathan Powell took the trouble of introducing Colbeck to the guard so that the detective could travel to London in the guard's van. The man was happy to help in any way that he could.

Victor Leeming, meanwhile, had watched their suspect getting into a first-class carriage and settling down. Producing a newspaper, Jeremy Keane opened it and began to read the morning's news. Leeming trotted to the guard's van and was able to give details of where Keane was sitting to Colbeck before the train began to move. Somewhere on board it was a man with a large amount of stolen money who was completely unaware that he was being followed all the way back to London.

Starved of the latest news about the case, Superintendent Tallis was seated at his desk in a belligerent mood. He had put a lot of thought and energy into the theft of a silver model but had very little to show for it. More to the point, no new information had been sent from Lincoln. Yet something important must have happened. He was tempted to head for King's Cross and to buy a ticket to Lincoln. Tallis wanted to have an important role in an investigation to which he had already contributed valuable evidence. But he was being deliberately ignored. It was an insult. There would be repercussions.

There was a tap on his door, then it opened to reveal a young constable in the uniform of the Metropolitan Police Force. The newcomer handed him a telegraph.

'This came for you, Superintendent,' he said.

'Thank you,' said Tallis, taking it from him then getting rid of his visitor with a dismissive wave of the hand. He glanced at the message, then exploded. 'All the money stolen from the cathedral and not a single arrest! What, in God's name, are you doing up there, Colbeck? You were supposed to stop any further crime happening there.'

Having read his newspaper, Keane had closed his eyes and pretended to be asleep in a compartment that was almost completely full. His travelling companions wondered why he had such a broad smile on his face. What none of them could see was the leather satchel in his lap. It contained his share of the theft from Lincoln Cathedral. And it was taking him from one life to an infinitely more enjoyable one. Even when he drifted off to sleep, the smile remained firmly in place.

Back at the farm, Patrick Farr and Silas Weaver were rewarding themselves with a glass of beer apiece. Everything had gone exactly as Keane had predicted. By taking chances, they had left the cathedral clergy red-faced, evaded the riders at their heels and got back to the protective shield of the farm. Each of them had enough money to transform their lives completely. Farr felt that a toast was in order. He raised his glass.

'To my cousin, Jerry Keane!' he said.

'He showed us what could be done if we had the guts to do it.'

Laughing aloud, they gulped their beer down.

Colbeck took no chances. Every time they stopped at a station, he left the guard's van and walked along the platform to the first-class compartment in which Keane was travelling. One glimpse of the man was all that he needed. Whether asleep or awake, Keane was grinning at his success. Once in the huge sprawl of London, he obviously felt that he would be safe, and so would the leather satchel clasped so tightly in one hand.

Back in Lincoln, the mood was very different. When Alan Hinton and Eric Boyce returned there by train with the horses and the policemen who had ridden them, they felt obliged to report to the Dean and Bishop. Both men sat stony-faced as they were told about the failure of the chase. For them, only one question dominated.

'What has happened to our money?' asked the Bishop.

'It's in the hands of the men who stole it,' admitted Hinton.

'Then it's gone forever,' sighed the Dean.

'Don't give up hope, Dean Courtney. Wherever their leader is, he has Inspector Colbeck on his tail. I sense better news in due course.'

Dean and Bishop exchanged a look of disbelief.

Jeremy Keane felt able to sleep comfortably for the bulk of the journey to London. Before he left his compartment, he checked that his leather satchel was securely locked. He then left the train and merged with the mass of passengers surging towards the exit. So confident was Keane that it never occurred to him to glance over his shoulder. All his attention was fixed on the next stage of his plan. As he left the station and joined the queue at the cab rank he felt a sense of elation. When he eventually climbed into a cab, he took great pleasure in giving his destination to the driver.

'Lombard Street, please,' he snapped.

'Very good, sir.'

As he settled back in his seat, it never occurred to him that the driver of the cab behind him had been told to follow his cab. Determined not to lose sight of him, Colbeck had already guessed where Keane would be going.

Edward Tallis was throbbing with anger. Seated alone in his office, he looked back on his contribution. In Lincoln itself, it had been largely ineffective. He acknowledged that. Since he had returned to Scotland Yard, however, he had worked tirelessly to gather information relevant to the crimes they were investigating. Tallis had sent a stream of vital information to Inspector Colbeck. The least he expected in return was an account of the latest developments in Lincoln.

A tap on his door brought him out of his anger for a moment.

'Come in!' he roared.

The door opened and Colbeck stepped into the office. At least he thought at first glance that it was the inspector, then he realised he that he was looking at a guard from the Great Northern Railway.

'Who the devil are you and what do you want?' demanded Tallis.

'I've come to deliver my report, sir.'

Tallis gulped as he recognised his visitor. 'Why on earth are you dressed up like that?'

'It was a necessary disguise,' explained Colbeck. 'The gang who handed over Gregory Tomkins's gift to the cathedral snatched the money in return and made a run for it. We pursued them all the way to Peterborough. I felt certain that one of the first things their leader would do was to return to London with his share of the booty. In order to follow him, I borrowed this clothing from the stationmaster.'

'Well, it doesn't suit you at all.'

'It seems to have fooled Jeremy Keane, the man whose name you discovered. When he left the station, I took a cab and followed him to Lombard Street.'

'What was he doing there?'

'What else would he be doing but adding a huge amount of money to his account? That was all I needed to witness. I came straight here so that you could be present at his arrest. It was only because of your detective work that we even knew that he existed.'

'I'm glad that someone remembered that,' grumbled Tallis.

'If you'll excuse me,' said Colbeck, 'I'll change out of these clothes and into the spare suit I keep in my office. Then the two of us can go to Lombard Street.'

'Why?'

'We can confirm that a large deposit was made by Keane then demand his home address. I think that the honour of arresting him must fall to you.'

'Thank you. But what exactly happened at midnight in Lincoln?'

'I'll tell you on our way to the bank.'

'Good. I'll be glad if you get that dreadful coat off. It stinks.'

'Give me time to get changed,' said Colbeck, 'and you'll be able to recognise me properly at last. You found Jeremy Keane for us. It's only right that you should be the man to snap the handcuffs onto his wrists.'

'I agree wholeheartedly,' said Tallis, rising to his feet. 'I feared that you'd forgotten my contribution to this investigation.'

'It was decisive, Superintendent. You were an example to us all.'

Now that they had escaped from the armed pursuit, Patrick Farr and Silas Weaver felt entitled to boast amount their triumph. It had been exhilarating.

'I'd forgotten how exciting a good chase could be,' said Farr.

'It certainly made my blood race.'

'We owe everything to my cousin.'

'Yes, Jerry controlled the whole thing. As a result, we end up with more money than we've ever dreamt of having and Inspector Colbeck is made to look a complete fool.'

'There's something so exciting about breaking the law.'

'What's exciting, Pat, is getting away with it.'

'All we have to do is to follow Jerry's advice.'

'He deserved having the largest amount of the money,' said Weaver. 'I wonder how he's going to spend it all.'

* * *

Jacob Hibbert was the manager of one of the many private banks in the vicinity of Lombard Street. He was a sleek individual in his fifties with a neat moustache. When told that two detectives wished to speak to him, he had no idea why. Hibbert ordered that both visitors be sent immediately to his office. Tallis and Colbeck soon arrived.

'Inspector Colbeck?' said Hibbert. 'Where have I heard that name before?'

'If you are ready to cooperate with us,' Tallis told him, 'you may read that name in tomorrow's newspapers. The inspector will explain why.'

'A case of murder and theft took us to Lincoln Cathedral,' said Colbeck. 'Thanks to the sterling efforts of the superintendent, we discovered the culprits. What we did not anticipate was how evil these men were. They not only injured people indiscriminately, they stole a large amount of money from Lincoln Cathedral.'

'Some of that money was deposited here today,' said Tallis.

Hibbert's face reddened. 'Surely not.'

'Inspector Colbeck witnessed it taking place.'

'That's not entirely true,' explained Colbeck. 'I followed this man to London disguised as a railway employee. When I trailed him to your bank, I saw him placing a very large deposit here. When he left the premises, he was glowing.'

Hibbert was horrified. 'Can this be true?'

'It's the reason we are here, Mr Hibbert. We know this man's name. What we need to find out from you is his address.'

'Is he liable to arrest?'

'On several counts, sir,' said Tallis. 'His name is Jeremy Keane and he lives in the capital. We must ask you to give us his address, please.'

'I need to verify some details,' said Hibbert warily.

Tallis got to his feet. 'I'll come with you while you do so,' he insisted.

Back in Lincoln, all that the Bishop and Dean could do was to pray together before discussing the situation. Bishop Jackson was forthright.

'Do you think that we'll ever get the money back?' he asked.

'I don't believe in miracles, Bishop,' replied the Dean.

'How could the inspector and his detectives be so easily deceived?'

'We may never know.'

'They not only failed to catch the thieves, those who came back from the chase did so as if they'd been soundly beaten. Inspector Colbeck was no longer with them.'

'I was told that he was following a new line of enquiry.'

'Will that be any more successful than the earlier ones?'

'I doubt it,' replied the Dean before rallying. 'But I am still sure that the inspector will continue to pursue these devils wherever the trail leads him. He will never give up. Superintendent Tallis told us what a remarkable detective the inspector is. Somewhere, I believe, Colbeck has devoted himself to a search for those devilish individuals.'

When the two of them returned to the manager's office, they looked as if all the information that had been checked had been accurate. Hibbert apologised for his doubts.

'Instinct is as important in the world of banking as it is in your world. We need to be good judges of character. Until today, that is what Daniel Cooper has always been. He's the man who accepted the deposit from Jeremy Keane.'

'Are such large amounts routinely deposited here?' asked Colbeck.

'Unfortunately, they are not.'

'How long has Mr Keane had an account here?'

'He's been a client for several years,' said the manager, opening the ledger in front of him. 'All of his previous dealings with us appeared to be completely legal.'

'Do you have his address?' asked Tallis.

'I have more than one, Superintendent. It seems that he has moved around.'

'Have you any idea why?'

'No,' said Hibbert, 'but he was a good client. He put regular deposits here and had occasional withdrawals. His address is in an area of the city where you need money to live.'

'Please give us the details,' said Tallis.

'We'll pay him a visit immediately,' said Colbeck.

They waited as the manager copied the details onto a piece of paper, then handed it over to Tallis. He looked up at the detectives.

'I have to say that Mr Keane has been a model client,' he said.

'You may be about to lose him,' warned Colbeck.

CHAPTER EIGHTEEN

Unaware that her husband was safely back in London, Madeleine Colbeck had decided to devote herself to Lydia Quayle. She sensed that what her friend needed most was the love and company of someone in whom she could confide her anxieties. That afternoon found the two of them strolling through the park together.

'How do you feel now?' asked Madeleine.

'It's wonderful to be with someone I can trust,' said Lydia.

'But you do that every day. You share a house with two excellent servants. Each of them is so supportive, Lydia.'

'It's a former servant that I worry about,' admitted her friend. 'I simply can't get Kitty Piper out of my mind.'

'But it's years since she stopped working for you.'

'I know, Madeleine. To be honest, she disappeared from my

mind completely. Then, out of the blue, she popped up outside my house.'

'I'm still not entirely persuaded of that.'

'I saw her standing on the opposite side of the road.'

'Have you seen any sign of her since?'

'Once was enough, Madeleine.'

'Yet you thought you saw her early this morning. When you looked more carefully, you realised that it was not Kitty Piper at all, but some unknown young woman with a dog.'

'Don't remind me. It was a mistake on my part.'

'Could the other time have been a mistake as well?'

'I wish that it had been,' said Lydia, 'but it wasn't just Kitty. There was this man with her, and she was pointing out my house to him. My immediate thought was that she was explaining how he could get into the house. It really shook me.'

'Then why has there been no sign of Kitty since then – or of the man she was with?'

'I can't answer that question, Madeleine. But I have been brooding on it ever since. London is a huge city. The chances of someone stepping out of my past are very slim. Yet it did happen. There had to be a reason for it.'

'Kitty Piper seems to have taken over your life.'

'I know – and it frightens me.'

'But you've seen no sign of her since.'

'That one sighting of her has burnt itself into my brain.'

'How can we get rid of it altogether?'

'I wish that I knew, Madeleine.'

'Do you still feel threatened by the thought of her?'

'Yes, I do, I suppose.'

'You immediately jumped to the conclusion that the man with

her was a burglar, getting his instructions. Yet he might just simply have been a close friend of hers. Nobody has tried to break into your house and nobody suspicious has been seen lurking there.'

'That's true.'

'So why are you letting this woman from your past cause you so much grief?'

Lydia came to an abrupt halt. 'I wish that I knew.'

'Until recently, you hadn't seen or heard from her for years.'

'That's true, Madeleine.'

'So why did she suddenly turn up in your life?'

Lydia needed a few moments before answering the question. Then she turned to her companion as a memory surfaced in his mind.

'I think that Martha mentioned her name to me,' she recalled.

When their cab reached the address, it went on past the house and parked on the next corner. After asking the driver to wait for them, Colbeck went down a side street so that he could cover the rear exit of the property where Jeremy Keane lived. It was a small, well-built house in the middle of the terrace. Tallis gave his colleague plenty of time to get into position before he walked to the address they'd been given. He knocked firmly on the front door and waited. There was no sign of movement from within the house. Tallis used the knocker once more, producing a louder noise.

After a long wait, Colbeck appeared from the rear of the block.

'There's nobody at home,' said Tallis, disappointed.

'We can come back.'

'Where do we go meanwhile?'

'The jewellery quarter is not far away,' said Colbeck. 'That's his stamping ground. We can get the cab to take us there. We'll find him eventually.'

'Wherever he is,' said Tallis through gritted teeth.

Back in Lincoln, the detectives had reported to Dean Courtney. Victor Leeming was now nominally in charge of the trio. He, Alan Hinton and Eric Boyce described the failed chase to Peterborough. The Dean winced at some of the details.

'In short,' he decided, 'you failed miserably.'

'It was not for want of trying,' insisted Leeming.

'In return for bringing us the silversmith's gift, they got away untouched with an enormous amount of our money.'

'I like to think that we gave them a scare now and then, Dean.'

'What about the scare that we had?' demanded the other. 'Our finances are very limited. Because of your failure, we are now in financial peril.'

'It's unfair to blame us,' said Leeming, 'and you forget that Inspector Colbeck is trailing the leader of the gang to London. He won't be shaken off.'

'What about the money?

'Jeremy Keane has a large amount of it and will put it in a bank in London. Once he's done that, there'll be a search led by the inspector and an arrest. Keane may think that he got away with it, but I guarantee that he will soon be under arrest.'

Edward Tallis was going over old ground. During his search for Jeremy Keane, he had visited several people in the jewellery quarter and been given useful information by some of the area's denizens. Back in the area, he went to the same people again. Nobody was surprised to hear that the police were searching for

Keane. A man who owned a large jewellery shop was particularly helpful.

'Have you been to Jerry's house?' he asked.

'It was empty,' said Colbeck.

'Then he's gone off to celebrate.'

'What do you mean?' asked Tallis.

'Have you never put a large amount of money in your bank account?'

'Of course I haven't.'

'Then you'll never have had that feeling, Superintendent.'

'What feeling?'

'The urge to celebrate – with a woman of your choice.'

'Don't be ridiculous, man,' snarled Tallis.

'Where might Keane have gone?' asked Colbeck.

'I can think of a few places,' said the man with a grin.

'Give me the names and addresses, please,' asked Colbeck, producing a notepad. 'The sooner we interrupt his celebrations, the better.'

Left alone at her house, Lydia had much to think about. Her walk with Madeleine had produced a change of mind. Hitherto, she had persuaded herself that a former servant of hers, Kitty Piper, had been planning to burgle her house. Having disappeared completely from her mind, the woman had suddenly monopolised Lydia's attention. Then Madeleine asked her friend a direct question. When had Kitty come back into her life? It took Lydia some time to find the answer and it came as a shock.

The person who first mentioned Kitty Piper was her cook, Martha. Realising that had had a profound effect on Lydia. It made her stop and think.

* * *

On the train journey to London, Jeremy Keane had planned each of his three moves. The visit to the bank was the first and he had the satisfaction of paying a sizeable amount of money into his account. His next port of call was a jewellery shop where he purchased a necklace that he knew would delight a close friend. Bella Vincent was overjoyed. After tearing off her clothes, she put the necklace around her neck and let it dangle between her breasts. Keane was naked in less than a minute, and he dived on the bed with her. It was a precious moment, and he took full advantage of it. He was rich, free and able to live the life he had always wanted. Bella Vincent was simply a first stage in that new life.

They were so caught up in the joy of their reunion that neither of them heard the sound of the doorbell. Getting no reply, Colbeck put his shoulder to the front door and exerted pressure. It took time and patience, but he was eventually rewarded with the sound of the lock giving way. Entering the house, they had a quick search of the ground floor then dashed upstairs. Keane and Bella were totally unaware that they had visitors. It was only when the door of the bedroom was flung open that they came to their senses. Bella's scream was matched by a mouthful of abuse from Keane. Colbeck stepped in to restrain the woman so that Tallis could have the satisfaction of putting handcuffs on his naked prisoner.

Dean Courtney was alone in the cathedral with the Bishop when the telegraph arrived. Glancing at the message, the Dean was overwhelmed with joy.

'Inspector Colbeck has followed the leader of the gang back to London and, with the superintendent's assistance, has arrested the man.'

'What about the money?' asked the Bishop.

'A substantial share of it is under lock and key in a bank near Lombard Street.'

'Thank heaven for that!'

'They are confident that the rest of the stolen money will also soon be recovered.'

'We were wrong to lose faith in the inspector,' said the Bishop.

'It appears that we also owe an apology to the superintendent. He seems to have made the significant arrest.'

Lydia Quayle was very conscious of the fact that she had let a former servant of hers dominate her thinking. Memories of Kitty Piper were always in her mind. Fears of what the woman might do had caused her sleepless nights. She agonised over the memory of having seen Kitty with a man studying her house from the opposite side of the road. One simple question from Madeleine had changed everything. When had her former servant come back into Lydia's life? When she thought about it, Lydia realised that it was her cook, Martha, who had first introduced Kitty's name. Why had the woman done so?

As she brooded on the situation, Lydia began to have uncomfortable thoughts about Martha, a woman who had been so important in her life for years. What was the cook's reason for mentioning Kitty Piper? It was one of many questions that Lydia was now asking herself. When would she get the answers that she craved?

Back in Lincoln, the detectives were also looking for answers. A troubled Victor Leeming was discussing the failed chase through the darkness with Alan Hinton and Eric Boyce. All three of them sat around a table in an inn. Now that he was in charge, Leeming was anxious to go over the details of their visit to the neighbouring county.

'I think that we made a mistake,' he admitted.

'What do you mean?' asked Hinton.

'It's that farm we visited. We were half-asleep when we were there and didn't really take a close look at the place.'

'Everything seemed as it should be,' Boyce pointed out. 'To be honest, I felt that we were intruding.'

'I've been thinking about that farmer,' recalled Leeming. 'He was so surly with us.'

'Can you blame him? asked Hinton. 'We were in his way.'

'The one who interested me,' said Boyce, 'was the man who worked there – Silas something. Did you notice the shoulders on him?'

'Yes, Eric. I saw how easily he moved those heavy sacks around.'

'That raises an interesting question,' said Leeming.

'Does it?'

'We know for certain that someone stole the heavy box containing the silver model of the cathedral. He carried it from the train to a waiting cart. Do you think that Silas would manage to do that?'

'Yes, I do,' said Boyce. 'He was as strong as an ox.'

'Then perhaps we should take a second look at him,' decided Leeming. 'Only this time, we don't have to ride all the way there on horses in the rain. We can take the train to Peterborough and get some help from the chief constable. Agreed?'

Hinton and Boyce nodded enthusiastically.

In his early days in the Metropolitan Police, Colbeck had often taken part in raids on some of the city's brothels. They were always lively affairs involving scuffles and bad language. Edward Tallis was less used to the sight of a naked woman screaming at him. Grabbing her clothes, he flung them at her. Colbeck, meanwhile, was trying to get some trousers onto Jeremy Keane, a difficult exercise when the man's wrists were handcuffed behind his back. Having pulled on her clothes at speed, Bella had the last word. Holding the necklace in both hands, she spat out her warning.

'Nobody's touching this,' she warned. 'I earnt it fair and square.'

Lydia Quayle decided to speak to Martha about what the cook had suggested.

'Do you remember what happened when I heard someone leaving the house?'

'Yes, I do,' replied Martha.

'I told you and Pamela what had happened.'

'It had clearly upset you.'

'You came up with the answer.'

'It was only a suggestion,' said Martha warily.

'You thought it might have been Kitty Piper. Why was that?'

'There were two reasons, Miss Quayle. The first one was that you told us how quiet the sound of the door closing was. That meant it was likely to be a woman. We know how to be gentle.'

'That's a fair point.'

'The second reason was that this intruder had somehow got into the house. How did she do that? Kitty used to have a key. Before she handed it back to you, she could easily have got a copy of it cut.'

'I never dreamt that Kitty would do such a thing.'

'I only put her name forward as a suggestion.'

'I'm beginning to wish that you hadn't done so, Martha.'

'Why is that?'

'It's caused me so much pain and discomfort.'

'That wasn't my intention,' said Martha. 'I was only trying to help.'

When Colbeck and Tallis delivered their prisoner to the nearest police station, Jeremy Keane was still denying that he was involved in any way with the crime. Even when they found details in his pockets of the substantial amount of money he had put into a bank account, Keane kept protesting his innocence.

'You let your grandfather down,' said Tallis, waving a finger at him. 'Percy Gull is very fond of his grandchildren. He expected better from you.'

Keane was shaken. 'How do you know about Percy?'

'I met him in Pentonville Prison.'

'What did he tell you?'

'He was too cunning to say it but my guess is that he wanted you and Patrick to live decent lives. But neither of you could do that, could you? Both of you wanted to follow in his footsteps.'

'Our grandfather was a wonderful man,' argued Keane.

'He was a wicked man who led the pair of you astray.'

'And where is he now?' asked Tallis. 'He's locked up in prison and finding it hard at his age. I spoke to him in person. I can tell you his cell number, if you wish. Percy Gull is the eldest and most cunning prisoner in Pentonville. How can you admire a man with his appalling record?'

'He's our grandfather! We love him.'

'He's a lifelong criminal.'

'He helped to bring us up.'

'And look where you've ended up,' said Colbeck. 'You're facing the full rigour of the law. That's what your admiration of your grandfather did for you. Percy Gull corrupted both of his grandsons.'

'You don't understand, Inspector!' yelled Keane.

'We understand only too well, Jeremy. Using your grandfather's name on that telegraph was a big mistake on your part. It gave us something to work with.'

'I led the search for Percy Gull,' said Tallis, 'and I ran him to earth behind bars. That's where he belongs in my view. That kind old man has an evil streak. Unfortunately, you inherited it from him.'

Keane's head fell to his chest. As he thought of his future, he quailed.

When the train took them to Peterborough, the three of them hailed a cab that took them to police headquarters. Hinton and Boyce had already met the chief constable. When they were admitted to his office, they introduced Victor Leeming.

'It's good to meet you, Sergeant Leeming,' said Marcus Napier. 'You are welcome to draw on any of the resources that we have.'

'We'll need horses and the support of half a dozen men.'

'Let's call it five men, shall we? I'll make up the half a dozen myself.'

'You'll be most welcome,' said Leeming.

'And don't worry,' added the chief constable with a smile. 'You will remain in charge of the operation. We will simply provide good, reliable men.'

Victor Leeming beamed.

* * *

Back at the farm, Patrick Farr and Silas Weaver were having a rest. They were still floating on the sheer excitement of having deceived the police and stolen a large amount of money from the cathedral. Their futures were now secure. After a wait of some weeks, they could go their separate ways and enjoy their wealth at leisure. Weaver was ready to salute the contribution made by Jeremy Keane.

'Your cousin is so clever, Pat. Thanks to him, we rang rings around the police.'

'There was a nasty moment when those men ran us to ground. We took Jerry's advice and started our usual morning round here while he was safely hiding in one of the outbuildings. The police found nothing untoward. We're safe, Silas.'

'We're safe and we're rich!'

'Thanks to my cousin.'

'How will you get word to your grandfather?'

'Jerry will find a way somehow. Percy has been languishing in prison for too long. When they finally let him out, we can have a family celebration.'

'Am I invited?'

'Yes, Silas. You're one of us now.'

Madeleine Colbeck was so used to seeing her friend turn up on her doorstep that she could not resist making a joke of it. After letting her into the house, she gave Lydia a welcoming kiss.

'I can see that I will have to get a front door key cut for you,' she said. 'Then you can come and go as if you live here.'

'I'm sorry to be an inconvenience, Madeleine.'

'You're always welcome.'

'I've only come to offer an apology,' said Lydia.

'No apology is needed. You're a special friend.'

'I'm horrified at the way that I've taken advantage of our friendship.'

'In what way?'

'Can we go into the drawing room?'

'Yes, of course.'

Madeleine led the way into the room, and they sat opposite each other.

'What's this about an apology?' asked Madeleine.

'I've taken up so much of your time,' said her guest, 'and I'm ashamed when I look back on it. I was very upset when I was alone in my house, and I thought I heard someone slipping out of the front door.'

'You had every right to be alarmed.'

'It was Martha who suggested that it might have been Kitty Piper. It was only a guess on her part, but I let it fester in my mind. The very idea that a former servant could let herself into my home was alarming. It was the reason I had the lock on the front door changed.' She gave a hopeless shrug. 'But it wasn't enough to keep the demons away.'

'What demons?'

'One in particular – Kitty Piper. I couldn't stop thinking about her and wondering what reason she would have to let herself into my house illegally. Then, of course, I saw her looking at my house – or, at least, I thought I did.'

'Are you starting to have doubts, Lydia?'

'Yes, I am. Did I really see Kitty – or were my eyes letting me down?'

'Only you can decide that.'

That's why I need to say sorry to you. I pestered you day after day about my former servant, and I persuaded myself that she really had been studying my house with a man beside her.'

'I was unable to change your mind about it.'

'Well, I've decided to stop tormenting myself. The idea that Kitty and the man had designs on my house kept me awake at nights. It was agonising – and I passed on that agony to you.'

'That's what friends are for, Lydia.'

'I've thought it through and decided that I never did see Kitty Piper outside my house. It was Martha who first mentioned Kitty's name to me, and it seemed to explain everything. I began to fear that it was Kitty who let herself into the house and who sneaked out when I was there alone.'

'Do you still think that?'

'No, Madeleine. I've resolved to forget all about Kitty Piper. She's a ghost from my distant past. When I heard someone leaving the house, it was not her.'

'Then who was it?'

Martha went to the market alone that afternoon, though it was not to do any shopping. She went to meet a friend. As soon as he spotted her, a skinny, middle-aged man left his brother to take care of the fruit stall, and he sidled across to Martha.

'I was hoping you'd turn up one day,' he said.

'It was a mistake,' she told him.

'I thought you enjoyed it.'

'I did – but it nearly cost me my job. It can't happen again, Frank.'

'I can be patient.'

'It's too dangerous in every way,' she said. 'When you left the next morning, you were heard shutting the front door. That frightened Miss Quayle. She went on and on about it. I had to pretend that a servant she employed years ago had got into the house – a woman named Kitty Piper.'

'Were you so ashamed of me, Martha?'

'Not at all,' she conceded. 'It was a very special time . . . but it can't happen again.'

'Are you quite sure about this?' he asked, squeezing her hand.

'Yes,' she said firmly, pulling away. 'Goodbye, Frank.'

'Give yourself time to think about it,' he pleaded.

'I've already done that.'

When they got to the farm, they split up so that they could approach it from different directions. The chief constable was with them but happy to let Victor Leeming retain command of the operation. As they converged on the courtyard, they found Patrick Farr and Silas Weaver seated on an old bench. Seeing the policemen approach, the two men got to their feet at once.

'We need to speak to you,' said Leeming.

'You did that earlier,' complained Farr, 'and you found nothing at all here.'

'We'd like to take a second look, if you don't mind.'

'We do mind,' warned Weaver, rising to his feet.

'I should warn you that the police are all armed,' said Leeming. 'And so is the chief constable.'

'That's correct,' added Napier.

'We've nothing to hide,' boasted Farr.

'Then you won't object if we examine your horses,' said Leeming. 'They are probably still resting after that long gallop from Lincoln. We will be able to tell if the animals were ridden to a standstill.'

'Leave my horses alone,' warned Farr.

'We can't do that, Mr Farr. They are witnesses to what happened last night,' said Leeming. 'Or is there a reason why you are afraid to let us see them?'

'This is my farm. Leave us alone.'

'We'll be happy to do so – once we've examined your horses.' Leeming turned to the policemen and pointed towards the stables. 'Take a close look, please. And before you try to stop us, Mr Farr, I need to pass on information that we received in Lincoln by telegraph. Your cousin, Jeremy Keane, the leader of your gang was arrested in London earlier. The money that he stole will be confiscated in the same way that yours will be.'

Too shocked to reply, Farr wondered what to do next. In the end, he decided on instant flight, but he got no more than a dozen yards before he was arrested by two policemen. Silas Weaver put up more resistance, knocking out the first man who laid hands on him and kicking the next one. But he was soon overpowered when Hinton and Boyce joined in. Securely handcuffed, all that he could do was to curse the police in foul language. Hinton confronted him.

'There were four of you,' he said. 'The leader of your gang is already under arrest, and we've just added two more members. Who is the fourth man?'

Having returned to work that morning, Tim Redshaw was going through his usual routine. Every so often, he kept yawning. Thoughts of their midnight triumph kept him firmly awake. He was now a rich man. A whole new future beckoned. When he saw two riders coming out from behind some bushes, he challenged them at once.

'You're trespassing on private land,' he warned.

'We've come to arrest you for your part in the theft of money from Lincoln Cathedral,' said one of the men with a grin. 'All three of your partners are also in custody. Your dreams of a happy life have just turned to dust, Tim.'

Redshaw's immediate reaction was to flee but, when he swung round, he saw that two other riders were backing up the others. He was hopelessly outnumbered.

Edward Tallis was so happy at the outcome of their investigation that he celebrated by smoking a cigar. Standing in front of his desk, Colbeck and Leeming were equally delighted that all the men involved were now awaiting trial.

'I think that congratulations are in order,' said Tallis.

'Your own part in the investigation was critical, Superintendent. You unearthed valuable evidence here in London. Without that, we would have struggled.'

'Yes,' added Leeming. 'You even managed to find Percy Gull.'

'He has a nasty shock coming,' said Tallis. 'When he learns that his grandsons have been arrested on a charge of murder, he'll realise that he'll never see them again. He led them astray at an early age. The law has finally caught up with them.'

'Thanks are due to the telegraph system,' noted Colbeck. 'Without that, we would have been severely handicapped.'

I just wish that I'd been there when Jeremy Keane was arrested,' said Leeming with a grin. 'It must have been a wonderful moment.'

'We were just doing our duty,' said Tallis, unsettled by the memory. 'Well, we have eternal thanks from Bishop Jackson. He was thrilled to have the money returned to the cathedral. And Gregory Tomkins's masterpiece is to be installed at a special ceremony. I have accepted an invitation from the silversmith to go with him to the occasion.'

'You deserve that honour, sir,' said Leeming. 'Congratulations!'

'It seems that I may still have some useful years ahead of me.'

'We agree wholeheartedly,' said Colbeck. 'You are indispensable.'

Tallis felt a surge of pride. He knew that he had earnt their praise.

PRAISE FOR EDWARD MARSTON

'A master storyteller'
Daily Mail

'Packed with characters Dickens would have been proud of. Wonderful [and] well-written'
Time Out

'Once again Marston has created a credible atmosphere within an intriguing story'
Sunday Telegraph

'Filled with period detail, the pace is steady and the plot is thick with suspects, solutions and clues. Marston has a real knack for blending detail, character and story with great skill'
Historical Novels Review

'The past is brought to life with brilliant colours, combined with a perfect whodunnit. Who needs more?'
The Guardian

EDWARD MARSTON has written well over a hundred books and was shortlisted for the CWA's Dagger in the Library award 2025. He is best known for his hugely successful Railway Detective series and he also writes the Bow Street Rivals series featuring twin detectives set during the Regency; the Home Front Detective novels set during the First World War; and the Ocean Liner mysteries.

edwardmarston.com

Printed in the United States
by Baker & Taylor Publisher Services